AIN'T LIFE GREAT!

A Series of Short Stories

by

Don Melbourne

Copyright © Don Melbourne

All rights reserved *2015*

AIN'T LIFE GREAT!

A Series of Short Stories

by

Don Melbourne

ISBN 978-1-326-26414-7

Published by AudioArcadia.com 2015

This book, which includes text and cover artwork, is sold on the condition that it is not lent, resold, hired out, performed, recorded, distributed, circulated or handed out by any other method in whatever format to any other party, including third parties, agents, retailers or any other source of distribution without the prior consent of the publisher. The publisher can be contacted by email at info@audioarcadia.com

CONTENTS

	Page
The Woman Who Knew Absolutely Everything	5
The Italian Job	8
Tom	21
What Are Friends For?	24
Lost Loser	29
The Vase	33
Daddy's Girl	36
Her Islands	47
Georgy Porgy	57
I Don't *Believe* It!	67
The Disappearing Man	74
Land of Hope and ?	86
The Pretty Green Shoes	98
Who *Is* Running The Country?	105
The Darkness	111
Twitched	118
Just Another Day	124
Spatz Foster, Private Eye	131
The Dragon Girl	141
The Final Challenge	146
The Price of Fame	179
The Red Necklace	186
The Footballer's Wife	193
Morgan	200
How to Play Chess	208
Happy Birthday	216
Double Dutch	220
Jonas	230
A Girl's Best Friend	243
Beautiful, Isn't She?	246

The Butcher	253
Charity Begins	261
Mirror, Mirror …	269
The Plot	273
Artistic Licence	280
Billy No Mates	283
My Percy	300

THE WOMAN WHO KNEW ABSOLUTELY EVERYTHING

The mechanic slowly raised his head from inside the car engine and looked up at her.

"You what?"

"Just make sure you use 15W-40 viscosity oil," Audrey repeated.

He muttered a curse. She could tell that her superior knowledge had embarrassed him. He'll learn.

On the way home, in the park, she also helped a young woman feeding her baby.

"Don't let the bottle tilt down, dear, else he'll be sucking air."

"Yes, I *do* know."

The woman gave her a look as if to say *"And how many children have you got?"*

Well none, as it happens, but that's not the point, is it?

"That football's soft son, it needs pumping up."

"*Thank you!*" said next door's fifteen year old. Rather too belligerently she thought, but he'll learn.

Audrey knows these things, you see. Tells it like it is. Well, it's for their own good, isn't it?

Some people are quite rude - what the dustman replied when she told him there was a better way to empty the bins couldn't possibly be repeated here.

Others think she's just showing off. Like the pilot when she suggested he could land just as safely with less reverse thrust, *and* reduce his carbon footprint.

Sometimes it's sarcasm: she only casually mentioned to the young woman in the High Street

5

café that if she pulled the handle down more slowly the coffee quality would be improved.

"Oh," the young woman replied. "I didn't realise *you'd* been on the Gaggia training course as well."

That's sarcasm, isn't it? She'll learn.

Her frail neighbour, Flo, is ninety-five. The doctor is no help, so Audrey visits her to give advice. She can't believe Flo hasn't a clue about keeping healthy; she told her that if she wants to live to an old age she should take some whisky every day.

Flo seemed bewildered, so Audrey bought a couple of bottles of the strong stuff for her.

"It stands to reason, Flo, that if a little a day does you good, then a lot will work miracles."

She also told Flo about olive oil.

"The people on the Med — that's the sea — swear by it," she informed her. "They cook with it, you know."

"I know." Flo was unenthusiastic.

Fortunately for her, Audrey remembered the Indian take-away had left some oil out near the bins.

"I know it's not from the Med, Flo, but it's near enough. Look at those Yogis, they live nearly forever. Look how supple they are and how they grow long beards."

Flo looked bewildered again, poor thing.

"Don't worry, dear, with my help you'll learn about these things," said Audrey, "and go on to live to a ripe old age."

Audrey mixed the oil and whisky together and gave Flo a good half pint a day.

There was no immediate improvement but these things take time, don't they?

Unfortunately for Flo, she died the following week. Shame. Must have had something seriously wrong with her.

The medical term is 'pre-existing condition' she told the Coroner. She could tell by his look that he was grateful for her advice.

Audrey advised the man at the Crematorium to turn down his oven because Flo was full of olive oil and that burns fiercely. She explained that Yogis make do with just wood when they go up in smoke and they have no problems. He'll learn.

In Court, Audrey defended herself. The Judge must have been having an off day. She was really shocked how little he knew about the law. When she told him so, his face turned quite red.

"Don't get so upset," she told him. "Stress is bad for your heart at your age. Take a 75mg dispersible aspirin each morning, get some daily exercise and relax more."

He'll learn.

Do you know what he said!? Well do you!?

He said she was dangerous. A menace to society. But name calling will get him nowhere, will it?

Then he gave her a six year prison sentence for Manslaughter.

"But I can't possibly do that long," she told him.

The Judge peered at her over his glasses, and gave a wry smile.

"Don't worry, my dear, you'll learn."

THE ITALIAN JOB

His eyes bulged, making the flab on his fat red face even more grotesque in the half light.

"You're nothing but a bleedin' waste of space, woman. I want you out of my house. Out of my life."

I was determined to keep calm, to be ladylike and show character. To win the argument by intellectual superiority.

"Oh yeah. And what about you – you lazy, drunken, ungrateful fat-arsed waster. After all I've done for you. Kept you afloat financially, cooked and cleaned and nursemaided you, as well as holding down a job. It's you who should go. Go and crawl back into your hole."

I could tell that my restrained, rapier-like language had riled him because he actually tried to move his body from the horizontal to the vertical, his hand ready to hit me as usual.

He didn't quite make it and slumped back on to the couch. Unable to physically bully me, he shouted. His voice like a loudhailer: "Get lost, you moaning cow. It's my house and I want you out of it by the morning. Understand?"

I was furious.

"Understand. Under-bloody-stand! The only thing that I understand is that you are an overweight loud-mouthed brute. I could say you are an accident waiting to happen but in your case it already has. They ought to lock you in the zoo with the rest of the apes."

Knowing I would probably regret it, I pulled the tabs off his last two lager cans and emptied the contents over his head. It felt good. Oh Yes!

"I am sleeping in the caravan tonight," I said, "and when you stir yourself at midday tomorrow I shall be gone. Forever."

I flounced out, leaving the lager running down his face and staining his string vest.

I had emptied the caravan of clothes the day before, ready for the winter. So I padded out in my Mickey Mouse pyjamas, wearing my Bunny rabbit slippers, with a sleeping bag under my arm. And, oh yes, a bottle of red wine and a few chocolate bars for company.

I was asleep before you could say "Ooh look, this bottle of Hardy's Shiraz is empty."

I dreamt a lot, as I always do after a bottle of wine. Voices, one of them squeaky, bumpy roads, fruitbats, metal doors clanging shut, apes and cats, and heart-throbs.

All jumbled up.

I awoke with a start, feeling sick.

It was still dark. I reached for the torch and looked at my watch. *Can't be.* I shook it and looked again – nine a.m.

Why isn't it light? Why is it so quiet? Why am I rolling from side to side?

What's happening!... Am I still drunk...or dead? I closed my eyes and pinched myself. Yes, still functioning.

Fear and dread slowly crept through my body like a dose of senna pods.

This is real. What's happening to me!?

I switched on the torch again and let its beam drift around.

Yes, still in the caravan.

Moving to the window I shone the beam through, blinked, and then looked again – a luxury 4x4 and various expensive looking paintings and bits of furniture. Beyond it all just metal walls.

I waited for my brain to catch up. Sit down, girl, and think it through – the caravan in some form of container (tick), with expensive stuff (tick). Slowly rolling, like at sea (tick), dreams of shouting and bumpy roads (tick), heavy door clanging shut (tick).

Good Heavens, girl... you've been hi-jacked while asleep. Kidnapped!

Control yourself. Keep calm. You used to be a Girl Guide; what would Arkala do? – probably her hair. God knows it needed it.

No, be serious. Check food stocks – plenty of bottled water under the sink. Six chocolate bars, a packet of unopened Frosties. Assorted tins, tuna, beans etc. A Portaloo, recently cleaned.

Try the door – locked. I could climb out of a window in an emergency. *Ha, who are you kidding.*

Where are we going and how long until we get there? Could be weeks. More likely a couple at most. Europe, Africa, the Med. Count the days.

Look on the bright side – what an opportunity to lose a bit of weight.

Two days later, as I was dozing, a series of new movements – bumping, swinging, ears popping, jolting...then traffic noises as though the container was on a lorry.

After several hours, all movement stopped. Meal break? Final destination?

Better get ready. No make-up. Hair all over the place. I look a real mess.

It was half an hour before the container doors opened. I peeped through the curtains and saw men starting to unload things.

Spanish? Italian? They all look the same to me. Moving their arms about like windmills when they speak. Then I heard "Hey, Mario."

I hid in the toilet and clung on tightly as the caravan was offloaded. I heard the door open. How did they get the key? Someone came in, looking, opening cupboards and draws. I held my breath.

When he opened the toilet door, I was standing there waiting, resplendent in my Mickey Mouse pyjamas and my Bunny rabbit slippers.

"Buen gurno!" I said loudly, my face only inches from his.

I had heard the term 'abject terror' but until then never knew what it looked like – white face, staring, unbelieving eyes, mouth dropped open but unable to produce a sound, rigid body, unable to move.

Confidence surged through me. I was definitely in charge of this exchange.

"Bella Italia," I exclaimed (my favourite Italian restaurant) as I stepped out of the toilet and pushed him back. I must have broken his trance. He turned and ran out as though he was on fire, shouting lots of Italian words.

I moved to the doorway, sunlight hurting my eyes, watching him.

I know I must have looked a bit of a sight but the three men standing outside had no need to stare and point at me like that. I mean it's not good for a lady's self-esteem. And anyway they didn't exactly look like Al Pacino or Dean Martin.

More like Silvio Whatsisname, their ex-Prime Minister. Goodness knows why he's such a hit with the ladies.

I gave them my alluring smile, the one that usually attracts men like lemmings. Well, it has done on a couple of occasions. Admittedly we were drunk at the time.

These Italian fellas seemed more interested in my mode of dress, which I must admit, on reflection, might be described as a teeny-weeny bit bizarre.

Then they all went into a huddle.

Knowing nothing about Italian culture, I wasn't sure whether it was a prayer meeting, a rugby team talk, or a pizza deliveryman training session.

When they had finished, one of them said, "You go!" and pointed to a nearby busy road. He insisted on escorting me, arm in arm, to a bus stop.

In normal circumstances I would not have allowed this to happen. Obviously.

But it seemed like part of the holiday package and it was romantic in a way, so I went along with it.

And, of course, walking arm in arm with an Italian man, even though his looks left something to be desired, would be a topic I could brag and dream about later.

When the bus came he said "Milano" to the driver and paid my fare.

"Arrivederci," he said, as the bus pulled away. His smile and wave seemed genuine, as though I was his fancy-dress attired demented aunt who caught this bus every week.

"Scusi, Senora."

I must have nodded off. The bus had stopped and it was dark outside.

Standing in front of me was a policeman.

"Scusi," he repeated. Then he went into Opera mode, jabbering on and emphasising his words with dangerously close waving arms.

I stared at him like the lunatic he obviously thought I was.

I mean what could I say? "Have a nice day."? It didn't seem appropriate somehow.

That was when I saw his gun. I don't like guns. So I screamed. Very loudly.

The next thing I knew, someone gave me an injection and through the haze I saw people in white coats carrying me off the bus.

Had it not been for the crazy people, the hospital would have been okay. A room of my own. Locked, of course. A nice view of gardens through the bars. But clean enough.

I was back in my MM pyjamas which had been washed and pressed, and in my Bunny rabbit slippers.

Then, what I presumed was a psychiatrist, a little man with a beard and a dirty mac, came in. He looked like a cross between Columbo and Danny DeVito.

He was smiling and rubbed his hands together as if to say *"Ah, we've caught another one."*

My silent gaze followed him as he walked around the room. I bet he felt paranoid.

He stopped by the window.

13

"Marco Inocetti," he said. I presumed it was his name but it could have been the latest Italian scooter.

I don't know what made me do it – possibly the excitement of the moment, or the ambience of being in a crazy place – but I unloaded on to him my entire Italian vocabulary: "Bella Italia, Lambretta, pizza, Pavarotti. Chianti. Risotto."

Well, not all my vocabulary obviously. I left out words like spaghetti and lasagne.

He gave me *that* look, the one psychiatrists all over the world use – Number Forty-Five in their Charm Manual – which conveys in crystal clear terms what they are thinking, "Trust me, you daft insane person."

His eyes lit up in Euro signs, like a cash register, with the wording 'A new Mercedes Benz'.

Obviously a private hospital. Correction – Clinic.

He walked over and stood in front of me, then started saying words slowly and clearly with a pause between each one. I finally realised he was going through all the countries in Europe.

He left the UK until last, which, as we all know, is our normal position these days in the Eurovision Song Contest, despite the heroic efforts of that talented prat, Andrew Lloyd Webber.

I nodded and said, "Yes."

"Ah," he exclaimed and dialled a number on his mobile. Then he gave me a tablet to make me sleep. Great, I can escape into my dreams again.

When I awoke I was confronted by a little man sitting by my bed. He had his briefcase on his knees, his hat on top of his briefcase, and his hands, as if praying, on top of his hat.

He looked like a subservient pixie, or possibly a pompous twit. Obviously English.

His eyes conveyed the message to me: 'seriously deranged woman'.

"Ah, Miss Kathleen Simmons, I presume."

I nodded. (Where had he come from, darkest Africa? Was he a chum of Livingstone?).

"Date of Birth: 6th June 1979."

I nodded again.

"Address: No.12 Pontefract Close, Walsall WS2 4HP."

Another nod. He wouldn't give up.

"Telephone 01922 424615. National Insurance Number AD/44/24/09/A."

He paused, so I got in quickly. "Where did you get all this information from?" I was suspicious.

"From you, Kathleen. When I came in yesterday."

I gave him my seriously deranged look.

"Don't you remember? I'm Humphrey Holmes-Brown from the British Consul's Office in Milan. You told me the whole story."

"Of course you are," I said. "Sorry, I just don't remember. Must be the tablets."

He studied me carefully for what seemed a long time. "We have somewhat of a problem," he declared.

"Humphrey," I replied, "that is a diplomatic understatement of the first magnitude."

He smiled. "Sorry, I'll try and talk like a normal human being instead of some patronising pompous twit."

I returned his smile. "Okay, what's the problem?"

"You told me that Vic Blake of that address would vouch for you."

15

All this nodding was hurting my head. "And…?"

"He says he has never heard of you…"

I shook my head, unable to believe it. "We had this argument. He threw me out."

"Yes, you told me…then I checked with the local police and they had a report from Mr. Blake of his caravan being stolen on the night you say. And," he chuckled, "neighbours identified you by your Mickey Mouse pyjamas. Bit of a Trade Mark, eh?"

I had to agree, but didn't show it.

"So that's it then, Humphrey – all solved."

He gave an exaggerated groan. "Apart from you being in a mental hospital, in a foreign country, mingling with the Mafia, being involved in the theft of a caravan, having no passport, no money and no clothes, you mean?"

The silence drifted between us like Titanic lifeboats.

He smiled and put his hand on mine. "But don't worry, Kathleen, my dear. Uncle Humphrey is on the case. It's all taken care of. You can leave here when you feel well enough, then I'll take you shopping for clothes and then you can fly home."

"You mean I haven't won on some Ant & Dec reality show?"

"'Fraid not, but whoever is convicted of stealing the caravan will have a hefty bill to pay – plus all the consequential expenses."

A week later I was back in Walsall, staying with my so-called caring mother.

"In trouble again I see. Mickey Mouse pyjamas indeed. I'm a laughing stock, girl."

16

She showed me a copy of *The Sun* newspaper – a picture of me standing in the caravan doorway, hair like a fairground clown. Face haggard and furious at the same time. The headline was **Don't Get Carried Away, Kath.**

One of those Italian guys must have taken the photo and sold it to the press.

Christ! Give me sunglasses and a new hair colour... or is it my fifteen minutes of fame?

Mom broke my thoughts. "*The Sun* reporter rang. He'll be here to see you at twelve."

Just then the doorbell rang. It was Billy, the seventeen year old who had been my neighbour for the five years I had been with Vic. A nice lad. We got on well.

We did a high five. "Cool, Aunty Kath." I gave him his usual hug. "You knocked 'em dead."

I gave him a 'Don't be silly' look.

"Got some info for you on my iPhone."

He touched a few images and there on the screen was Vic and his new dolly bird, in the garden looking at *The Sun* newspaper. Vic was laughing. "Best place for her – loony bin in a foreign land. What do you think, Gloria?"

"Two birds with one stone, Vic. A backhander from the Mafioso for setting up the theft of your caravan, plus the insurance money. *And* getting rid of Mickey Mouse. Ha. Ha."

I recognised the squeaky voice immediately. She must have been part of the gang who transported the caravan on to the container.

"You are brill, Billy," I said. "Can you email the video to the British Consul in Milan?" I gave him Humphrey's card. "And to the Walsall police, in

Green Lane. Just put a note with my name and this address, and the names and address of the two people in the video."

Billy was nearly jumping up and down with excitement. "No prob," he replied.

"And Billy, could you wait half an hour and transfer that stuff to *The Sun* reporter's iPhone. I'll make sure your name is kept out of it."

"Will do, Aunty K." He was gleeful.

"And even more news!"

He was clearly on a roll. "Vic told Mom he's got another caravan coming later. Bought it off some gypsies. Said he'll pay them tomorrow when the insurance cheque comes."

The Sun reporter got a bigger story than he was expecting. I laid it on thick – how I could have died with no food or water for several days, hence my 'near death' appearance in the photograph.

"The uncaring beast could have killed me," I stated as he took a photograph of me, all dolled up, in front of Mom's Jesus on the Cross picture.

I also played the patriotic card. "Had it not been for the Herculean efforts of Humphrey Holmes-Brown, the British Consul in Milan, I would still be languishing in a stinking rat infested hell-hole of a mental asylum, drugged up to the eye-balls and mixing with deranged serial killers."

My fee from *The Sun* was five hundred pounds. I gave it to Billy.

When he had gone, I rang the insurance company explaining that the owner of the caravan had been involved in its theft. They said the cheque was in the post but that they would put a 'stop' on it so that it couldn't be cashed.

Humphrey phoned me to thank me for the e-mail. Tomorrow Vic would be getting a registered letter from the Government with a bill for twenty-seven thousand pounds. This was for Consular fees and consequential expenditure – clothes (Milan designer shops are *very* expensive) and air fare. Plus the private clinic fees for my treatment.

He chuckled. "Lost in it will be the one thousand pounds spending money I gave you – that's just between the two of us, of course."

He paused. "Payable in thirty days, otherwise property to its value will be seized."

Good old Humphrey!

After enjoying Mom's famous lamb casserole – the best meal I'd had in ages – (I lie ... the meal Humphrey had treated me to in Milan was fab ... and *very* expensive), I dressed in black trousers and a dark hoodie and made my way to Vic's house. It was dark.

The new caravan was on the drive. I knew he was too lazy to have insured it yet, or to have fitted any security devices. The legs weren't even down.

All I had to do was ease off the handbrake.

You need to know that Vic's house is at the top of a hill. A very steep one.

I watched from a distance as the caravan careered down, gathering speed, before toppling on its side into the water-filled quarry at the bottom and disappearing from sight. Gurgle, gurgle...

Oh dear. What a shame.

The Beast Who Tried To Kill His Devoted Girlfriend

Thus ran *The Sun*'s headlines the next day, with a picture of Vic and Gloria. It reported that he and his new girlfriend were to be charged with the theft of a caravan, defrauding an insurance company and attempting to endanger life.

'Kathleen,' the paper reported, showing a flattering view of me in front of the religious picture, 'is recuperating slowly at her mother's after her dreadful ordeal'. *Poor dear.*

The following day, straight after breakfast, Mom answered the doorbell. I stayed in the kitchen.

She came back, hardly able to contain herself. "It's Vic. Wants to know if you could help him out with some money." Snigger, snigger.

I smiled. "Vic who?" I asked. "Never heard of anyone by that name."

She went and told him. I heard her say "Good riddance!"

She was smiling all over her face when she came back.

"His new caravan has been stolen," she said. "And," she went on, "his new girlfriend disappeared at the same time. She was packing the caravan for a weekend away…"

Oh dear.

TOM

Broad Street is bustling. I mingle with the throng, breathing in their excited, boisterous, fun-filled pleasure. But I am not part of it, never have been, never will be.

My clothes give me away. Not for me the flimsy shirt – even in my overcoat I'm still not comfortably warm.

"Got a light, mate?" I ask a passer-by.

"Yeah, of course."

As he leans forward to give me a light I have this strange feeling; it's hard to explain – as though I'm looking at an old friend, myself even. *Get a grip, Darren!*

"Have we met before?" I ask him

He smiled. "In another life maybe...my name's Tom."

As I shook his hand a strange tingle ran up my arm... *I even recognise the voice.*

A nod, and then we wandered off in different directions.

Why am I so unnerved? The uneasiness stirred hidden memories and I felt myself drawn back in time. I was one of twins; I was told Thomas died after a few hours, as did my mother. Dad couldn't cope and I went into care. I had no one. I felt so alone. That is when I discovered Tom – a virtual friend they would call him these days. He helped me get through my difficult times, comforted me in my nightmares. He was the one I talked to in my secret moments.

Tom stayed with me when I left care, and when I was sacked from my first job. He disappeared for a while when the Army became my family. Then, in Iraq, my Land Rover was hit by a roadside bomb. The driver by my side was killed instantly. I was thrown out, injured and stunned. Small arms fire was hitting the track only inches away. *This is it,* I thought. Then I heard Tom's voice. Clear as a bell it was.

"This way, Darren, roll into the ditch."

Tom? I murmured, then passed out.

My head and leg injuries got me invalided out of the Army. I couldn't settle in civvie street and gradually drifted into a downward spiral, eventually ending up in a hostel, and then on the street.

You can see now why I feel so unnerved by this... this...*stranger?*

Preoccupied, I wandered back to my pitch – my tarpaulin lean-to on the canal behind Broad Street. Cramped, damp and dismal. *Oh, how I hate it!*

As though compelled, I pulled out the loose brick – the secret hiding place for my treasure – two twenty pound notes, all I had in the world.

The same compulsion drew me back to Broad Street. Pleasure oozed out of every doorway – fun, laughter, enjoyment – a parallel world to mine, just a few yards away.

Ahead I saw a small crowd outside a wine bar – a body on the floor, people side-stepping it. As I drew closer I saw it was Tom, the man who had given me a light.

"Can't you help him?" I asked the doorman.

"Too right, son," he said. "He's a load of bother, collapses all the time. Shouldn't be allowed."

Under my disapproving stare he modified his tone: "Don't worry, he'll come round in a minute."

As he started to move, I dragged him to the side and eventually on to his feet.

"I'll get you home, Tom...where do you live?"

He looked at me. "I don't have a home," he replied weakly.

"Look, you need a good meal and a bed for the night. Have this." I pushed the two twenty pound notes into his coat pocket.

His pale face gave the flicker of a smile. "Thanks, mate, but..."

Before he could finish he collapsed again, out cold.

"Coming with him, sir?" the ambulance lady enquired. It was the least I could do.

Straight into a cubicle with doctors rushing in and out. After twenty minutes one came over to me: "We couldn't save him, I'm afraid," he said. "You a close relative?"

I shook my head. *No, my closest was my twin brother, Thomas. He died.*

Back at the lean-to, as I went to replace the brick to conceal my hiding place, I noticed the two twenty pound notes were back in there.

"Anyone been in my pitch?" I asked a nearby rough sleeper.

"Oh yeah, about an hour ago. Pale faced bloke...looked a bit like you. Said his name was Thomas..."

WHAT ARE FRIENDS FOR?

Di was brazen. "You owe me, Vicki, you *know* you do."

Vicki's pretty face, still young looking despite her thirty-eight years, looked puzzled: "Oh yes, and on what warped logic do you base that, my precious."

Di, who was a perpetual but unsuccessful dieter, looked her best friend up and down enviously.

"Well, here *you* are – single desirable, sexy, with blokes lining up…"

Vicki tossed her head theatrically, causing her long auburn hair to fall over one shoulder. "And…?"

"And here's *me,* married to boring old Phil, who never compliments me, or takes me out, and who thinks sex is redundant now he's forty." She sighed. "I'm stressed out and frustrated, Vicki, I really am."

Vicki lifted her eyes skyward. "Poor old you. Your Phil's okay, I can think of worse. And *you* chose him remember. We all thought he was a hunk, and were as jealous as hell."

Reluctantly, Di nodded at the truth.

Vicki looked solemnly at her friend, her green eyes large on her tanned face.

"So why should I lie for you? Going off on holiday with some toy-boy and saying it's me you're going with. I mean, it's a bit much, Di."

Di touched her friend gently on the shoulder and shook her head.

"Come on, Vicki, you can see I'm suffocating here," she said gravely. "If I'm to save my marriage I need to escape for a while, recharge my batteries."

She paused, her eyes pleading. "You'll do it for me, won't you?"

"It's not that easy Di. If I cover for you *I'll* have to disappear too, just in case Phil or one of his mates sees me."

Di lifted her eyebrows and smiled, sensing victory: "But you'll do it?"

Vicki hesitated just long enough to see her friend's smile falter. "Yes, Okay, I'll do it."

Di was overjoyed. She wrapped her arms around Vicki and gave her a big hug. She had known her best friend wouldn't let her down.

Phil knew he should be doing more to keep his relationship with Di alive, but the constant slog of a demanding job meant he had no energy for anything else. His good intentions always became submerged in a sea of lethargy. He was content with just lying on the settee watching TV most nights, while his wife busied herself with cooking and running the house.

They hardly spoke any more, but he thought she seemed content with the situation...well, she didn't complain.

Di had prepared herself: she would act naturally, as if it were true. Phil would never detect that she was lying.

But she had hardly got through the door from work when she went to pieces and blurted out: "Vicki's asked me to go on holiday with her. What do you think, Phil?"

She turned away from him to steady her nerves, then kissed him on the cheek, their normal after-work greeting.

Phil, already in his lounging clothes, with matching attitude, half turned his head from the television. His eyes were looking at her but she could tell his mind was still tuned into the programme.

"Eh?"

She repeated herself, this time more believably, just as she had practised. She looked at him, fearing he would reject the idea, a forced smile hiding her apprehension.

He raised his eyebrows. "Where to?"

"Majorca. Santa Ponsa, I think. Vicki's made all the arrangements."

She thought his brown eyes had a sympathetic look as he returned her smile.

"Sounds great, love. You need a break anyway. Just go and enjoy yourself… and don't worry about me. I'll manage." His eyes glazed over as he turned towards the TV again.

Like an incoming tide, guilt gradually began to wash over her. She knew he would struggle – microwave meals, unwashed clothes, unmade bed, beer cans everywhere. The place would be a tip. She hated herself for the deception, but it was too late now to pull out. In any case she was determined to escape from the matrimonial cage and get two weeks of sun and sex.

Di consoled herself with one thought. "Perhaps my being away will be a wake-up call for him." But she knew, deep down, that she was deluding herself.

The phone line from Majorca crackled. "Hi Phil, it's me. How are you coping?"

Her emotions were rampant; even in the middle of her love-nest Di couldn't help worrying about him, but she thought he sounded cheerful enough.

26

"I'm okay, love. Missing you, of course. How are you and Victoria getting on? Drinking the place dry, I expect."

"Don't be daft, Phil. It's great here and very relaxing. Vicki's even left off her inhaler, her asthma's disappeared. We've been by the pool most of the time, getting a nice tan. Must go, love, the card's running out. I'll ring again next week. Take care."

Even though she had kept the call short, the accompanying feeling of guilt dampened her mood and made her strangely anxious – until she returned to the romantic company of her temporary lover, that is.

When Di arrived home, relaxed and fulfilled, she was dreading the household chaos that awaited her. To her great surprise, and delight, the place was immaculate – not a beer can in sight and all the washing-up done.

"What happened, Phil? Been on a *Good Housekeeping* course?"

Phil shook his head and produced a big smile. "Didn't want you coming home to a mess, love. Wouldn't be fair, would it?"

He gave her a lingering kiss. "You look lovely by the way. A million dollars."

As he looked longingly at her, his eyes twinkled in a way she had not seen for years. A reminiscent flutter stirred inside her. Instinctively she moved closer and he put his arm around her shoulder.

"Fancy going out for a meal, love?" he murmured "Save you cooking."

She couldn't believe how he had changed. Was she dreaming?

"Yes, I'd love to. I'll just have a shower and stick some clothes in the washer first. You got anything?"

"No nothing, love. It's all done," he said proudly.

He was right, even the bedclothes. She *was* impressed.

She smiled as she noticed he'd forgotten to empty the waste bin in the bathroom.

"Ah well," she chuckled to herself, "I'll soon train him to do that."

As she pulled out the plastic bag something inside clunked against the metal bin.

When she looked inside she felt her heart stop. There at the bottom she saw an inhaler – the type Vicki used.

THE LOST LOSER

The smell of beer entered my nostrils; his leering face only inches away. "Don't mess with me, son, I'm as hard as nails and just as deadly." His face came closer.

"If I ever see you again, you're dead! Got it?"

I staggered back as his fist thudded into my chest and I crashed noisily against the wall, slowly sliding to the floor.

His bulk stood over me, a shaved head catching the dim light. I noticed the thickness of his neck.

Silence.

I cowered, breathless and in pain. "Okay, okay. Sorry about your drink, an accident…"

A self-satisfied smirk crossed his face as he moved away to join his mates.

Unsteadily, I got to my feet and dusted off my clothes. The small crowd of drinkers parted silently as I made my way towards the pub door, my eyes lowered and my dignity in tatters.

Sure, I'm out of shape. That's a joke. I've never been in it. Shape, that is. My real problem is that I'm scared stiff of conflict. Have been since bad experiences at school.

I am your archetypal victim. People instinctively know it. It's as though I have a flashing sign on my head. Or perhaps they can smell my fear. Even my name says it – Cecil.

I avoid conflict and confrontations like the plague. And competition. People are *always* better than me. Always. Better at sport, better at their job, better conversationalists, better lovers. You name it, I'm the worst.

My life is infected by the disease of failure. I walk, afraid, in the shadows of life, and every experience, like the one in the pub, confirms it. I am a loser, a born failure. God, it makes me so angry!

Of course I delude myself that one day I'll escape from this strait-jacket. One day I'll find the other me lurking inside, someone brave and bold who wants to break out.

Yes, one day I'll show them!

The bloke who followed me out of the pub must have read me like an open book.

"Wait a minute, young man, I can help you."

I looked at him cautiously and something about him made me stop. He was holding a business card: "Take it, please…"

I did. It read 'Ed Birch – Life Coach'.

I nodded, without enthusiasm. "Thanks, but I'm a hopeless case. One of life's failures."

"No such thing. Well…?"

"Cecil."

"Well, Cecil, my friend, today is the first day of your new life."

And it was.

Under Ed's guidance, I learned that damaged people *can* heal themselves. Over weeks and months I started to believe in myself, to like myself. I was liberated from the yoke of failure. I literally grew in stature as well as in confidence. My constant desire to do well overwhelmed me and, much to my amazement and joy, I became a winner.

No longer was I afraid of confrontation or competition. In fact, I sought them as a way of honing my new found confidence. My self-belief became unstoppable. I could do no wrong. I couldn't fail.

"I'm amazed, Cecil. I truly am," Ed said. "There is nothing more I can do for you. It's in your own hands from now on."

I stood tall and proud. "You got me started, Ed. The rest I did for myself."

He nodded. "Now, how do you feel like doing something for me in return? I'm away next week and stuck for someone to run a life skills seminar for me. You could do it – just tell them about your own experience. Inspire them."

I knew it would be a piece of cake. "Yeah, why not."

As soon as I entered the seminar room an overwhelming aura of negativity enveloped me. It stuck in my throat and stifled me. I looked at the faces sitting before me and saw a roomful of pathetic losers – no enthusiasm, no ambition, no desire – just hollow, useless, empty shells.

I stared each one of them down until they looked away, and then asked why they had come. I felt myself resenting their weak and pitiful excuses.

"You're a crowd of neurotic no-hopers," I told them. "Wasting your own money and, more importantly, my time. You'll never change. *Never*. I can tell."

I had no sympathy for their snivelling little lives as I sneered at them. "You're all a waste of space. Get back down to the bottom of the pile where you belong. Back to your insignificant existence, and stop bothering the likes of me. I live in a different world. Another planet. One that you'll never inhabit. Thank God."

I felt ten feet tall.

Heads down, they slowly shambled out of the room. A skinny blonde-haired woman was nearly out of the door when she turned half-heartedly and started to remonstrate with me: "You can't say that to us…"

Her feeble whining really irritated me. "What! Who do you think you are, you nasty little slag."

I'd had enough. I stepped forward and hit her across the mouth with the back of my hand, then punched her in the stomach and, as she crumpled on to the floor, I put the boot in. Ha! That soon shut her up, the snivelling little nobody.

The Magistrate looked poker-faced at me. "You were in a position of trust and you carried out a particularly nasty and unprovoked attack on this vulnerable young woman who you were supposed to be helping."

Yeah, yeah. Yawn, yawn… Who does this bloke think he is? God. Can't he see the little wretch deserved it.

"Your solicitor has said you were under the misguided notion that you were somehow superior to the lady you attacked but, in reality, you are nothing more than an egotistical bully."

He glared at me again. "You will go to prison for six months."

"Another friend for you, Smithy," the prison officer said, as he pushed me roughly into the cell.

The other occupant had his back to me as he spoke. "Whoever you are, you need to know that I'm as hard as nails and …"

My nightmare had begun.

THE VASE

I am sitting here looking at the vase.

It's black and red. And tall. Sitting on a little doily.

I'd rather be with you. Of course I would.

If I were...Ah well, who knows what I'd be doing? We might well talk about getting a hamster from Fortnum and Mason's or some other juvenile nonsense.

Like when we very first went out together and wanted to keep our romance secret – we walked hand in hand. You wearing your high viz vest! Half the neighbourhood could see us. Possibly passing aeroplanes too.

The vase is looking at me now. I don't mind. I mean...what can it see? An oldish bloke, with thinning hair and a 'lived in' face.

It's more elegant than I am. Sitting there straight, stately and superior, while I slouch on the settee, my thoughts scurrying around.

How did it get here? The vase I mean. All the way from China? Come to think of it how did *I* get here, all the way from my roots – tin baths, horse manure, outside loos, black-leaded grates, German bombs, evacuation. Rationing...

Oh yes, I remember glimpses of it now. It's been a long, long journey; a struggle sometimes. Full of happiness and heartache. Mainly happiness.

It seems like five minutes, not seventy odd years.

Here I am sitting on my settee. Still looking at the vase. Thinking how the hell did I end up living in my little flat, alone. The two loves in my life gone forever. Dead. Finito. Caput. Laid to rest in their little boxes. Cried over by us all, until the tears slowly wash away the hurt, the helplessness we feel.

Now, only out-of-focus memories ebb and flow. Part of me went with them; part of my spark. I know it will never return.

You know, don't you. You have been there too. Perhaps we both should be standing on doilies to soak up the tears and sadness that occasionally explode within us without rational cause.

Strange, isn't it. How life captures our emotions, juggles them around and gradually wears them down like stones on the shore, their intensity diminished. We may act like teenagers at times but without their exuberance, their vitality. Without their loud shouts of excitement and wonder.

These days our recklessness is measured.

But although we have become more subdued, more cautious, the passion for life still bubbles within, fuelling the engine that keeps us going.

Inside we know what really matters in life. Know it is not material things. We know what happiness is. What contentment is. What love looks like.

How lucky we are to have found each other, and connected. To have found love again, when so many sit alone, dwelling on the past, sharpening fading memories into what might-have-beens.

They can only dream about being with someone like you, or me. To experience love again. Having someone to live for. Someone close, to care for.

I can sit here and say to the vase, "That's enough."

Put on my coat and walk to be with you. Hear your voice. Feel your warmth. Taste your lips.

Others may continue to sit and watch the vase.

Not only does it see them, it may also speak. "Stop looking at me," it will say. "We vases were born to be silent, unattached, unapproachable. Made to stand alone. You humans are not like that. Life goes on for you. It changes. Grasp its opportunities. Go and find someone to love. All the other lost souls are waiting. Waiting for your love."

DADDY'S GIRL

"Best steer clear of Tod," they said. "He's a weirdo." Everyone in the village knew it. "He's joined at the hip to his mother. Real close they are, except when he's in the psychiatric unit." And he often was.

But I didn't care; his reputation didn't scare me.

I'm El by the way. Short for Eleanor.

Tod was twenty-two, my age, and good looking. Correction – he was a magnificent hunk of man. I'd watched him working in his garden and I knew he'd noticed me too. I could feel his hungry eyes stripping my clothes off, leaving me walking naked. Oh...it felt good.

I dream about him most nights. Fantasise about romance, and other things. Respite before my black nightmares start. I can't click back to him after that; I just curl up trembling, trying to erase the powerful thoughts that take over my mind. You don't want to know about them, you really don't – all that blood and viciousness. Not done *to* me, you understand, done *by* me.

Daddy pays for my Psychiatrist. Dr. Stone says my disturbance is caused by Daddy leaving Mommy and me when I was eight. He says that I am an innocent victim.

Mommy has MS and Daddy pays for all her treatment, a special car and everything. The divorce and her condition make her vulnerable. But that's her problem, not mine. She's good at squeezing loads of cash out of Daddy. Without it we'd be penniless.

Dr. Stone says because I need Daddy to keep bankrolling me I have transferred all my hostility on to his new wife. Mommy and me call her The Slut.

Dr. S. says that the hate I feel, and the damage I do to her in my dreams, is perfectly normal. My self-mutilation, he says, is because I feel so guilty about wanting to kill her that I am punishing myself.

Mind you, I think he changed his diagnosis somewhat on the day he called The Slut my stepmother. *Stepmother!* I saw red and hit him with the paperweight on his desk, breaking his nose. After that he said I had psychopathic tendencies.

A look in my full length mirror each morning tells me I'm beautiful – face, eyes, hair, figure; every detail is faultless. Thanks to Daddy I have plenty of cash; he tries to buy back the hurt he caused me and as far as I am concerned he succeeds – nice car, holidays, expensive clothes, a credit card. I don't need to work, of course.

I really love Daddy, and his money. It's The Slut I *hate*.

The only thing missing in my life is a boyfriend. Don't get me wrong. With my looks they are queuing up. *Keeping* one after the first date is the problem. One even said I was weird – to my face. Would you believe it – *to my face!* I paid a couple of blokes in a pub five hundred pounds to break his leg. As it worked out they must have misheard me: they broke both legs and an arm as well. Well, it serves him right, the creep. A lady should be treated with respect.

My ordeal started so innocently – let me tell you about it. It was a lovely sunny day, all blue skies and vapour trails. I put on a cool flimsy dress, intending to walk through the village to the river. As I passed Tod's house I saw him in the garden, back towards me, bending over, in shorts. *Wow!* He looked so powerful and magnificent. I stopped and said something schoolgirlish like "bottoms up." I could feel myself blush as I said it.

He straightened up, smiled, and walked towards me. Oh what a fine specimen of manhood – I would have swooned had I known how.

"Hello," he said. "What's a beautiful woman like you doing chatting up a fella like me? Don't you know my reputation?"

I fluttered my eyelids. "Of course I do, that's what makes you interesting."

Next thing I knew I was sitting in his kitchen drinking a glass of red wine.

We got on well. He didn't seem weird at all. Not until I went to leave, that is.

"Sorry, El. I can't let you go," he said, just like that. "You're so pretty I want to look after you forever."

I was not totally surprised. In fact I was banking on something like this happening. But I couldn't let him know that, could I? No way was I scared, rather flattered, in fact.

I intentionally misunderstood. "Okay, Tod, I'll stay a little longer if you want me to."

"No, you don't understand." He looked anxious. "Mommy is in Australia for a month, so we have the house to ourselves. After that you can live in my room, Mommy doesn't go in there."

Mommy?

I sobbed into my hands. "You mean... I'm a prisoner...?" A good performance I thought.

"No...no, more a guest, staying as my friend." He was trying to reassure me. "But..." his face suddenly hardened and he flicked open a lethal looking knife "if you try to escape I will have to cut your face or kill you." His eyes became vacant as he waved the knife in the air. "I use it to kill cats and dogs all the time, then I bury them in the garden. Killing a woman would be just the same, just more blood..."

Ugh! I didn't know whether to laugh or cringe; I thought it sensible to do the latter. Hand over my eyes, I looked at him through slatted fingers.

"I'm sorry, El," he said. "Haven't been taking my medication since Mommy went." He was smiling again. "I don't want to hurt you – you are my friend." He put the knife back into his pocket.

I asked Tod to show me round the house. His bedroom was all subdued lighting. The dark blue walls were covered with posters and magazine pages, each depicting someone killing or being killed. *And I thought I had problems!*

"These people were my friends." He pointed to the posters. "But now I have you."

Oh well, that's okay then.

Then he became all sheepish and said hesitantly, "Can I kiss you, El? I have never kissed a woman before."

Oh yes! I gave him a gentle kiss, something I had been longing to do since we met, then more passionately, pulling his body towards me. I broke away when I was sure he was aroused.

"Enough now, perhaps more later," I said, smoothing my dress over my body.

He stood there, overawed. Gobsmacked. Like a kid in a sweet shop for the first time.

His mother's room was fab – all frills and chintz; cream silk sheets, with delicately patterned duvet and curtains. Persian rugs covered the oak floor. Mirrors everywhere. It was a dream. Just like a film star's boudoir.

"Right, Tod," I said, in the most commanding voice I could find. "As your friend and guest, I'll sleep in here."

"No, you can't...this is Mommy's room..." His voice tailed off, unsure.

So I helped him. "What a pity. This is a ladies' room. You could watch me undress in here. I could pretend to be your Mommy, like this..." I slipped the straps off my shoulders and let my dress fall to my waist.

There was a little hesitation, but not much.

"Yes, yes, I would like that," he whispered as he stepped forward and touched me.

I kissed him on the cheek and moved away. "Off you go then and fetch Mommy some tea."

He went, like a lamb.

The wardrobes and drawers were full of expensive dresses and underwear – my size as it happened. Most look unworn. When Tod returned with the tea, I was posing, reclined on the bed in one his mother's more revealing negligées.

He looked totally confused seeing desirable me wearing his mother's clothes, sitting on her bed – well, who wouldn't be? I thought he might be angry, so I quickly guided his emotions by putting his hand on my thigh. "Come to Mommy." I kissed him passionately. Just enough to get him going, no more.

Then I turned my back on him, let the negligée fall to the floor, and walked naked into the bathroom.

"Mommy will be down for dinner at six," I said, closing the door.

I wore a stunning off-the-shoulder red dress, with diamond necklace and earrings, hair done up. His mother's Chanel No. 5 surrounded me. I had seldom looked so good. A real knockout.

As I walked into the dining room I heard the breath leave his body through his open mouth. I could see the eager desire in his eyes.

"Give Mommy a kiss," I murmured.

He moved across the room as though mesmerised and went to kiss me on the cheek.

"Silly boy. That's not how to kiss Mommy, is it?"

I gave him a lingering kiss, persisting until our lips melted together. Oh what joy; my stomach began to flutter. Oh, how I wanted him...but no, not yet. Not yet.

"Good boy. Now let's have dinner, shall we?"

Afterwards we did what Tod and his mother did most nights – played cards, watched TV, held hands, and talked.

At ten o'clock I announced I would be retiring to my bedroom and didn't want to be disturbed until he brought me breakfast in the morning. Now that's what I call self-sacrifice. I craved to have his body close to mine, touching me, making love. Ah well, that would come.

The pattern continued for a week or more – cosy flirting and brief sexual arousal. Tod was an enthusiastic carer; I could tell he was beginning to worship me, just like he worshipped his mother. Well, why not? I was worth it wasn't I?

Yes, things were working out well.

We often talked about death and killing – subjects that fascinated us both. What would it be like to kill a human being, a real person?

"Would you really dare to?" I asked him one night.

He was unsure, but I could tell the idea attracted him.

Then the crunch question:

"What if someone had hurt *me*, Tod, had caused me great pain – someone I hated and wanted dead. Would you kill them for me?"

"I would do anything for you, El, you know that."

"Me too." I lied.

We celebrated this pledge by cutting our wrists and letting the blood mingle together. No big deal. Cutting was not a new experience for me.

That night as I went up to bed I said to him, "You can sleep in Mommy's bed tonight, Tod, that's if you want to."

He was clad in just pyjama bottoms as his bare feet padded into my room.

I stood in front of him and pulled the cord. It was like setting off an explosive charge – a great unleashing of passion. He was magnificent. Oh God, what pleasure! All my fantasies come true.

Before I sent him back to his room, I told him about The Slut, how I hated her and how I wanted her killed. If he did it, I said I would stay with him forever.

Next morning when he brought my breakfast, he asked me for all her details and then said he had arrangements to make and would not be returning until late.

When he did return he was elated. Hyper. On such a high he was shaking. He rushed in, shouting "I've done it, El!.I've killed her for you! I've killed her!" He was ecstatic, jigging around the kitchen.

I joined in: "Tell me, tell me..." I shouted excitedly "Tell me how..."

He told me in great detail how he had cut the brake pipes on her car and tampered with the petrol tank so that it would explode on impact. Then he waited. It was dark when she drove away from the house. He followed her for about a mile until on a sharp left hand bend her car crashed into a wall and burst into flames.

His eyes lit up. "It was an inferno, El," he said, "nobody could have survived that ball of fire! Nobody!"

"Hallelujah!" I blurted out. "The Slut is dead!" *Now my nightmares can stop.*

We hugged each other and danced around the kitchen like mad people. Tod whispered in my ear, "Now you can stay with me forever."

"Yes, I will. And Mommy has another treat for you. One you will never forget." I had prepared everything.

We went into my bedroom and I undressed, standing naked before him.

"Tie me to the bed and I will be your slave for the night."

He tied my wrists and ankles to the bed rails. "Tighter, tighter..." I was urging him on.

What happened after that was the most satisfying experience of my life – we were both high on adrenalin, both steeped in our own powerful emotions – *my* tormentor was dead. *He* had killed his first human being.

Drained, at the end of our celebration, he untied me. The Slut was dead! We lay in bed revelling in every detail of the killing, again and again.

I leaned across him and picked up his knife from the bedside table. "Could you have killed her with this?"

Tod nodded excitedly. I handed him the knife. "How would you have done it?"

He put the point of the blade just under my left breast. "Just there," he said, nicking my skin.

We watched as the drops of blood slowly trickled down my stomach.

"My turn." I took the knife from him and put the point over his heart.

"Just there?"

As he nodded I pushed the handle with all my strength. I felt the blade slide smoothly between his ribs. He didn't realise what had happened until the blood spurted out. Then it was too late.

"Thank you, Tod," I said, "for killing The Slut."

But I doubt if he heard me. Probably too preoccupied with other thoughts.

As I stood up, his blood was soaking into the cream silk sheets. His open eyes had a look of surprise. Perhaps we are all surprised when we die...?

I ran out of the house screaming. A passing motorist took me to the police station. Hysterically I told them of my ordeal – of being held a prisoner, being kept tied up, and being forced to dress as his mother, of being his sexual slave.

Tonight he had raped me and said he was finally going to kill me. I was desperate. I picked up his knife and somehow found the courage to stab him. I had no choice did I? Is he badly injured?

The Police Surgeon confirmed I had been raped, and noted the rope burns on my wrists and ankles. He even found the cut on my wrist, and on my chest at the spot where he was going to knife me. He said I was in shock and gave me a sedative to make me sleep.

I woke up in the hospital, feeling groggy but otherwise okay after my ordeal. The police lady told me that unfortunately Tod had died of his injury. *Oh dear.* I cried and she put her arm around me. There would be no charges brought against me, she said. I was an innocent victim. He had a long psychiatric history and was known to be sadistic and a weirdo. I would hear no more about it.

They said I should remain in hospital for a few days in order to properly recover. I did.

Mommy came and took me home by taxi. She looked and talked funny, as though she was having one of her bad days. Perhaps that's why she wasn't driving.

When we arrived home I noticed my car was missing from the drive. A man was hammering a 'For Sale' sign into the front lawn. I looked anxiously at Mommy's pale exhausted face for an explanation. "Mommy...?"

She put up her hand to stop me; tears were rolling down her cheeks. She was finding it hard to speak.

"I'm sorry to tell you this, El, dear, after all you have been through...Daddy has been killed in a car accident. Burned to death. His Will says he left everything to The Slut. Absolutely everything..."

HER ISLANDS

"Thirty-five years, Malcolm. Thirty-five bloody years! That's how long I've put up with your sodding ultra-cautious, introverted and boring behaviour. And yes, before you say it, I know, I'm a flighty airhead with a tendency to drink and swear too bloody much."

He raised his eyes to the ceiling. "And don't I know it, Pam, my dear."

Her voice became assertive.

"Well, *I've* decided we are going to do something about it! *We,* my darling stick-in-the-mud husband, are going to swap personalities. I'll be you, you be me. Then we'll bugger off on holiday to try it out."

Malcolm took a deep breath, knowing the futility of arguing. "Okay, you're on, my dear." His impulsive reply was immediately followed by an enveloping apprehension: he just knew his cosy, conservative world was about to be blown apart.

Pam fancied 'Her Islands' for the holiday.

"Where the hell's that?"

She showed him the brochure. "There…"

It read: *Greek Mainland and Her Islands*………..

They fell about laughing.

Two weeks later, in their hotel, they sat soaking up the fading rays of the evening sun in the small terraced dining room. It was typically Greek – simple, with just enough refinement to avoid being an archaeological site. Hungry cats wandered silently beneath the tables seeking scraps from cat-lovers, unsettling the other diners.

"Just arrived, have you?"

They turned towards the sound and were met by two eager smiling faces at the next table.

Malcolm wasn't sure his transformed personality was ready to meet anyone yet. His hesitant "Yes" triggered an immediate response: their hands shot out, waiting to be shaken.

"Ya Soo. I'm Derek, and this is Karen, my wife."

They smiled self-consciously.

"Malcolm and Pam...nice to meet you."

Pam ran her practised eye over them: they were about mid-forties. She, once pretty, was battling to retain her looks. Her revealing cleavage was arranged to create a distraction from her face. It almost succeeded.

His handsome good looks were complemented by expensive, well-chosen clothes. He reminded her of a younger Malcolm – reliable, fastidiously boring, but a real gentleman.

Malcolm too ran his eye over them. All *he* noticed was Karen's gaping top.

When coffee came, Derek leaned across. "Fancy a drink in the bar after coffee?"

"Thanks, Derek, mate, but we're bloody knackered after the flight. Thought we'd stretch our legs and then have an early night. Perhaps tomorrow, yeah?"

Karen winked at Malcolm. "Don't do anything we wouldn't," she giggled. "We don't want any heart attacks do we, Malc?"

Laughter all round.

Back in their room Malcolm and Pam fell into bed, happy with their first night and surprisingly at ease with their newly adopted personalities.

In the soft sunlight of Zante's early morning, they enjoyed breakfast on the terrace, sharing a table with their new acquaintances, Karen and Derek.

Karen admired Malcolm's lively Hawaiian shirt, which he wore with long baggie shorts and sandals; for the first time in his life he wore them without socks. His eyes spoke volumes as they ogled her low cut blouse.

Their partners, by contrast, sat primly, giving each other knowing and sympathetic glances. Karen's hand brushed Malcolm's leg under the table.

"Sleep well, Romeo?"

"Like a dream, my Treasure."

Her face screwed up, unsure of her new title. Malcolm laughed. "Oh sorry, love – it's because of your big chest. Treasure...Chest. Get it?"

They smirked like two teenagers.

Derek looked embarrassed. "Is he always like this, Pam?" he whispered, his dark eyes full of understanding.

She nodded.

"I sympathise," he said quietly. "I keep telling Karen that all those low-cut flouncy clothes will...well, you know."

"Give the wrong impression?" Pam offered.

Pam knew she was falling under Derek's spell; she was attracted to him. She felt they had an unspoken bond.

All four of them seemed to accept the situation naturally. They became closer, slipping in and out of each other's company like life-long friends.

A couple of days later, on Derek and Karen's balcony, Pam lazily flicked through a pile of magazines as they waited for pre-dinner drinks. She pulled out a glossy brochure and was about to open it when Derek hurriedly put the drinks on the table and took it out of her hands.

"It's nothing," he said defensively. "Villas in Cyprus. Friend of mine built them."

His curt manner cut the topic dead.

"Crisps and things..." Karen breezed on to the balcony. "Oh, he's showing you our bargain holiday home is he?" She beamed at them both. "Got it at cost you know. One hundred and fifty thousand instead of two hundred. It'll double its value in two years."

She picked up the brochure and waved it. "And you know what? There's a guaranteed rental income of twelve thousand pounds each year for five years. That's why we're here – it's booked solid for the next two months."

Pam and Malcolm felt obliged to look interested. Pam gave an envious smile. "We never seem to have that kind of luck, do we, Malcolm? Cyprus sounds lovely."

Derek, they noticed, put the brochure back into the pile. As he did so, Karen grabbed his arm. "If they're interested, can't you get Gerald to let Pam and Malcolm have the last one?"

Derek waved her quiet, his tone sharp. "No. Out of the question. He won't want to do that, you know what he's like." He glared at her. "Let it drop, Karen."

Karen's smile retreated as she glared back defiantly.

"You're as bad as he is, you old grump. These are our friends." Her voice became demanding. "Ring Gerald now!"

Derek didn't move.

Pam tried to diffuse the looming row. "Look, it doesn't matter. Really. Don't fall out because of it." She took Malcolm's arm and walked him away. "We'll give you some space."

"Yeah," Malcolm was clearly upset. "We'll be in the bar."

He was downing his third pina colada when Karen burst into the bar and rushed over to them, breathless: "Wonderful news. I persuaded my blockhead husband to call his friend. The last villa on the site is sticking and he's anxious to get over to Florida to start his next project..."

Malcolm, still upset by Derek's off-hand behaviour, cut her short. "Drink?" he snapped.

Karen didn't answer. Instead, she jumped up and down and screamed "Gerald's agreed! You can have it!"

At this point Derek strode in and, after ordering a round of drinks, began to apologise.

"I'm sorry, you two. Gerald insisted I keep it to myself, you see. But I've explained that you are friends of ours, and he's happy for you to have the last villa...that's if you want it, of course." His face broadened into a smile. "And the good news is: he's prepared to let you have it for a hundred and fifty thousand! But he needs to know quickly."

They looked at each other, then at Derek, and then at Karen as she spoke: "If you don't feel it's right for you, fine, we'll understand, no harm done." She shrugged her shoulders as she smiled. "But we thought it would be nice to give you first refusal."

Derek laughed. "No pressure folks."

Pam admired his ability to mix business with pleasure so easily. He was genuinely trying to help them.

"It sounds wonderful. Thank you, but we are naïve in these things. Do you have any more details? Service charges, how the rental system works, that sort of thing?"

"You're in luck. As it happens they're all in my notebook in the bedroom," Derek replied. "Come and have a look. Have the brochure as well, then you can sleep on it."

They were just finishing their coffee at breakfast next morning when Derek and Karen joined them. "Okay you two, what's the verdict?" Karen asked eagerly.

"Seems bloody fantastic to me, Treasure," replied Malcolm raising his eyes momentarily from her plunging top, "but Pam's the one who's a wow with figures. Me, I like the other kind..." He winked at Karen.

"Behave yourself, Malcolm. One of us has to be sensible." Pam was irritated, but all eyes were on her.

"Well," she finally said, "the place looks magnificent. It's up and running so all the figures are accurate – a wonderful opportunity for us to make some money for the rest of our retirement."

She looked at Derek, her face becoming serious. "We appreciate you doing this for us, we really do, but I'm afraid the answer has to be no. I've spoken to our bank and when we scrape everything together we are still twenty thousand pounds short." She shook her head and began to cry. "I'm really sorry...we so wanted to be part of it. We feel we are letting you down."

Malcolm too shook his head, as he muttered, "Another bloody dream down the drain. Story of our lives."

It was Karen who broke the silence. "Come on, Pam, it's not the end of the world. I can't bear the thought of you losing the chance of a lifetime. There must be a way around it."

After a moment's thought she turned to Derek. "We're not short of a bob or two, can't we...you know...lend it to them?"

Derek suddenly came alive. "You're a marvel, Karen! Not just a pretty face, is she?"

Pam shook her head. "No. We couldn't possibly. I don't like going into debt, particularly from friends. No. No, thank you all the same."

Malcolm got up and walked away, shoulders slumped.

Derek bent down in front of Pam and took her hand. "Oh, come on, Pam. It isn't like a proper loan – you can pay us as and when from rental income or when you sell." He looked up into her tear stained eyes. "We all have our pride but please don't forfeit the chance of a lifetime, my dear. You'll only regret it, you know you will."

Pam knew he was right. She put her head into her hands and began to cry again.

"Look," said Derek, "if we give you a bank draft for twenty thousand pounds, and you give us one for a hundred and fifty grand, that's all it needs. You will have to clear ours first, of course, to top up your account but, what the hell, we trust each other, don't we?"

53

Pam turned to Malcolm, who was standing apart from them, twisting a handkerchief in his hands. He looked such a forlorn figure she couldn't help smiling through her tears as she steered him back to his chair.

"I can't have him looking like this forever, can I. Not in his Hawaiian shirt..."

"So the answer is ...?" Derek asked expectantly.

"Yes. It's yes! Thank you, Derek, and you, Karen. Thank you," Pam said simply, putting her hand on Derek's suntanned arm. "But I insist we do it properly, draw up a proper loan agreement."

"Well done, you won't regret it. I'll ring Cyprus and have them draw up the deeds and I'll send payment as soon as your bank draft clears."

Malcolm's mood changed dramatically: he became animated, a man transformed. "Well, what are we waiting for folks, let's get bloody cracking!" He looked at Pam. "When can we be ready, sweetheart?"

"Well, straight away, I suppose. The money's there and waiting. When do you think, Derek? Bank drafts the day after tomorrow?"

Derek nodded his agreement.

"I'll drink to that!" shouted Malcolm excitedly. "Champagne all round."

"Just a mineral water for me." Pam tried to calm his eagerness.

"And for me," added Derek laughing. "We financial wizards need to keep a clear head."

"Looks like a whole bottle of bloody champers for you and me then, Treasure," said Malcolm, as he headed for the bar.

As soon as Pam confirmed that the twenty thousand pounds was in their account, she gave Derek their bank draft for the full amount, kissing him on the cheek as she did so, hoping it would convey her feelings towards him.

"Thank you," she said tenderly, "you're so wonderful."

He gave her a hug. "My pleasure, Pam, dear. I'll order a taxi to take this into town and wire the money off to Cyprus."

Malcolm stuck his head into the open taxi window. "See you in the bar later, folks. Champers this time, I insist... then we can plan our trip to Cyprus."

They laughed, smiles of joy all round.

When Karen and Derek returned two hours later, they were certainly not smiling. Devastated and fuming would be more accurate. They had been told the bank draft was counterfeit. Counterfeit! They couldn't believe it!

They rushed back to the hotel, only to find that Pam and Malcolm had checked out. No forwarding address.

Reception said a note had been left. They read it together:

DEAR KAREN AND DEREK,
WE WERE PRACTISING *THAT*
SCAM WHEN YOU WERE
STILL AT SCHOOL.
BETTER LUCK NEXT TIME.
LOVE, PAM AND MALCOLM. xx

The ferry to Kefalonia – another one of 'Her Islands' – was half an hour late.

"I think I'll complain about the delay, Malcolm."

"Keeping the same roles are we then, sweetheart?" he chuckled.

Pam nodded. "Yes, of course we are."

"Suits me fine," he said, smiling. "I'm bloody enjoying it!" He winked at her. "How do you fancy flying on to Cyprus, my little Treasure?"

Pam's face showed a pained expression. "What do you mean 'little'?" she exclaimed, thrusting out her chest.

GEORGY PORGY

"Don't Mommy, please don't... No. Noooo. Aaah!"

It is my first childhood memory, the one that still triggers my horrendous nightmares. My Mommy is pushing my naked body into the icy cold water of the garden pond. Her hand on my head, pushing. Pushing me right under the freezing water and holding me there until I run out of breath and am forced to take in mouthfuls of the stinking water.

The memory is still vivid – our footsteps in the snow covered garden, the crack-crack as she breaks the ice with a hammer.

I was about three years old.

As I try to climb out, half drowned, my small body shivering and convulsing, she grabs my hair and pushes me under again.

Her words then, and repeated throughout my childhood, chill me to this very day. *"Remember, Georgy, my child, you will always belong to Mommy."*

When I finally climbed out, coughing and spluttering, totally exhausted, Mommy had gone. Gone into the house and locked the door.

I was alone. Shivering and sobbing uncontrollably.

My childhood was dominated by these cruel sadistic 'punishments' – being locked in a tiny cupboard, bent over for hours. Being deprived of food for days, being put into icy or scalding baths, being beaten with a stick until I couldn't stand. Sometimes she would wake me up in the middle of the night and make me stand in the corner of the bedroom, naked, with my arms above my head. When I put them down, which I had to do eventually, she would beat me. Her cruelty towards me was relentless.

Each episode seemed worse than the one before and the fear of what was to come and the words preceding it: *"Remember, Georgy, my child, you will always belong to Mommy"* made me wet myself. Every time.

Something Mommy seemed to take a delight in.

As I grew older I began to realise that the reason I was made to endure her sadistic behaviour was because she had wanted a girl, not a boy. She *hated* little boys. Despised them. And men. The pain and humiliation I suffered throughout my childhood was her way of showing me that, as a boy, I meant less than nothing to her.

When I was ten I found my father hanging from a tree in the garden. He was just hanging there, swaying in the breeze, a rope around his neck. His body was loose and his face pale. He seemed to be smiling in a funny lopsided way. He didn't respond when I spoke to him and, when I held his hand, it was cold.

I wondered whether Mommy had killed him and whether she would try to do the same to me. I knew she was capable. When I went into the house to tell her Daddy was dead, hanging from the apple tree, Mommy picked up the stick and beat me until I was bleeding all over and then threw me, whimpering, into the little cupboard. At that moment I longed to join my Daddy in death.

Although we were not a wealthy family, my father's job in the insurance industry meant that his death, even by his own hand, ensured Mommy was well provided for.

As soon as she received the money, she packed me off to Boarding School and paid extra for them to keep me at holiday times. I saw this as her final act of rejection.

From then on my only contact with her were the periodic letters she sent me. They all said the same thing. *"Remember, Georgy, my child, you will always belong to Mommy."*

Nothing else.

I didn't write back.

I know it sounds strange, but I had somehow come to believe that Mommy's vindictive behaviour was normal. Because I knew nothing else, I suppose. It wasn't until I started Boarding School that I discovered the truth – that the other boys had mothers who didn't beat them senseless. They were to experience it now, of course, from the older boys and the Masters. It made them feel afraid, upset and homesick.

I felt none of those emotions. I was hardened to worse. Much, much worse.

As I got even older I realised that bullying the younger boys, which was the custom, gave me a sense of power. It was also my experience that very occasionally a boy seemed to *enjoy* being beaten. It gave him some sort of perverted pleasure and he would come back willingly for more. I could never understand the psychology of it but I began to recognise the subtle signs in the new boys, the ones who were fawning and submissive, and who would let you do anything to them. It was as if by hurting them I somehow made them whole.

In a way I envied them, for they knew their place in the world.

Sheltered from Mommy's violent outbursts I began to do well at Boarding School. I gained six 'A' Levels and at eighteen I won a Scholarship to Bristol University to study English Literature.

Money was always tight and in my second year, to supplement my income, I embarked on a small enterprise giving discreet massages to older women. I called it 'Massage to Heaven'. Financially it was a huge success and I became proficient at giving full-body massage. Most wanted just that – to be pampered and de-stressed for half an hour by the soothing hands of a young man. Some, I could tell, and they invariably asked, wanted sex as well and these I passed on to a rota of my University chums, operating from a tastefully furnished bedroom above the shop I rented. Either way, the ladies loved it.

My gentle massage technique for new clients included a tentative pinch on the buttocks. Nothing too severe. When they complained, as most did, I would apologise profusely and blame it on cramp in my fingers, and then resume my usual soothing style. Very occasionally there was no complaint and I repeated the pinch more sharply. These women seemed to tolerate it, even enjoy it, just as the boys at school had. Using the instincts I had built up there I would subject a few women to increasingly greater pain on each visit. I knew full well that in doing so I was getting rid of my pent up feelings of hostility towards Mommy. Acting out my 'revenge', if you like, on these vulnerable women. Because they enjoyed being hurt, I could justify it by saying I was not harming them. They *wanted* to be punished. No one was forcing them to attend my sessions. They chose to, knowing the increasing pain, degradation and humiliation I would inflict. I had no conscience about it.

It was about this time I learned from the family solicitor that Mommy had died after jumping from the roof of a psychiatric hospital. According to the police she had been shouting abuse at someone called Georgy just before she jumped. I chose not to attend the funeral. I couldn't face it. Surprisingly, I felt angered by the news. At the manner of her final rejection of me, I suppose – killing herself while still abusing me verbally. But despite everything she was my Mommy, the only one I had. And now she was gone. And I was upset.

The unfortunate lady who felt the backlash of my feelings was called Mary. She was my mother's age and had similar looks. I subjected Mary to the most cruel things I could think of – degrading sexual acts, cigarette burns, cutting, beatings. I even sent her, terrified and naked, into the rat infested cellar. She was a quivering wreck, although she still came back for more. But I couldn't oblige. It was as though I had worked all the revenge and hatred out of my system. I had no more left. And no Mommy to hate. I continued inflicting pain, yes, because for a few it was an expected part of the service they had paid for, just as massage was. But not malicious or cruel. I no longer felt the need.

About this time, perhaps coinciding with the extinction of my anger towards Mommy, I came to consciously realise, for the first time, that I gained no sexual pleasure from massaging naked middle-aged women. What I wanted, what I *needed*, was a girlfriend of my own age who could satisfy the intimacy and sexual feelings which were now emerging within me.

During Mary's early visits, she had told me, with great pride, about her daughter, Francesca. Even showed me a photograph. Now, months later, as I was beating her with a cane, I asked Mary if she would arrange a date for me with her daughter. I felt her stiffen.

"No way!" she said. "No way am I introducing my Francesca to a monster like you. You would ruin her innocent life."

I suddenly became angry and Mary's body jerked as I laid a harder than usual thwack on her bottom.

"That, my dear Mary," I shouted, "is the last pain I shall ever inflict upon you. I never want to see you here again."

"But I can't. She's my only child. You will destroy her life. I don't want her turning out like me. Surely you can see that…" She was crying.

I threw her clothes at her. "Out!" I shouted angrily, "and don't bother coming back."

She did, of course. Come back, that is. We both knew she would.

She had set up a date for Francesca and me at a local restaurant.

Francesca was simply beautiful. She had her mother's slender build, was softly spoken and shy.

She blushed when I first spoke to her.

"Has your mother told you anything about me?"

I tried to appear casual.

"No. Nothing. Only that your name is George and that she met you at the health club she goes to."

She paused and her lovely green eyes sparkled. "I have a little flat of my own and work funny hours in an old people's home, so we don't really see much of each other these days."

I nodded my understanding.

"I'm at the University. In my final year. I might stay on for a doctorate if I do okay."

"I wish I was brainy like that. I live a very sheltered life, I'm afraid." Her eyes looked down in embarrassment. "I've never really had a boyfriend," she said softly.

"Me neither." I laughed nervously. "A girlfriend, I mean…"

She gave me a gorgeous genuine smile. "This is new for both of us then. That's nice."

The intimacy of the small restaurant and the wine, helped to reduce our nervousness and we chatted throughout the meal. In fact we got on very well together. A surprise to us both I think. I somehow felt attracted to Francesca. Feelings I had never encountered before – protectiveness, tenderness… others I couldn't put a name to; all mixed up. I wondered if this was how love started.

My past was now behind me – my disastrous childhood, the pent up feelings of anger and revenge. It was all gone

And being replaced by what I think are normal feelings. The ones everyone has. I can't wait to settle into normality and this evening with Francesca is a perfect start. The absolutely perfect dawn of a new life for me.

It was still early when we left the restaurant and as we stood outside I could tell Francesca felt as awkward and as lost as I did.

"Fancy another drink, or something?" I asked her tentatively. "Sorry I can't invite you back. Uni rules and all that…"

Francesca nodded. She hesitated for a moment as though trying to weigh up the situation. "Well, if you don't mind drinking coffee in a tip, my place is just around the corner." She smiled. "Or another bottle of wine if you want…"

"Thanks. That sounds great – if you're sure?"

She nodded with a smile.

At that point, for the first time in my life, I felt totally relaxed around another human being.

We ended up drinking another bottle of wine. It had the effect of giving me the courage to kiss her.

She responded cautiously, blushing and shy, but obviously willing.

Even though we were both nervous, we gradually became increasingly passionate, leading to us starting to undress each other, our inexperienced, excited fingers fumbling with buttons.

"Sorry, George," Francesca whispered, "but I feel so shy, a man seeing me undressed for the first time. Can you shut your eyes, please?" She reached behind a cushion. "Or better still, put this sleep mask on?"

I put it on willingly, feeling it would, somehow, protect my embarrassment too.

We continued to undress each other, kissing passionately all the time, until we were both naked.

I was obviously sexually aroused and my heart was pounding as my hands explored her body. I began to shake uncontrollably in anticipation of the ecstasy that was soon to come. I was losing control...

Francesca took my hands in hers, steered them away from her body, and said softly: "Sorry again, George, but I feel you are about to explode, to lose it."

I knew she was right. Knew that the urge I was feeling would soon be unstoppable.

Francesca gave a little embarrassed laugh. "We women need a little more time to get aroused. Here, let me slow things down. It will be more enjoyable for both of us. Turn over." She helped me turn over on the settee and gently tied my hands behind my back with her scarf. "There, that's better, isn't it?" she said.

The next thing I experienced was a sharp pain on my buttocks, as though from a burning cigarette or candle. It was immediately followed by the thwack of a cane across my feet. It was excruciatingly painful, then my calves, my buttocks and my back, all in quick succession. The pain brought tears to my eyes.

What was happening?

It was unreal, unbelievable. Was it a dream, turning into a nightmare?

The room fell silent, charged with emotion. Neither of us spoke.

I curled up into the foetal position anticipating another blow. But it never came.

Instead, I felt Francesca put something around my neck and tighten it. She took my blindfold off and I could see it was a dog collar. It was attached to a long chain which she used to pull me off the settee on to the floor.

Her voice broke the spell. When she spoke, her words sent a chill right to my heart.

"Now, Georgy, Mommy is going to take you for walkies. I shall untie your hands. If you utter a sound Mommy will beat you. Do you understand?"

My timid "Yes" was followed by an almighty lash across my back by the chain.

"Mommy told you not to speak, didn't she? Get on your hands and knees like a little doggie."

I got on all fours.

"Now bark," she commanded.

I did so, loud and without hesitation.

She led me into the bathroom by the chain and told me to drink from the toilet bowl. I did, lapping water like a dog.

Francesca crouched down in front of me, her beautiful face only inches from mine. When she spoke, her voice was cold and cruel: *"Remember, Georgy, my little one, you will always belong to Mommy."*

I wet myself. I couldn't help it.

I was a child again.

I DON'T *BELIEVE* IT!

"I know desperate times deserve desperate measures," he said, "but it's a stupid idea, Daf. You know we are broke."

They locked eyes. "Exactly, Henry." Her voice was defiant. "A *Superstition* weekend could bring in new business. It's worth a try, surely?"

Mentally she had stamped her feet and he had caved in. They were running out of time and the bills were piling up. "Okay," he muttered. "But no one these days believes all that superstition rubbish do they? I certainly don't."

"No, well of course *you* don't, the high and mighty Henry Brown, owner of the Belvedere Hotel." The sarcasm was tempered with a knowing smile.

"Don't be like that, Daf. You know it's just meaningless twaddle for the feeble minded."

She touched his arm. "Wait till the bookings come rolling in, Henry, then you'll become a believer."

He winced at the thought; he had endured too many disappointments to suddenly become enthusiastic about this latest idea.

Their relationship had always been a verbal battlefield, mostly good natured, but always competitive. It had spurred them on to buy the hotel five years ago. Then, they were full of ideas, but devoid of money and experience. The recession had hit them hard.

Nevertheless, as a team they worked well together and the plan for the coming weekend was soon completed – self-help workshops, a visit to a local haunted house, a quiz and a themed menu. The planning had racked up their optimism, as did the surge of bookings. They could have filled the place twice over.

He put his arms around her and gave her a peck on the cheek. "You're a genius, Daf, my dear," Henry said, as they waited for the guests to arrive. It was Friday the thirteenth.

Henry was relieved that the first guests he welcomed seemed reasonably normal. However this cosy notion evaporated with every phone call saying yet another guest could not possibly travel on Friday the thirteenth. They wouldn't be starting out until after midnight, they said, meaning that the bell in their bedroom rang regularly throughout the night.

"I feel like a bloody yo-yo." Henry was tetchy as he climbed out of bed for the fifth time.

"Can Basil have some milk? It has been a long journey for him, poor thing."

The voice came from under a large hat. He leaned over the counter to see a little old lady and an extremely large black cat.

"I'm afraid we have a policy of no..." Before he could finish, the hat moved hurriedly away.

"Never mind, I will get it myself. This way is it?" She scurried off towards the kitchen, the cat ambling behind in that superior rhythm cats have. What else could he do at three o'clock in the morning. He couldn't throw them out. Henry let them get on with it.

Breakfast time arrived far too quickly.

"What would you like?" asked the man at table number two.

Henry blinked. He knew he was tired but...*I just said that*, he thought.

"I beg your pardon, sir?"

"I beg your pardon, sir?" the man said.

Oh God, the fool's repeating everything I say. Just show him the menu and point to something. Henry let his finger dwell on scrambled egg on toast.

The man nodded, looking relieved. "And coffee, please."

As he moved away Henry noticed the couple in the window table had taken all the crockery and cutlery off their table and were in the process of re-laying it; both wore white gloves. When he returned with scrambled eggs they were folding and unfolding the napkins obsessively.

He was at the other side of the dining room when the smell hit him. *Ugh. Blocked drains* flashed through his mind but his nose told him it was coming from table eight. As he approached, the smell enveloped him. "Eh, Miss Turner, can I see you in the foyer for a moment, please?" He addressed her face, not daring to glance at the offending body. She was perhaps thirty-five and quite pretty in an austere way.

"Yes, of course." Her voice sounded educated.

Henry moved away swiftly, drawing in some fresh air as he went, only to be overwhelmed again when she caught up. *There is no easy way to do this,* he thought. "I'm sorry, but your smell will put the other guests off their breakfast," he said firmly, too embarrassed this time to look at her face.

She hung her head down. "I'm sorry, Mr. Brown. I know I smell." Her eyes searched his, pleading. "But I am so afraid that if I wash and change my clothes something terrible will happen. I just can't do it on my own."

Despite her bizarre behaviour, Henry felt sorry for her. "Why don't I arrange for you to have breakfast in your room and then I will ask my wife, Daphne, to come up and help you with your problem. Say about nine-thirty. How's that?"

Her smile and her eyes were full of gratitude. The smell accompanied her up the stairs. *Oh, Daf will love me for this. Serves her right for inviting a load of cranks.*

As he got to work with the air-freshener, he became aware of a dithering man glued to the bottom stair, desperately clutching the pillar as though his life depended on it. The man had the look of someone about to commit suicide. Henry rushed across. "Everything all right, sir... Mr. Clarke, isn't it?"

The man's shrill reply reflected his body language. "No...No...I can't...I can't..."

"Can't what, sir?"

His wide eyes were full of fear. "It's the wooden floor. I can't possibly step on the cracks. I just can't." He was looking decidedly suicidal again.

"No problem, Mr. Clarke. Just stay there a moment." Henry tried to keep his voice low and steady; he even smiled reassuringly. *God, I can't stand much more of this. Just walk on the floor like me – see, I don't drop dead, do I, when I walk on the cracks?*

He gathered several small carpets from the bar and laid them in a line between the stairs and the dining room. "There you are, sir. You can use them as stepping-stones. How's that?"

The man's manner changed immediately. "Oh, thank you, thank you so much. People don't understand."

Henry thought the man was about to kiss him in gratitude.

"Please have this charm. Keep it with you always for good luck."

Henry looked in his palm. The man had given him a rabbit's foot. *A bloody rabbit's foot!* As Mr. Clarke bounded across the floor, Henry imagined himself succumbing to suicidal tendencies...or even homicidal ones. He went into the kitchen, poured himself a cup of tea and slumped on to a chair. "Do you want the good news or the bad, Daf?"

Daphne pulled her hands out of the sink, picked up a towel and looked at him wearily. "I need cheering up. Give me the good."

He told her about laying the stepping stones.

"Come on, Henry, you're making it up."

"Am I? Well, how about this then – the bad news."

Her face dropped as he told her about the state of Miss Turner in Room Eight. "Think I'm exaggerating? Go up and see for yourself."

She did. He wasn't.

By the time Saturday dinner was over, Henry Brown was distraught. His dream of an efficient, smooth running hotel, full of happy smiling guests enjoying themselves, was in tatters.

"I can't stand much more, Daf," he declared, banging his head down on the kitchen table. "We're having to cater for every obsessive, neurotic, crazy and delusional whim they have in their tiny heads." He raised his head, exhausted. She had never seen him like this before. "They are all deranged.

Absolutely doolally. Have you seen that stuffed owl on table three? She says it's her dead husband."

"You don't have to tell me, Henry. I had to clean up Miss Turner, remember?" Daphne clenched her fist up to her face. "She's dosed up with valium as well. Scared something terrible will happen now she's in fresh clothes. I came very close to fulfilling her delusion, I can tell you."

"It's like a bloody neurotics' convention out there," he said quietly.

Daphne shook her head and gave a weak smile. "And we're in charge, Henry. What does that make us look like?"

When all the guests had departed on Sunday morning, Henry and Daphne spent the rest of the day getting the hotel spick and span again. They fell into bed that night ready to sleep for a week. Soft murmurings, then something silky kept passing over his face…and again. It floated across his dreamlike state. And again. Then a claw ripping down his cheek, piercing his skin, hurting. Suddenly he was awake, eyes struggling to focus. Now he could see it, inches away, sitting on his chest, purring loudly – the big black cat. *Christ Almighty.*

He shot out of bed, a reflex action, his mind still in shock. He felt a strange compulsion to follow the cat…through the door and up the stairs. It stopped outside Room Eight, its luminous green eyes looking up at him.

As Henry opened the door, smoke and flames jolted him wide awake. He rushed into the corridor, found a fire extinguisher and aimed it – Whoosh. The foam spread like a blanket across the flames, suffocating them. Only a haze of smoke remained.

Daphne was by his side, an arm on his shoulder. "Whatever happened, Henry?"

"It's okay, love. A fire, but it's out now. Could have burned the whole place down though. Luckily the cat woke me, brought me to this room."

Daphne frowned at him as she wiped the blood from his cheek. "What cat?"

"The big black one...you know...belonged to the little old lady."

"Oh, come on, Henry, wake up. They went off after breakfast. You saw them leave, remember?"

Henry, suddenly weary, tightened his grip on the rabbit's foot.

THE DISAPPEARING MAN

Karen Sharp was fighting back tears as she looked up at the Solicitor. She struggled to smile. "It's the best thing he's ever done for me. He's gone! Disappeared from my life!"

Dennis Blake, the senior partner, handed her a tissue from his Asda value box. He waited while she dabbed her eyes, noticing the black mascara streak on the white tissue.

He knew the emotional bombardment would continue, so he eased himself back into his padded leather chair, put on his "I understand" face and prepared to nod encouragingly. He had seen it all before.

"He was a real bugger, Mr. Blake." She put her hand to her mouth. "Oh, sorry. But he was. A womaniser, a bully and a drunkard. My life with him was a living hell. I hope he's dead."

He nodded and handed her another tissue.

"Have you reported his disappearance to the police?"

"Yes, weeks ago. They put him on the Missing Persons database – said I was well shot of him. Said it wouldn't be an active case."

She stared at him, his nodding, sympathetic expression was irritating her. She wanted help and advice, not an imitation of the Churchillian dog on TV. "Mr. Blake…?"

"Uh, yes…Right then, Mrs. Sharp."

Silence followed as he gathered his thoughts.

"You may believe he has disappeared for good, or even think he is dead but, in law, I can assure you he is very much alive, until proved otherwise... and therefore still your husband."

It was not what she wanted to hear. The disappointment must have shown in her face. "Sorry." His concern sounded genuine. "I am afraid you cannot get a divorce until he has been missing for seven years, and you certainly cannot touch any of his assets, nor claim on his Life Insurance, nor sell the house until then."

"But I can't wait seven years, Mr. Blake." She began to cry.

"That's the law, I'm afraid. Unless you can persuade the Coroner that your husband is dead, you are stuck with being Mrs. Karen Sharp."

He picked the last tissue out of the box, and blew his nose on it.

Sleep wouldn't come. "Prove he's dead" battered every corner of her mind throughout the long disturbed night.

Morning found her searching through Yellow Pages. She needed to find someone who knew how to investigate these things.

Her high heeled shoes clattered all the way up the two flights of stairs to his office. The sign said 'Samuel Doyle – Private Investigator'. The glass in the door rattled as she knocked it.

He stood with his hand outstretched. "Ah, Mrs. Sharp, come in..."

He was a big man, overweight, sporting a beer belly and a day's stubble. His crumpled shirt needed a wash. A perfect match, she thought, for the shabby surroundings. Her notion that his image may be a sophisticated camouflage was soon destroyed. "Now, my lovely, what can I do for you?"

His leer gave the words another meaning.

She resisted the temptation to walk out again. He moved some papers off a chair and waved her on to it. She was careful not to distract his attention by crossing her legs.

"It's my husband. He's disappeared."

"Want me to find him for you, do you, love." It was more a statement of intent than a question.

"Good God no!" she blurted out "I want you to find evidence that he's dead, and then to persuade the Coroner."

Doyle raised his eyebrows in surprise, but he was already hooked: a pretty woman, lovely perfume - *and* a mystery. "You'd better tell me the whole story, love."

She did.

"What I can't understand, Karen, love, is why you think he's dead?"

She sighed. "I just have this feeling. I can't think he's disappeared on purpose. He would have taken clothes, his credit card, passport, wouldn't he?"

"True," Doyle conceded, with a nod.

"And if he'd had an accident I'd have heard by now. I've checked all the local hospitals."

"Was he the suicidal type?"

"Joe? Christ, no. Thought too much of himself. And bullies are cowards, aren't they? He'd be too afraid to top himself."

Doyle leaned forward and put his elbows on the desk.

"Okay, my love, I'll try and find out what's happened to him. I have a contact in the Coroner's

Office. If I can find evidence that he's dead, I should have no trouble persuading them."

Karen Sharp smiled for the first time.

"If he's dead, I'll have a Life Insurance payout; I'll pay you five thousand pounds for your services."

Doyle leaned closer, taking in her pale blue eyes, and more of her perfume. He returned her smile. "Look, Karen, love, this is how it works: *I* do the bloody work, *I* set the bloody fee." He continued his friendly smile. "If I work my arse off and get nowhere, it costs you nothing – but it still costs me a packet."

He paused to take in her expression.

He could see she understood.

"Good. Now if I can prove he's dead, you stand to make a fortune, right? I think my fee should be at least ten grand, don't you?"

He held out his hand. "Deal?" She took it.

"Yes, it's a deal Sam," she said.

Sam Doyle was an ex-police detective. The general consensus among his colleagues was that he was not a very good one. He had survived in the job for ten years by cutting corners, planting evidence and setting up criminals. Nothing corrupt, as he saw it, no taking back-handers, but he lived on the murky edge of scandal and deceit.

But this was not his downfall, nor the time he spent in his precious garden when he should have been on duty. No, it was someone noticing his face on television, at a Test Match fifty miles from his patch, when he should have been working.

They threw the book at him; dragged up every minor misdemeanour of his career – and there were many. He was lucky to get out on 'health grounds', with his pension intact. It was about this time that his wife left him.

He sank his savings into setting up as a freelance, in a town by the sea, and he rented a flat. He missed his beloved garden. He was just about keeping his head above water financially, always on the lookout for the big break – the super-rich client. Karen Sharp would be a step up the ladder...*if* he could find evidence of her husband's death.

Doyle trawled through the list she had given him – haunts, routines, acquaintances. Locals told him that the *Hope & Anchor* on the list was a thriving pub in the days when the harbour was busy. Now, with no fishing fleet, it looked rundown. When he put his head inside, even at nine o'clock at night, it only had a handful of drinkers.

The landlady looked in her late forties. Despite the hard times she had kept up her appearance – make-up on, hair neatly tied back, and a flouncy blouse that showed enough to catch the eye, but not enough to encourage lusty thoughts. Doyle thought it was all wasted on the assortment of blokes who were tonight's clientele, as they sat huddled and silent over their drinks.

He smiled as she handed him his pint. "And one for yourself, love."

"Thanks. I don't very often get that these days." She glanced around the bar. "This lot hardly know I'm here."

He lifted his eyebrows. "Pity to see such beauty going to waste..."

She shook her head in what he took to be a gesture of scepticism. Then she smiled at him knowingly. "I bet your next line is 'And where have you been all my life?'"

Doyle laughed and looked at her over the glass as he took a sip of beer.

"No, really, I mean it. You've obviously put a lot of effort into looking gorgeous."

He transferred his glass to his left hand. "Anyway, I appreciate it."

He held out his free hand. "I'm Sam."

"Norah." Her hand was warm to his touch and lingered a fraction longer than necessary. "I run the place. Have done for the past fifteen years, so I know bullshit when I hear it."

She looked him straight in the eyes. "Now, Sam, what was it you really wanted...?"

He noticed her dark eyes glistening in the dim light of the bar.

"Just some information, Norah, my love. There could be a slap-up meal in it, if you can help...with a very sophisticated bloke. No strings."

She laughed. "Okay, I'll fall for it..."

Doyle smiled. He knew they were on the same wavelength. "Joe Sharp, a regular of yours, I'm told. He's disappeared."

"Can't say I'm surprised. He was a Jack the Lad. Not that he got anywhere with me..." She looked Doyle up and down "I'm particular. Heavy drinker too."

"I'm trying to find out what's happened to him, that's all. Did he have any mates?"

"I don't really know. Only had one in here – Darren Lowe. He's an okay guy, not Joe's type at all. Should be in tomorrow."

Norah leaned across the bar, her mouth breaking into a grin. "I'm free on Thursday. So when will I get to meet this sophisticated man who's taking me out?"

"I'll get him to pick you up at seven. But he may need more favours."

Norah raised her eyebrows. "Oh yes?"

"No, nothing like that...just to do with Joe Sharp."

He thought she looked a little disappointed.

It had been a spontaneous gesture on Doyle's part. He hadn't had a real date since his wife divorced him. *I could do worse,* he thought.

The following night Doyle was propping up the bar, chatting with Norah, when she nodded to a man who came through the door.

"Hi, Darren. Usual?" She started to pull a pint of Carlsberg. "Sam here wants a word..."

"I'll get that, Norah." Sam put out his hand. "Sam Doyle..."

Darren was in his early forties, clean shaven and smartly dressed. The handshake was firm, the smile genuine.

"Hi, how can I help?"

"It's about Joe Sharp. Can we talk?" Doyle carried the drinks to a corner table.

As they sat down Darren Lowe said, "I don't know if I can help. I haven't seen Joe for a couple of months."

"That's the point really, Darren. He's disappeared. His wife's hired me to find out what happened to him."

Darren nodded to show he understood. "Never met the lady, but I knew Joe." He smiled as he shook his head. "Bit of a character, our Joe."

Darren tapped the side of his head. "Slightly crazy. Does things without any thought of the consequences."

"Remember when you last saw him?"

"Yeah, I do, as it happens. It was my birthday, February 15th. A few of us in here celebrated the fact, including Joe. We'd had a skinful. Joe got a bit rowdy and Norah cleared him out."

"See him again?" asked Doyle.

Darren took a drink and nodded. "I left a few minutes afterwards and, when I got out on the quay, I saw Joe in the distance, right at the end of the breakwater. Then he just dived into the sea..."

Darren looked into space. "Suppose I should have reported it...but Joe, well, he was a bit of a daredevil. Had nine lives. It never occurred to me." Doyle concealed his excitement. He knew he had a breakthrough.

"Any idea why he would go into the sea?"

The other man was thoughtful for a moment, then he whispered, almost to himself "No, it can't be, surely..." and then to Doyle: "Now I think about it, we did have a fairly heated discussion the week before – about swimming across the bay. I said it had never been done because of the strong currents. Joe bragged that he would be the one to do it. I bet him he couldn't."

Darren shook his head, his face grim. "Never thought any more about it. We'd both had a few – you know how it is ...?"

Doyle placed his large hands on the table. "Yeah, I do. Could solve the mystery of his disappearance though, couldn't it? Anyone else witness the bet?"

81

Darren shrugged. "Not sure. I could find out, if you like."

"Thanks, yes. Can you write down what you have told me, Darren. There's a hundred quid in it for you. Get me corroboration of the bet and there's another hundred in it, plus fifty for the witness."

Darren nodded his agreement. "I'll do my best, Sam."

Norah looked stunning in a long blue dress that showed off her reasonable figure. The chunky necklace was a statement: she was definitely a modern woman, still in the mainstream of life.

It was the best she had looked for ages, certainly since her partner left her for a younger woman two years ago.

"Sam Doyle won't stand a chance," she said, as she admired herself in the mirror, "but don't be too pushy, girl, you're not desperate. Well, yes, you *are* actually – this is the first date you've had in a long time."

The doorbell interrupted her thoughts. Sam Doyle was standing there in a smart dark blue suit, holding a bunch of red roses.

"For you, Norah, my love…"

As she went to kiss him on the cheek, he moved his head and their lips met, tentatively at first, then melted into a passionate kiss. It was another hour before they left for their meal. Norah's dress and Sam's suit looked slightly crumpled. Neither minded, nor even noticed. They felt like teenagers again.

After the meal and a couple of bottles of wine, Doyle reluctantly returned to the subject of Joe Sharp.

"I need your help, Norah, love."

She smiled. "And here was I thinking it was only my body you wanted."

"Darren's birthday – you threw Joe out when he was drunk, yes?"

"Yes, I did."

"Darren tells me that a week earlier he bet Joe he couldn't swim across the bay…"

"I don't know…"

Doyle cut her short. "What if I suggest to you that you remember Darren telling you about it on that night, saying what a bloody fool Joe was?"

He took her hand. "Would you do it as a favour for me?"

Norah smiled. "Is that all, Sam? Of course I will." She emptied her wine glass. "Now, Mr. Sophisticated, back to my place for a nightcap?"

He squeezed her hand. "Whatever makes you happy, babe…"

Within a week, Doyle had all his witness statements. The bet was corroborated, as was Joe's drunken state when he left the pub on the night he disappeared. Doyle also found an old fisherman, who, with a little financial persuasion, remembered, when he was out walking his dog, seeing Joe on the breakwater diving into the sea.

Karen Sharp confirmed that her husband was not a strong swimmer, and the Met. forecast that particular night indicated high winds and rough seas.

Doyle made the case to the Coroner's Office. The Coroner himself took evidence on oath from Karen

Sharp, Darren Lowe and Norah, and then asked to see him.

"Mr. Doyle, you have assembled persuasive evidence of Mr. Sharp's probable death." He looked up from the papers in front of him. "But disappearance without a body always leaves some doubt, as you well know."

Doyle used his solemn Court voice: "Yes, sir, I know."

"As an experienced former Police Officer, I rely on your judgement and your integrity in this matter."

"Well, sir, my professional opinion is that he drowned. We have proof of his drunken state, his certainty that he could swim across the treacherous bay, his diving into the sea, and the fact that he was a poor swimmer. We know also of his foolhardy character. The prevailing currents and the rough state of the sea for the following few days could have carried his body well out into the Atlantic, never to be found."

"Indeed. Yes. That would be my conclusion too, Mr. Doyle." The Coroner closed the file in front of him. "I shall therefore return a verdict of Death by Misadventure, and issue a Death Certificate accordingly. Thank you, Mr. Doyle, for your help."

They shook hands.

Karen Sharp was overjoyed. She was now officially a widow. The Death Certificate enabled her to release her husband's assets and to claim the Life Insurance.

She invited Sam Doyle round for a celebration, and to pay him his fee. When he arrived he found Karen and, to his surprise, Darren Lowe, sitting cosily together on the patio of her small garden.

"Ah, Mr. Doyle, Sam. Glad you could come." She rose, reached into her handbag and handed him a cheque for twelve thousand pounds. "Your reward for convincing the Coroner...and a little bonus." She kissed him on the cheek. "Thank you so much."

She paused and looked at Darren. "Of course, you couldn't have done it without Darren's help. We didn't know whether you would believe his story..."

Doyle looked puzzled as he took the cup of tea Karen offered him.

"I hadn't realised you two knew each other."

They smiled, and then at Doyle. "Oh yes, Sam. We're getting married next month," Karen said. "Darren's been living here since Joe died, and we were – how shall I put it – 'very close' for a couple of years before that. Joe had no idea, of course."

Doyle began to feel uneasy. He didn't want to know any of this, particularly now he had his fee. He stood up. "I'd better go. Norah's waiting..."

"Before you go, Sam..." Karen took his arm. "You're a keen gardener, aren't you? Let me show you my pride and joy."

She raised her arm and pointed to a corner of the garden where the flowers and plants were thriving.

"What do you think?"

Doyle was impressed. It was a magnificent show.

"Horse manure?" he enquired.

"Not exactly, Sam. We call it Joe's corner..."

85

LAND OF HOPE AND ....?

A waster, that summed him up beautifully.

A luckless, self-centred, juvenile loser.

No personality. No talents. No qualities worth mentioning. And definitely no money.

Inside he felt useless and miserable. One of life's rejects. Prone to dark thoughts and depression. Well, who wouldn't, in his situation.

He was living proof, if any were needed, that life isn't fair. That we were not all born equal.

However, like many to whom life has dealt a bad hand, he made a fine job of hiding the awful truth he felt inside. Yes, that's right – he compensated. He bragged. Exaggerated. Put on a happy face and bought people drinks on his tab.

Everyone thought he was a fine, fun loving extrovert. Everyone, that is, except his creditors, of whom there were many. They had other names for him.

Nowhere was his make-believe charm and charisma appreciated more than by the ladies. Like moths to a flame they were. Jostling to be 'the one' seen out with him.

The reason, you ask? Well, Michael St. John Blake's solitary saving grace was that he looked remarkably like Prince Harry. Yes, that one. The spitting image, in fact. Uncannily so. Even the hair colour.

Being his one and only virtue, Michael played on it. Of course he did.

He courted the popularity it gave him. He refined his accent to reproduce Harry's manner of speech. He put his heart and soul into it, he really did. No messing about. He was, he often said to himself, a *genuine* fake.

One of his many girlfriends was so taken with the similarity that she insisted he spoke to a firm who would trace his family history. 'History 4U' – can you believe the name? He went along with it to keep her happy and even signed a contract to pay them two grand at the end of their research.

Once again, he knew he would not be able to pay. But this never worried him. He did it all the time: cars, clothes, holidays, mail order, bar tabs, gambling, credit cards – you name it, he avoided paying for it. It was all part of his make-believe lifestyle.

His debts, which of course he never bothered to count, were somewhere in the region of a quarter of a million pounds.

Occasionally he found a girlfriend who had money. This one was called Cindy.

"Daddy's a banker," she said.

"A what? A wanker?"

"No silly, a banker. You know, he runs a bank."

"Yeah," he replied dismissively. "Probably a wanker as well. Most of them are."

Cindy was therefore loaded. Both figuratively and figuratively, if you see what I mean.

If you don't, it relates to her shape and her dosh.

One day, she said to him, "Michael, my love, how do you fancy some hols in the sun. Somewhere romantic like Monte Carlo. I'll pay."

He shrugged. "If we must, but I'll need some new clothes and stuff."

So off they went to Harvey Nics. They welcomed Daddy's card like manna from heaven.

All the clothes and suitcases were in the style Prince Harry used. Of course they were.

"I want to stop here..." Michael pointed to Monte Carlo Casino. "Try my luck."

He flashed his newly whitened teeth at Cindy. "My lucky day," he declared.

The taxi drove around the square and stopped at the entrance. A liveried attendant opened the door. Behind him, sheltering in the shade of the building, looking bored with life and trying to conceal a sneaked cigarette, stood the Duty Manager.

Cindy emerged first from the taxi and the flash of her long legs cancelled out the boredom the Manager had felt.

Michael followed and stood there expectantly, looking cool and regal. He put on his sunglasses and looked around.

The Manager's eyes nearly popped. He stubbed out his cigarette, straightened his tie and rushed down the steps.

"Your Highness," he said, with a slight bow. "Welcome to Casino de Monte Carlo."

Michael nodded casually, acknowledging the welcome.

The Manager shoo'd the taxi away, escorted the couple to the VIP lounge and opened a bottle of champagne. The room was a cool relief from the heat outside. The champagne even more so.

"Impressive, my dear," Michael mimicked his best Prince Harry voice.

He turned to the Manager. "Yes, one is most impressed."

Cindy was nearly wetting herself with the excitement of it all.

The Manager bowed his head in gratitude. "Are you staying with His Highness, Prince Albert, Sir?"

"Not on this occasion, no. This is a personal visit. Can you recommend a hotel?"

"The Ritz, Your Highness, is the best. With your permission I shall book a penthouse suite overlooking the harbour and the Prince's Palace in Monaco. For as long as you wish."

"Thank you." Michael smiled at him. "As this is a personal visit one does not want any publicity or paparazzi. You understand?"

The Manager bowed slightly. "You can rely on our complete discretion and that of The Ritz, Sir."

He waited for them to take another sip of champagne before he continued: "The Casino's Rolls-Royce will be at your disposal for your stay, of course. Or, if you prefer something a little less eye-catching, perhaps a Mercedes, a Porsche, or a Ferrari?"

He winked at Cindy. "Yes, my man, a Porsche 911. Black. That would be splendid."

"Of course, Your Highness. A 911 in black it shall be."

The Duty Manager had never met royalty before but he had been well trained in the knowledge of etiquette and that all expenditure incurred would be efficiently reimbursed by Buckingham Palace. The Ritz, the car, everything.

"How much would Your Highness like to start with at the tables? One thousand Euros, ten thousand? Any amount you wish."

"Ah yes, the tables. I think five thousand will do for now. We may return this evening should we feel inclined."

"Of course, Sir. I will arrange for five thousand Euros in chips to be waiting for you at the tables." He pointed to the other end of the room. "Through those green doors... in the meantime, please enjoy your champagne."

The Manager bowed his farewell and walked toward the entrance, then stopped and returned. "I apologise for overlooking it, Sir, but would you like me to arrange a yacht and crew to be put at your disposal for your stay. I can recommend the mv *Prince Michael*, a superb vessel."

Michael tried to hide his excitement. "Yes, one would appreciate that."

When they were left alone, Michael put his finger to his lips. "Be careful," he whispered, "hidden bugs and cameras."

"How exciting!" Cindy exclaimed.

He took a swig of champagne, kissed her and fondled her bottom.

"Nice one, Your Highness," she giggled.

The Blackjack table let him down and his five thousand Euros stake soon disappeared. Inside he felt, once again, betrayed by life. Felt the familiar uncaring world gnawing at his soul. But only momentarily.

"I'll be back," he said to the croupier. "To win."

She smiled. *Just another dumb punter,* she thought. "Naturally, Your Highness."

The two weeks they stayed provided them with every luxury money could buy. Not their money, of course. They didn't have to pay a penny.

It was Cindy who suggested they move on, before the half a million Euros she calculated they had spent caught up with them. She was right, of course.

Michael, who was getting a little bored with the place anyway, said, "Let's sail down the coast of Italy to Portofino, shall we? Use the yacht we are paying a fortune for."

"Oooh, lovely," she replied.

Cindy and Michael were the only passengers on the yacht and the Captain and crew of ten pampered them lavishly. They spent five heavenly days at sea – eating, drinking, making love and sunbathing. This life of luxury, where he never had to lift a finger for himself, was becoming normal for Michael; he took it for granted. No longer did he see it as a cheeky pretence but his, by right. He *was* a Prince and deserved to be treated like one.

"Captain, have you made arrangements for a hotel in Portofino?"

"Not yet, Your Highness. I can radio ahead. Do you have any preferences? If I may recommend the Hotel Bristol."

Michael gave a brief shrug of his shoulders. "Very well, Captain. The best suite they have."

"May I ask how long you wish to stay, Sir?"

"Oh, I would think at least two weeks, wouldn't you, darling?"

Cindy looked up from her book and raised her sunglasses. "Yes, at least."

Again they lived luxuriously, their hosts assuming normal Palace protocol would guarantee payment. As usual in these cases, each one had inflated their prices to compensate for the bowing and scraping they had to endure.

Towards the end of the second week in Portofino things started to go wrong.

Michael was getting tired of Cindy. Of her sharing the limelight that was his alone. Tired of her calling him Michael. Of her being a constant reminder that he was Michael St. John Blake.

He was now Prince Harry and didn't want a mere commoner reminding him otherwise.

And there were many other females queuing up for his royal favours. Just wanting him, no matter how briefly. It would be their claim to fame; their passport to success.

Two things happened almost simultaneously that pulled the royal rug from beneath him.

"You are the most wonderful man I have ever known," the Italian woman said, from beneath the sheets.

Michael smiled graciously. "One does one's best," he declared.

At that moment Cindy returned early from the hairdresser.

"You brute!" she shouted. "I'm going to the police." She threw her handbag at him and stormed out of the room, slamming the door.

"Off you go then, my dear." He bundled the woman out of his bed. "Get dressed. I will see you for dinner this evening."

When she had gone he emptied Cindy's handbag, found Daddy's credit card and the PIN in her diary. The front page, would you believe.

He packed quickly, asked for his cases to be put into the Porsche and informed the hotel manager that he would be in Rome for a couple of days and to keep the room until he returned.

"Of course, Your Highness, that will be our pleasure."

Once out of the hotel, Michael made for the nearest cash machine and drew the maximum on Daddy's credit card. It was a miserly amount. He didn't know how people lived on so little.

The newsagents next door had just received yesterday's British newspapers and, in order to change a large denomination Euro note, he bought one.

Calamity! There on the front page was a photo of Prince Harry with his leg in plaster following a skiing accident in the Alps.

No man deserves such luck, do they? Once more the world was conspiring against him. Trying to put him down.

Michael ditched the Porsche, bought himself a crutch and caught the overnight train to Paris. Once there, with his Prince Harry crutch, he tried to gain a suite at the Hotel Lyon. But the jungle telegraph had preceded him and the Manager attempted to detain him before contacting the Gendarmerie. A quick stab at the Manager with his crutch soon put paid to that and Michael was able to escape and buy a Eurostar ticket to London.

More bad news awaited him in London. His apartment had been burgled. Ransacked.

His dreams of a good life were shattered. And now this! He was as low as he could get and ready to give up on life.

There was obviously only one thing to do but Michael knew he was too much of a coward to contemplate suicide. The alternative he chose was to drown his sorrows in drink. To get into such a stupor that he would not give a damn about the demons in the world out to get him.

He settled himself against the bar of the seedy pub around the corner and began to drink. Each glass depressed him even more. He became distraught. He had nothing. No make-believe. No future. No money. Absolutely nothing ...

At least that would have been the case had he not got into conversation with the sharp-suited, weasel-faced little man who stood beside him. His name was Alan. They got on well and after several more drinks together he confided, much to Michael's surprise, and very quietly, that he was a professional assassin. Michael believed him. He had that distant cool look about him.

Michael caught his arm and limped over to a quiet corner table where he removed his hat and dark glasses and revealed himself as Prince Harry. The man was completely taken in, Michael could tell.

After a few more drinks, Michael moved in closer and lowered his voice even more.

"Could you do a little job for me, Alan?"

The man looked around before he answered. "It would be my pleasure, Your Highness. What is it?"

"A man is going around impersonating me. It is terribly embarrassing. One wants him stopped but one doesn't want to involve MI5... too much paperwork. You understand?"

Michael thought he saw a glimmer of a smile in the man's eyes.

"Stopped, as in dead, Sir?"

Michael nodded. "A clean kill, such as they taught us in Afghanistan. Can you do that?"

The man nodded. "It will cost ten grand, Sir. Normally I wouldn't charge such as you but I have some heavy bills to pay."

"Yes, of course. As you know, one doesn't normally carry cash but I happen to have five hundred pounds in Euros following a trip to Europe..."

Michael pulled out a wad of notes and slid them across the table. The man covered them with his hand and put them into his pocket. "The rest will be on completion."

"Right, Your Highness. I will make it clean and quick, like an accident and I will take a photo on my phone to confirm the death. Can you be here at ten tomorrow night with the balance of the cash?"

Michael nodded. "Yes, that will be no problem. Just one more thing Alan... we never met. Okay? And tomorrow night I shall be in disguise again."

The man gave a quick nod.

"Now," he said, reaching into his coat for a notebook and pen. "Give me the details."

"Name?"

"Michael St. John Blake."

"Address?"

"Apartment Twelve, Regency Mews, Prior Street. Just around the corner."

Michael smiled. "He will look just like me."

They lifted their glasses and clinked them to confirm the arrangement

Michael suddenly felt in his pocket. "Oh, nearly forgot, I managed to obtain a spare key to his apartment."

He slid it across the table into the man's hand.

Michael had a few more drinks after the man had left and then staggered around the corner to his apartment. He noticed the post was spilling out of his mail-box and emptied it, throwing the junk mail into the bin. He was left with one letter which he threw on the kitchen table with his keys and wallet before falling on to his bed into a deep alcohol fuelled sleep.

The sun shining through the window awoke him. It was ten-thirty.

He felt lousy. Too much to drink. He was not used to it.

He couldn't recall how he got home. Obviously not a woman: he was still fully clothed and alone. Something niggled in the back of his mind but he couldn't fathom it in the blur that was his brain. Not important.

Michael's head throbbed as he stood and made his way slowly to the shower. Then he pulled on his dressing gown and sat at the kitchen table drinking a glass of water, trying to pull himself together.

He reached for the letter he had found last night and opened it. Flashy notepaper headed 'History 4U'. Dated two weeks ago.

My dear Sir,

As requested we have researched your family history. Your bloodline can be traced

back to James II. His grandson, Charles Edward Stuart, (also known as the Young Pretender) had a son in 1740 named Charles St. John Stuart. The child was sheltered from the political and religious turmoil of the time by his mother, who feared for his life. She took him into exile and changed their surname to Blake.

In our opinion, which has been confidentially verified by other experts, you are the legitimate heir to the British throne, taking precedence over the House of Windsor and as such you would become King on the demise of Queen Elizabeth II.

If, however, as is likely, Parliament did not wish to disrupt the present succession, then you would be offered by Her Majesty the title of Prince Michael of Norfolk with a generous annual income. This arrangement has been informally agreed by the Palace.

It is with honour and humility that we convey this information to you, together with our congratulations.

Michael read it again. And again. It was a dream come true. He always knew he was different. Somehow special.

A real Prince...my word.

A warm glow began to consume him, starting inside, he could feel it reaching his cheeks.

He stood erect, looked at himself in the mirror, and smiled. A smile of contentment.

It was at that moment that Michael St. John Blake heard a key turn in the lock of his front door...

THE PRETTY GREEN SHOES

The warm water trickled out of the tap, through the bubbles, on to my toes. It tickled.

Momma knelt beside the bath to fulfil her daily ritual. I notice her knuckles turn white with anger as she grips the side of the bath. Her voice is soft, but filled with hatred. I can see it in her eyes. I can feel it.

"They are nothing but farmyard animals. Nasty, cruel, stinking vermin."

I nod, my chin just above the bubbles. "Yes, Momma."

"Keep right away from them, my child. Men and boys. They will steal your life, your dreams, all to satisfy their evil primitive urges. They need killing. All of them."

"Yes, Momma," I answer again. It is part of the ritual, for I know that to remain silent will only prolong her dire warnings. They had been going on throughout my childhood, every bath-time. Her words are ingrained in my mind and I became afraid of these evil monsters in case they savaged me in the darkness of the night, in case they crept up on me to do their wicked deeds. Voices in my head kept repeating Momma's warnings, like a scratched CD. I had never known my father. He had left us when I was a baby. Perhaps that was the cause of Momma's bitterness.

Then one night, when I was twelve, it all became real. Mamma's brother, Charlie, who was staying with us for a few days, climbed into my bed and lay on top of me. He had no clothes on. I could tell by the smell that he was drunk. I wriggled from beneath his suffocating, beer soaked body and screamed. Momma came and took me into her bed.

"I warned you, didn't I? They are all animals, not to be trusted." She said it as though it was somehow my fault.

It was about this time that I began to feel I had a special gift. I would see things in my head before they happened but was powerless to stop them. They always involved someone dying.

I had plenty of reasons to hate Charlie, but to kill himself using rat poison? What a horrible way to die. I foresaw it, of course. He was drunk, as usual. He stirred three sugars into a mug of tea laced with rat poison. I saw the whole agonising, lingering episode in my mind; the writhing, the retching. His desperate, pleading eyes. They were still pleading when I found him but it was too late to help. All I could do was sit and watch until his dreadful end came. It took about two hours. He left no suicide note; just a tin of rat poison under the sink.

Later, when I was at High School, some brainless, obnoxious youth took a fancy to me. He tried to grope and kiss me. Ugh! We travelled on the same bus home and got off at the same stop. I foresaw him falling under the wheels of a bus and getting his head squashed. Sure enough the next day, when we got off the bus together, he lost his footing and fell under the bus as it was driving off. There was nothing I could do to help and when the crane lifted the front of the bus, his head was squashed, just as I had foreseen, his brains splattered over the tarmac.

When I started work, I had a boss, old enough to be my father, who used to take liberties with all the young women in the office. He was creepy –

standing too close to me at the photocopying machine. Touching me whenever he got the chance, making lewd remarks and asking me to work over in his office when everybody had gone home. He was a real pest and he made my life a misery. One day I foresaw him jumping out of the office window to his death. And, believe it or not, it happened that very same day. The weather was hot and sultry and the windows were wide open. He asked me to help him close them before we left. He must have stretched too far out and lost his balance. I told the police there was nothing I could do to save him, it all happened so quickly.

I know this will sound strange, but last year when I bought a pair of pretty green shoes from a charity shop and wore them, they seemed to take me over. Instead of foreseeing things, when I was wearing the shoes I had the urge to actually be its *cause*. It was really weird. Each time I wore them, I felt this ripple of excitement run through my whole body and a compulsion to do dreadful things, as though something was possessing me, had a hold over me. I called them my 'ghost shoes'.

My behaviour changed. My thoughts grew darker and I was roused to anger more quickly. I began to hate men, all men, to see them as worthless, evil creatures who ruined women's lives, just as Momma had told me. For the first time in my life I began to dress provocatively — short skirts, low cut blouses, plenty of make-up. And gloves, I always wore cream leather gloves.

One dark night, I was roaming a couple of miles from home, all dolled up, when a car pulled up beside me. A large black BMW. The driver stuck his head out of the window. He was middle-aged, with thinning hair. Wearing glasses. "Want a lift, love?" His voice was demeaning, his manner arrogant.

I was ready. "Yes, thank you. I'm going that way." I pointed away from my flat.

"Hop in," he said.

The seat smelled of expensive leather. As I sank into it, my skirt became even shorter. I saw the man ogling my thighs as we drove away.

"How much?" he said, a slight quiver of excitement in his voice.

"For what?" I asked innocently. But I knew.

"For the full works, darling. On the back seat. In that Industrial Estate up ahead. It's dark. No cameras." He had obviously preyed on women before.

"A hundred quid."

He pulled out his wallet and dropped five twenties on my lap, his hand stroking my thigh as he did so.

Despite his fantasies, the thrust was mine, not his. My stiletto pierced his jacket, his shirt, his lung and his heart in one swift movement. I was surprised how little effort it took. There was no sign of blood, other than on the knife. I wiped it clean on the arm of his coat.

The man hadn't uttered a word, not a sound, nor struggled. His face showed a mixture of surprise and bewilderment as he sat there, mouth open, resting back on his soft leather seat. I felt elated but also had the feeling I needed to do more.

It suddenly came to me – I would cut off one of the fingers that had stroked my thigh. I chose the one with the wedding ring on. Again I was surprised at how easily it became detached; a swift slash, a twist and it was resting in my gloved hand. I stuck it in his mouth. Serves him right, the pervert.

As I opened the car door, the light came on. I wiped the make-up off my face, took a long plastic mac from my bag and put it on. Then I walked half a mile and caught a bus back to town. I felt happy with my evening's work. Satisfied. *Happiness is ridding the world of one of the evil monsters,* my 'ghost shoes' seemed to say. This time I hadn't foreseen the end of that animal's life, I had caused it.

I called them *my animals.*

The next one fell from a great height. We were on a funfair big dipper. He thought, because we were alone and out of sight, he could take advantage of me. I persuaded him that to do so he had to take his harness off. He was in such a state of excitement, so keen to grab me, he must have forgotten the ride turned upside-down at one point. I never heard the thud as he hit the ground, only the screams of the bystanders.

In all, I have slaughtered eight animals – seven men and one woman. All with my pretty green 'ghost shoes' on. It was wonderful!

At the office I was assigned to work on a project with Alan. He was funny and caring, like no other man I had come across. I didn't see him as an animal; I didn't feel afraid of him at all. We got on well together and he seemed to like me. I never wore my special shoes when I was with him. We confided in each other and I told him that I could foresee things. I think he thought I was joking until I proved it to him.

A woman in the next office fancied him; she was all over him, wanting him to take her out. He told me all the nasty things she had said about me, calling me weird and a witch. He was flattered by her attention, of course he was, but he seemed to lose interest in her when I told him I could foresee her being killed in a car crash one day soon. A steering fault I told him.

Sure enough, the following week, on her way to work she lost control of her car on the motorway and was killed. The inquest found that a nut on the steering mechanism had somehow worked loose. The experts didn't know how. But I did. With the help of my 'ghost shoes', the internet, and a spanner, I located the vital nut one night outside her house. At seventy miles an hour she stood no chance.

I became besotted with Alan, thinking of him every minute of the day. We started going out together – to restaurants, the cinema and all kind of places. One day he kissed me. Just a little peck on the cheek. I had anticipated it with fear and loathing but to my great relief I found the experience enjoyable, romantic. He began to kiss me every time we went out on a date. I looked forward to it. My mother had been wrong: not *all* men were animals.

Our romance blossomed and we began talking about the future, about marriage and children and where we would live. We were deeply in love. So relaxed was I about our relationship that I decided I would have no further use for the pretty green 'ghost shoes' and took them back to the charity shop.

I was the envy of all the women in the office. Alan was quite a catch, they told me. Hang on to him, they said, you don't know how lucky you are.

Unfortunately, a new woman, Sandra, thought she could take my place. She started flirting with my Alan. I knew he wasn't interested – he told me so – but the silly woman persisted. As I didn't now have the shoes I visualised her falling down the stairwell – all twelve floors to the basement. I could even hear her screams as she plummeted to her certain death.

A few days later I was working late, looking forward to a date with Alan. Everyone had left the building. As I was about to get in the lift, I noticed someone had forgotten to turn the light off in the stationery storeroom. I approached and heard whispered voices inside. One I recognised as Alan's. I opened the door and there he was with Sandra, both in a state of undress.

My world stood still. I must have fainted with shock. The next thing I knew, they were carrying me, face down, along the corridor towards the stairwell. I could only see their feet. To my horror, I noticed Sandra was wearing the green 'ghost shoes'.

The last thing I heard before they threw me over the banisters was Alan whispering in my ear, "Didn't your Mommy ever tell you that all men are monsters?"

WHO *IS* RUNNING THE COUNTRY?

Faces bobbed up and down expectantly. I read '*Help Us*' in their faces as they willed me to be their Saviour. Willed me to eradicate the 'Not Fit for Purpose' tag which was now attached to most Government Departments.

The Prime Minister was introducing me to top civil servants at the Home Office. "This is Barry Neilson," he said. "I cannot speak too highly of him. He has turned around the fortunes of eight global companies and one failing Asian economy." I smiled benevolently as he continued. "You will find him dynamic and inspiring but, be warned, he uses unorthodox methods."

You bet I do! Well, you have to in these tough circumstances, don't you?

"Mr Neilson has my full confidence. He will have full reign to alter anything and he will have full control of all budget headings."

He looked around the room, his impending threat bouncing off the walls and reflecting in people's faces. "I will expect each one of you to support him one hundred per cent. If you feel you cannot do so, leave the room now to write your resignation letter." His voice became more commanding. "Do I make myself clear?"

Their combined tension escaped in a unified chant. "Yes, Prime Minister." A round of applause as he left the room. *Was it for him or me?* I couldn't tell.

I was on a high. Anyone would be after that intro.

My "Call me Baz, folks" broke the ice and to my surprise the top brass seemed to welcome me with open arms. I suppose my appointment let them off the hook; from now on I would be the universal scapegoat. *Ah well, in for a penny...*

My PA, Penny, is a lovely woman. She says she will do anything for me, I only have to ask. I can tell she wants me to succeed.

"Penny, I want you to buy me some trendy clothes for work. No ties."

She smiled knowingly. "Yes, of course, Mr. Neilson."

"Baz, please, call me Baz." Her smile this time incorporated a nod. "Then, Penny, sweetheart, you will be delighted to know I am doubling your salary, starting today. How's that?" She nearly fell off her chair. "Take my word, gal, you will earn it."

Later, I addressed all the section heads. "Now, lads and lassies, I want you to ask yourselves *'What is my biggest problem?'* Put it on a single piece of paper and I will allocate one of my personally selected Special Advisors to come up with a radical solution."

I had chosen my Special Advisors with great care. "I want common sense solutions," I told them. "Talk to people in the street and, most of all, talk to people who are perceived to be causing the problem." They understood. Of course they did.

Mohammed had bored me often enough with his fundamentalist views, so I put him in charge of terrorism. Or, should I say, how to combat it. My faith was not misplaced. He came back with a stick and carrot approach. Every Mosque and every Church would join forces in their locality to draw up a petition to the Government. It would be signed by all congregations, their families and friends; it would also be available in schools, colleges, universities, in supermarkets, pubs and clubs, on trains and buses, be issued to Trade Unions and backed by radio, TV, newspapers and social media.

"I guarantee we will raise twenty million signatures to deliver to Number Ten and we will back it up with a million people marching into central London on the same day. The petition will urge the British Government to change its foreign policy of intervening militarily in Muslim countries and to withdraw British troops from any existing conflicts within three months," Mohammed said. "And I'll make sure every Member of Parliament will be warned that if they want to be re-elected they should support the proposal, and the associated one which says that the one billion pounds annual saving from the Defence Budget will be spent on the NHS and education."

"Nice Catch 22," I told him. "But I think your idea that the sons or daughters of MPs who don't support the proposal should be conscripted into the armed forces and sent to Afghanistan in a community-building role is a little *too* radical."

Mohammed gave a smile. "It would work though, wouldn't it, Baz?"

Yeah, it would.

Trev is my youngest Special Advisor. He has close links with the grass roots and understands deprived communities. I call him my 'Big Issue' man, so I gave him one – the job of ending yob culture. His answer was to set up contracts with known potential yobs on a neighbourhood basis, pay them a hundred pounds each week to behave themselves. Any infringement – no ifs or buts – would see them enrolled for two years into a new Civil Army, a

107

tough training regime which would send them to remote parts of the UK to dig ditches, clear snow, mend fences and dry stone walls, gather beach litter, make roads and paths, etc.. Doing all the harsh all-weather jobs that no one else wanted to do.

"Well done, Trev, my lad. But what about the hoodies?"

He smirked. "Simple, Baz. We recruit squads of elderly guys in each community and issue them with hooded tops. With their hoods up they will hang about the areas where hoodies are a nuisance." Another smirk, this time accompanied by a rubbing of the hands. "I guarantee, Baz, that within a week any self-respecting hoodie will have ditched the fashion."

"Brilliant!" I meant it.

"Hypocrisy" was the word Shirl always used to describe the current drugs policy.

"Go for it, gal," I told her.

And she did.

Drugs, she decided, would be treated the same way as the really big addictive killers – tobacco and alcohol. They would be decriminalised. As they came into the commercial mainstream, prices would drop drastically, the need for smuggling too, as would all the associated criminal activities, including drug related prostitution. As with smoking, drink and other addictions such as gambling, major educational campaigns and helping strategies would be set up.

"Wonderful, Shirl."

Devon looks a bit weird. Well, let's face it, he is. But he has *presence*. Considerable, intimidating presence. So I put him on the case of gun and knife culture. He came up with a zero tolerance solution. "If they're so in love with weapons, man," he said, "then anyone carrying a knife or a gun, no exceptions, man, will go into the armed forces: two years for a knife, five years for a gun." He shrugged his huge shoulders. "If they want to play with weapons, then they can learn to do it properly."

"High fives, Devon, my man," I said.

The five of us worked our socks off to get these solutions off the ground. The projects were welcomed by the general public and by the politicians. The media saw us as (quote) 'Saviours of the Country'. There was a stampede from other Government Departments to use our expertise to solve their intractable problems.

After nine months, the Prime Minister invited us all to Number Ten. He was over the moon. "Lady and Gentlemen," he said, with a broad grin on his face. "I cannot thank you enough. Your work has been an overwhelming success and my Party's ratings are at an all-time high. Because of you, we are in an excellent position to win the forthcoming General Election. Well done!" He shook us vigorously by the hand. "Tomorrow, as a token of the country's gratitude, the Queen will bestow on each of you an OBE – Order of the British Empire."

The brief silence was broken by a "Whoop" from Shirl. We all hugged each other and then the PM, much to his embarrassment. "Now gather round for a group photograph," he said. I reminded him of our 'no publicity, no personal photos' agreement. "Don't worry, Baz. I assure you it will just be for my personal archives."

Fair enough. I nodded my agreement and we all said cheese.

The following weekend one of the Sunday papers carried the said photograph under the heading 'National Treasures'. Who are these wonderful people who brought common sense back into Government and ended the scourges which were ruining our country? Within days our secret was out. The same Press pilloried us for 'Cruelly Deceiving the British People'. There was no mention of our successes, of course.

I suppose that now the cat is out of the bag I had better come clean – I had shared a room with the real Barry Neilson who had suffered a mental breakdown. He was about to start a new job advising the PM on a strategy to win the General Election but it had all got too much for him.

"Do it for me, please," he pleaded.

The others bet me a tenner I wouldn't do it. And that's how it all started – me and my Special Advisor friends. They're the ones with the OBEs, the same ones who had eradicated some of society's worst ills. They are all long-stay patients in a psychiatric hospital.

Ah well, back on the anti-psychotic drugs. Anyone for bingo?

THE DARKNESS

Total blackness. Indescribably dark. Frighteningly so. Darkness tainted with gritty volcanic ash and dust. You can touch it. Taste it. Die from it. Die in it. Many have.

Even in the daytime it is dark. Murky. No sun you see. But at night. Here. Now, outside the glow of our campfire, the darkness is like an impenetrable black wall.

The ash is a foot thick, building all the time. Like a grey snow. It covers everything. There are no colours anywhere. Just the colour of ash. A dull charcoal world.

There is no sound either. Not even the sounds that constitute silence. It has the stillness of an abandoned world.

Time stands still. We have lived with this volcanic blanket for three years now. Each day an increasingly desperate struggle. We have adapted as best we can. We wear masks and sweep the ash away from the fire and around our bedding, where we huddle most of the time from the numbing coldness.

Life as we knew it has ceased to exist. The infrastructure of our country is no more – no vehicles, no shops, no food production, no water, no gas or electricity, no phones. Nothing.

A State of Emergency exists. Strict curfews are enforced by the Army and the dreaded Curfew Patrols. To be caught is an immediate death sentence. Wham! An on the spot execution. It happens all the time. Life is no longer sacred.

One of us goes every week with our ration cards to the former splendour of the Baron's Court Hotel, now the local Feeding Station for a meagre amount of food and bottled water. Barely enough to keep us alive.

Our commune is a mix of twenty people. Men, women and children. We are former residents of a block of flats, burned out because some nuthead had an open fire in his room.

Mainly we survive in the open, in the courtyard, but, when it gets too cold or the black rain comes, we retreat into the bin store and a couple of garages that partially survived the fire.

We share what few possessions we have – scissors, a wind-up torch, a few tatty books, needles and cotton, an almost spent First Aid kit. Pathetic.

We each have a job. Mike (that's me) and Jen, my partner, are wood collectors. For the fire. Others cook, attempt to keep the place clean and sanitary, and some guard the commune from the vicious marauding gangs that burst in and steal everything. They kill if they feel like it. For fun.

Fear is our daily companion – fear of disease, fear of capture, or of an attack. Fear of a violent death for us both.

Jen and I are snuggled down on our mattress, fully clothed, with two duvets covering us. We are barely warm enough. Ever.

Jen is like a skeleton. Me too, I suppose.

I look at her blackened face in the firelight. At her dirty and matted hair. We don't wash. No point. No water. All our precious standards have long gone. We are fighting to survive. Right on the very edge. I feel my desire to live ebb away each day.

I could cry as I look at her but that will get us nowhere. We need to be strong. And ruthless. If we are to make it.

I nudge her. "Time to go, Jen, love."

"Right," she says wearily and reluctantly. "Where to tonight?"

"Goscote Valley. Remember? The shed I told you about – if we can find it. I can't think of anywhere else."

It was as though a plague of locusts had descended on the area and devoured all the wood There must be a hundred small groups like ours scavenging for anything. Everything.

The animals and wildlife have gone. Eaten. Now it is just fuel to keep us warm.

"I'll get the clubs. You got the string and the wind-up torch?"

Jen nodded.

We both knew this would be a long and dangerous journey. Well out of our area.

We hold the string loosely in our hands. This allows us to walk about ten feet apart in the pitch dark. We communicate in a crude way, to alert each other, by pulling it tight. If one of us was stopped by a patrol, we would drop the string and the other could possibly escape in the darkness. Possibly.

"We'll walk down the road, up the alley at Shelfield, then across the fields to the river."

"Okay," said Jen, "but not too fast, Mike. I find it hard to trample through all this ash."

"Don't worry, I haven't the energy, love. In any case we need to be very careful. The patrols are everywhere."

Jen gives me a hug. "They won't find us. We can't even find each other without the string!"

She gives a feeble laugh. The first time in ages. Humour is a distant memory. A casualty of our desperation. What would I do without her? I give her a hug.

We put scarves around our faces and set off. It is deathly quiet, the ash muffling our footsteps.

Every few hundred yards we stop and hug each other. Whether for comfort or reassurance, I don't know. Or perhaps deep down we know that if things go wrong this would be our last physical contact.

As we cross the fields in Goscote Valley, I feel a sharp tug on the string and stop instantly. Jen appears beside me and whispers in my ear: "Voices. To the left. Three, I think."

We crouch down and pull out the thick wooden staves we use as clubs.

I can hear them now, moving towards us

"Where's the river?" one says. "If we can find it, we can follow it home."

Jen pushes me, face down in the ash, then joins me, her gloved hand on mine.

Suddenly the glare of a powerful light silhouettes the three people. It is accompanied by a shout: "Curfew Patrol. Stand still, you scum!"

We are about a yard away from the pool of light and those who had been caught only a few feet further in.

They freeze. One shouts "Run!" and the three of them scurry away from the light.

Crack...Crack...Crack.

Three rifle shots disturb the peaceful night and the runners slump to the ground, each one sending up a cloud of ash as they fall. They don't move.

Jen clutches my hand even tighter.

One of the Patrol moves slowly into the circle of light, looking around. We hold our breath. Petrified he will see us.

"No more," he shouts as he walks over to the bodies. "Well done, lads. I'll see to them. Leave the light. I'll catch up with you at the bridge."

The man takes items from the bodies. This will prove their work and earn them extra food and other privileges.

Before I can stop her, Jen crawls forward and stands up just outside the pool of light. Then, as the man is kneeling over one of the bodies, she rushes forward, club in the air, uttering a low guttural sound. The man hears her too late and only has time to move his head. She hits him a powerful blow on the back of his neck. All her pent up hopelessness, frustration and anger seem to be concentrated into that first deadly blow.

She hits him again. And again. I knew he was dead. He had to be.

I rush across and put my arms around her. She is shaking.

"Search him," I say. "Quick, in case the others heard anything. I'll get the light."

Jen strips him of a rifle, a pistol, a hunting knife, his ID card.

"I can't believe it," she says. "Look. Four bars of chocolate! I haven't seen chocolate for years."

Together we strip him of his long leather coat, his scarf, a warm pullover, his trousers and boots. Then we drag him into the bushes and cover him with ash.

"Let's look at the others," Jen says softly.

Gently we turn them over. They are all dead. Shot in the back. One, a girl, no more than twelve years old. A child.

"Probably a family," she says. "Desperate, like us."

Then she threw up.

We agree to forget about the wood; it is more important to get the other stuff back. This time we walk together. Secure with the guns.

At last we approach the commune, exhausted. We sense something is wrong.

"We'll leave the stuff here, Jen," I whisper. "Guard it with the pistol. Use it if you have to." She nods.

I creep silently around the burned out buildings and look into the courtyard. By the light of the fire I can see everyone lying on the floor, hands on their heads. The children are crying. Four men with assorted weapons are searching them roughly. Our lookout, Roy, is sprawled on the floor, either unconscious or dead.

"Where's the food?!" one shouts, as he kicks our friend Charlotte in the ribs. Hard. She groans and points to one of the garages.

The man kicks her again. "Tell everyone Dr. Johnson's Mob have visited. We will come every week for food. If there is none, we will kill you one by one." He points to Roy. "You'll be dead, just like him." He laughs. They all laugh.

I am about to intervene, rifle at the ready, when I sense someone behind me. I turn to see the razor-sharp edge of a machete just before it splits open my skull. I feel the bone splinter.

A rope goes around my throat and tightens, choking me. *Can't breathe.* Blood runs down my face, into my eyes. *No way am I going to get out of this.*

Before losing consciousness I hear a sinister voice in my ear: "I'm Dr. Johnson..."

The sudden light is vivid. Startlingly white. Blinding. It penetrates my eyelids.

Then, a shadow in front of me cuts it off. A white figure moves in close.

"Wake up, Michael. I'm Dr. Johnson, the one who operated on your brain tumour. You're lucky. We got it all."

The darkness comes again...

TWITCHED

I've been married too long. Thirty years to be precise. I'm stifled. Everything is so predictable, the never-ending mediocrity of it all – his jokes, his birds, his friends, his work, his dress sense, his love-making. We have become a real 'Howard and Hilda' couple, sleepwalking through our marriage. That's my name by the way – Hilda. My husband is John.

I need an electric shock from one of those resuscitation machines to jolt me back to life. Some thrills. Some passion. To feel special again. I feel a need to do something outrageous.

Don't get me wrong, I don't hate my husband, he's always been there for me, treated me well and I know he's devoted to me. He'd be horrified to hear me talking like this. It's just that he's so wrapped up in his work and his damned birdwatching – yes, that kind. He is not the type to even look at another woman. He's a Twitcher. Spends all his spare time out there with his binoculars. Talks about nothing else, incessantly. Me, I can't tell a Grey Wagtail from a bloody eiderdown. It all leaves me cold.

Believe me, I didn't go looking, I'm not that sort of woman. Too reserved. But I was desperate. Just a fling, I thought, something to kick-start my life again, to recharge my emotional batteries.

I feel so ashamed, so guilty about feeling like this. It's as though I'm betraying him. Breaking our marriage vows. My mother, bless her, would turn in her grave. But it's a matter of survival, isn't it?

Pete is his name. He's not a hunk, just a normal bloke. We met by chance in a coffee shop. A woman had fainted and we both went to help. Fate? Who knows?

"Nothing serious," he said, when she came round. Her friend took her home.

"No," I replied, "but I'll have another cup of coffee to steady my nerves."

"Mind if I join you?"

And that's how it started.

We hit it off immediately and met in the same place for a week or two. Talking and sharing our lives, as friends do. But just being friends wasn't enough for me. It was a pleasant distraction, but not enough to revitalise my life. So I found the courage. "Pete...I'm mad about you," I blurted out. His face had a surprised look. "Can't we...you know...have a fling, or whatever they call it these days?"

He put his hand on mine and said in mock surprise, "You mean become an *item?*"

"Don't muck about. An under-the-counter item maybe, known only to the two of us. Unlike you, I have to be careful. People know me around here."

I looked into his wonderful dark brown eyes. "And I also have to do battle with my conscience. Although John is as stale as last week's bread I still care for him and he dotes on me. It would destroy him if he knew about us."

"Okay, Hilda, I understand. You want some clandestine passion." He winked at me. "Of the sexual variety, I hope?"

I felt so embarrassed and so ashamed. But, yes, that's what I wanted.

"You'd like some loving attention, without upsetting your marriage, is that it?"

I nodded.

"With no strings. I know it's a lot to ask, and very selfish of me."

"Cheer up, little lady. It suits me too. With my job taking me away, I can't afford to get too attached, wouldn't be fair. Tell you what, let's try it for a couple of months and see how it goes."

Fortunately, John worked late at the office one night a week and was out birdwatching most weekends. This gave Pete and me time together, and we used it well – very discreetly, of course. I felt liberated doing my own thing and having Pete lavish attention on me. And, naturally, by the sex. But at another level I felt the strong tug of the emotional umbilical cord which attached me to John and, in my quieter moments, overwhelming guilt tore me apart.

The dynamics of our marital relationship changed. I suppose, because I was in a more positive frame of mind, it encouraged John to be so too. He took more notice of me, we talked more and everything seemed to perk up, even our love life.

Barely into our third clandestine month, Pete dropped the bombshell: "Sorry, Hilda, my love, they're sending me to South Africa on a one year contract." He read the disappointment on my face and shook his head. "I've tried to wriggle out of it…"

"When?" was all I could say.

"This weekend, I'm afraid. Bit of an emergency."

"But it's Friday today…"

"I know. I'm sorry, love."

My mind raced, trying to take it in. I'd known it wouldn't last forever and, of late, the passion had subsided a little. Perhaps it had served its purpose, dragged me out of the marital mire. I felt more positive about myself, and my marriage was reviving. All this, thanks to Pete.

"I'd like to buy you something to remember me by," he said. "Some jewellery, perhaps? You choose. Money no object." He looked at me and laughed. "Within reason."

"Really, Pete, there's no need...although it would be nice to have something to cherish."

I chose an emerald ring. Large stone, with a diamond studded shank. A beautiful Victorian antique, a one-off. It cost two thousand five hundred pounds but Pete didn't seem to mind. It was just what I wanted.

I wore it as we said goodbye in our coffee shop. I placed my hand on his, the green stone sparkling. "It will remind me of you forever." I leaned across the table and kissed him.

They say parting is always difficult and I could tell Pete was struggling to find the right words.

"Keeping in touch will be difficult where I am," he said. I nodded. "What say we leave it at this. We both have fond memories and the ring will remind you. Wear it when you think of me."

"I will, I will." I squeezed his hand. "We both have new challenges ahead – your job, and me making a go of my marriage."

We hugged each other and parted as we had met – as friends.

I was determined to start the task of rebuilding my marriage that night, one of John's late ones. He looked exhausted when he arrived home, poor chap. My heart went out to him. I kissed him on the cheek.

"Go and have a shower and get out of your work clothes. Don't be long. I've cooked your favourite – spaghetti bolognese."

I had even put candles on the table.

Over a bottle of wine we talked and laughed like old times.

"You've changed, Hilda," he said. "Sort of found yourself again."

"You too, John. Much more your old attentive self. I'm so pleased."

He laughed. "Yes, I realised I'd become stale. Past my sell-by date perhaps?

I joined in, genuinely happy despite Pete's departure.

I had one problem. What to do with the ring? I desperately wanted to wear it. It symbolised a turning point in my life. But John would notice and I couldn't pass it off as cheap bling. It looked what it was – rare and expensive. I decided to hand it in to the police station as if I had found it.

"Nice ring, madam," the man behind the desk said. He smiled at me. "If no one claims it within a month, it's yours." He handed me a receipt. "Bring this with you."

All that was on it was the name of the police station and a reference number. Even better. I could tell John I had found the receipt, perhaps even get him to redeem it. And that's what I did: gave him the receipt and left it with him.

Wrapped up in my new-found happiness, I had almost forgotten about it, until John reminded me at the annual RSPB Branch dinner. We were among the guests of honour and had to greet everyone as they entered the dining room.

"Sorry, Hilda, I almost forgot..." John pulled a ring box out of his jacket pocket. "I finally got around to getting this from the police station. Looks great. I put it in a nice box for you."

I put my hand on his arm "Thank you, dear. What would I do without you."

I couldn't wait to put the ring on and a delay in the line allowed me to open the box immediately. I nearly passed out. Inside was a plain looking eternity ring! Surely there had been some mistake?

John nudged me. "Come on, dear, we're falling behind."

"What? Oh...sorry."

A lady was waiting to shake my hand.

"This is Amanda, our Branch Secretary."

I gave her a dazed smile. As I grabbed her hand, my thumb touched a large stone. I looked down. On her finger sparkled my beautiful antique ring...

JUST ANOTHER DAY

As I said to the Inspector, it started like any other day.

"Mommy, why isn't Father Christmas black?"

My four year old asking impossible questions again at the most awkward times.

"Shoes on, Cheryl, babe, or we'll be late for Nursery, and Mommy late for work."

Under my breath I cursed Cheryl's father, my ex-husband, for not being around to help out. He would know about Father Christmas, or perhaps the nursery staff will have the answer.

Then into work. I am the Security Manager at a new high-rise business complex – all tinted glass and high-tech security. Yes, I know. I have to pinch myself sometimes, a woman too, and black.

My staff are all men. Nine of them in total. They think it's all about brawn and uniforms, but I know it is about brains. I always wonder though if brains will be enough.

The day like any other was shattered when the phone rang.

"We have your daughter, Mrs. Robinson. Do as we say and she will be returned. Tell anyone and she's dead. Be near the phone at eleven."

The line went dead before I could speak. Practical joke? No, it can't be. A cold shudder ran through me. This is real. Oh God, don't let them hurt her. Then another phone call, this time from the Nursery to say Cheryl had been picked up by my brother. Just checking that it was okay.

"What?..Oh…sorry…I completely forgot. Yes, yes it's okay. Don't worry."

Don't worry? I am frantic. *I don't have a brother.* But what else could I say?

Eleven o'clock came: nothing. Stay calm. At five past the phone rang.

"Just listen: *One.* Take over the evening shift. *Two.* Switch off the CCTV at six forty-five. *Three.* Let us in through the back door at seven p.m. *Four.* Have the key to Jasmine Associates available. Tell no one or your daughter is dead."

I was trembling as I scribbled down the instructions. I pictured Cheryl hiding in a corner and crying…Oh God. Stay calm. Deep breaths. Be positive. Think!

Into the Ladies. I splash water on my face and sit down to think it through. What are they up to?

Jasmine Associates are overseas property consultants. Low security risk. One office plus toilet. Two men in and out a couple of times each week. No visitors. Nothing of interest. It doesn't make sense – what am I missing?

Then into their office. Nothing unusual – computer, photocopier, property brochures. Nothing hidden that I could see. No safe. One brochure caught my eye – a property development at Diamond Head, Hawaii. It triggered a spark – diamonds. We have a diamond dealer on the ninth floor. No obvious connection. I was still no wiser; my mind was working overtime.

As I went down in the lift, the answer suddenly dawned on me. Yes, I was sure.

At six thirty I checked that the building was empty, locked the entrance doors and quickly got to work. When I had finished, I secured the building by the remote control system – the lift, the stairs and the security doors at both ends of each floor were deadlocked. Wonderful system: a single switch. Impregnable, the makers say. But then again, so was the Titanic.

I was waiting at the rear door when they arrived. Two of them, both well built. Dressed in boiler suits and face masks. As they stepped inside one of them grabbed me roughly by the arm. "Your little girl will be released when we leave." I could almost feel his sneer.

He pushed me into the security office. "CCTV off?" he asked, looking at the blank monitors. I nodded. They seemed convinced, unaware that I had only disconnected the monitors but left the cameras recording. "Now open the security doors."

How the hell do they know about the system?

I keyed in the security code and flipped the switch to open all the deadlocks. I also handed over the keys to Jasmine Associates. One of them bound my hands in front of me with a plastic strap and then bundled me into the lift. As they pushed me into the office of Jasmine Associates, I noticed they left the keys in the door. I was dragged through the office and pushed hard into the toilet; I hit the wall and crumpled on to the floor.

"Stay in there and be quiet, otherwise you know what will happen. We will be finished in an hour."

After half an hour, I gently edged open the door a fraction and peered through the crack – one man was sitting at the desk, the other at the computer. Both had their backs to me. Ideal!

I opened the sink cupboard and pulled out the items I had put there earlier: a respirator and two canisters of CS gas. I struggled to put the respirator on and then pulled the tabs on the two canisters, waiting five seconds before throwing them into the office. They immediately exploded into billowing clouds of gas. It tore at their eyes and throats; they choked, retched and stumbled, totally disoriented.

I made a mad dash for the door and locked it from the outside, sinking down against the corridor wall, hardly able to breathe. Gas had crept into the ill-fitting mask. It was about ten minutes before I was able to make my way down to the security office.

Once there I threw the security switch, completely locking down the building, then I locked the rear door which had been left open when the men arrived.

"Which was when I called you, Inspector," I said.

Inspector Dave Kemp had taken the call. The caller's voice was hysterical and raw, her words punctuated by fits of coughing. He eventually understood that she had trapped two burglars and was frantic with worry about the safety of her daughter.

He mobilised the few resources he had and arrived at the building twenty minutes later.

"Don't worry, Mrs. Robinson. Cheryl is safe and well. She is with your mother."

"Thank God." I staggered back into a chair. The Inspector caught my arm and cut the plastic restraint on my wrists with his penknife. He looked concerned. "You okay?"

I nodded.

"Tell me what happened."

"They said they had abducted my daughter and would kill her if I didn't co-operate." I started to shake at the thought of it. "It was horrible."

"Where are they now?"

"Locked in a room full of CS gas on floor six. It's all on CCTV."

"Show me."

I switched on the monitors and reversed the recording to seven o'clock. It showed the two men entering the building, taking me captive and going into Jasmine Associates office. I was about to fast forward it when he pointed to the screen. "Wait a minute. What's that?"

I ran it again. The monitor showed that at the time we entered the lift, another man, scarf over his face, came through the unlocked rear door, into the security office, then up the stairs, eventually emerging on floor nine where he used a key to enter one of the offices.

"That's the diamond merchants!" I said.

I fast forwarded the disc. Half an hour later the man came out, back down to the security office and left the building. We looked at each other.

"What the hell was that?" I was puzzled.

"At a guess, I'd say it was someone stealing diamonds."

The monitor showed me slumped in the corridor on floor six, coughing and spluttering, with my wrists tied and looking the worse for wear.

Inspector Kemp shook his head in the silence which followed. He spoke hesitantly. "I'm sorry, Mrs. Robinson. You need to know that the people who kept you prisoner were from a private security firm, hired to test your security response. It was an exercise. Your daughter was safe at the Nursery all day."

"But the Nursery rang to say someone had taken her...?"

"All part of their plan, I'm afraid. The call wasn't from the Nursery. Your mother also had a call from them asking her to pick up Cheryl at the normal time." He shook his head in disbelief. "They said you had been delayed at work."

I couldn't help it, my hands instinctively went to my face and I began to cry. "I thought they would kill her," I sobbed.

"Best get you home so you can see her for yourself. Your Deputy is on his way. He can hold the fort while we see about releasing the animals who put you through this." A smile crossed his face. "I'll take my time looking through the CCTV footage again. They can stew for a bit longer..."

It turned out that one point two million pounds in diamonds had been stolen. The police had no idea who the thief was. I was exonerated from any blame, of course – even commended by the Company and given a bravery award by the police.

I told them I would resign. That I was not prepared to put myself or my family through such an ordeal again. They understood, and their guilt led them to pay me six months' salary in lieu of notice, plus five thousand pounds for the distress I had been caused.

Three weeks later, when the money had reached my bank account, I asked my mother if she could cope with Cheryl for a few days while I had a break. I had to get away, to re-charge my batteries. She understood.

The following morning I broke the news to Cheryl: "Mommy is going on holiday for a few days, babe. Is that okay? Nanny will look after you."

"Is it to the seaside Mommy? To St. Kitts, where Nanny goes?"

"No, darling, it is to a place called Amsterdam. Mommy will be meeting Daddy there. They have something to sell."

SPATZ FOSTER, PRIVATE EYE

It had overwhelmed him as a little lad. An only child.

Daniel Foster fantasised. About his abilities, his looks, his family – absolutely everything.

Daniel became all the characters in his comics. He swam the Channel, climbed Everest, rowed across the Atlantic, and had beaten up all the bad guys.

Often he could not distinguish between truth and fiction, between dreams and reality, between the real world and his imagination.

Daniel was happy in his dream-world. Very happy. Although alone, he was never lonely.

As he grew up he had no choice but to accept the imposition of the real world. School and work forced their unwanted attention on him but his fantasy world never died. It was alive. Thriving.

Dan's job in the railway ticket office was boring. He met scores of people every day. Imagined who they were, what they did. Some of the regulars would smile at him and say "Hello". He called them his friends. He had no others.

After work, back in his little bedsit, Dan conjured up images of them – became a Director of their Company, had mad passionate love affairs, played professional football with them, helped them solve their marital problems.

When he was thirty, Dan Foster's life took a dramatic turn. He won the Lottery – almost one million pounds. It was in the local newspaper.

This was his big chance. He could now do anything he wanted. Be anything he wanted. The world was his oyster.

He knew straight away what he must do. His long held ambition, gleaned from comics when he was a lad, was to become a Private Eye – a Private Detective. He would solve all the difficult cases. Have his name regularly in the crime section of the newspapers, have informants and influential friends in the police and in the underworld.

He knew he had all the necessary skills and talent. He had practised them over and over again in his fantasy life.

So here he was, watching as they erected the sign over his Office. It read 'Spatz Detective Agency. Friendly and Professional Service. We Solve Anything & Everything. Success Guaranteed'.

Dan had to wait three days before his first client appeared. Melanie Sparks was her name. She had phoned him to see if she could drop in.

Melanie Sparks. He heard her coming in the front door. She would be in her twenties. Drop-dead gorgeous. High class. Rich. Overburdened with a problem which he would solve.

The thought of meeting a famous Private Eye would turn her on. His magnetic boyish charms would be irresistible to her. They would become lovers. Now. Right there on his desk. Holy Moly!

The door to his office opened and in walked a forty-something woman. Her urge to diet was obviously defeated. She was trying hard to maintain her once good looks – unsuccessfully, he thought – dyed red hair, breasts escaping from a too tight blouse, tight skirt showing too much thigh. Crippling heels.

Sexual passion on the desk...? I don't think so. Perhaps she's a rich widow.

"I want to see the gaffer..."

Her raucous voice grated.

Dan held out his hand. "I'm Dan Foster, otherwise known as Spatz. I run the Agency."

Her hand was soft, damp, big. It held on to his for too long as she leant forward to parade her cleavage and waft her perfume in front of his face.

"Pleased to meet you, Dan. Call me Mel," she said.

Dan gestured to a chair and she sat down. She hitched her already too short skirt even higher. Then Dan made his first mistake.

"What can I do for you, Mel?"

She pounced on it, slowly uncrossing and crossing her legs in an exaggerated Sharon Stone movement that revealed...he wasn't sure what...but it unsettled him.

In a Marilyn Monroe sexy whisper she said: "That's the best offer I've had all day, love. I'm completely in your hands..."

Seeking damage limitation, Dan sat firmly back into the safety of his enormous black leather chair. He put on a serious face.

"Now, what's the problem, Mel?"

"It's Nancy, my daughter, Dan. She's gone missing."

She began to cry. Mascara streaks ran down her face. "She's only sixteen. She's all I've got now that her dad's gone."

His thoughts of her less than desirable appearance were undermined by her tears. She looked vulnerable. Desperate. Alone. Dan felt sorry for her.

Dan gathered her into his arms.

'Don't worry, doll. Relax. Spatz Foster is on the case. I will find her. No problem. They don't call me the town's best Private Eye for nuthin'.'

She melted into his arms.

'Thank you, Spatz,' she said, through her tears.

"I'm worried sick, Dan," she said. "She's probably off with that toe-rag boyfriend of hers. Gary Wade. He runs drugs and goodness knows what."

"You realise at sixteen she can choose her own life?"

"I know but I want the best for her; for her to settle down with some bloke who will look after her properly. To have a better life than I've had. Besides, she wouldn't just disappear without telling me. We're close. I think she's been abducted. Forced into white slavery...kept somewhere against her will."

White Slavery! He could be up there with the big boys – Major Crime Units, MI5 – help them pull down a cartel. He could become one of their undercover Agents. The Agency would become a front for their operations.

Her mascara now resembled an Army camouflage demonstration.

He gave her a Kleenex. Then another.

"How much?" she asked.

'Don't worry, doll. One of the rewards of being a rich, successful Private Eye is that Spatz can afford to be generous in certain heart-rending cases. Yours is today's, babe.'

"You're my first client, Mel. When I bring Nancy home safe and sound we can come to some sort of arrangement."

Clang again. She didn't pick up on it.

She smiled through her tears: "I might have won the lottery by then." She gave him a knowing wink.

Kleenex Number Three.

The following day Dan went to the boyfriend's address.

Spatz was tooled up with a Smith & Wesson .45 in his shoulder holster. His reflective glasses gave nothing away.

He casually leaned on the door frame as he knocked. It was opened by a vest-clad hoodlum. He looked as hard as nails, but not as sharp. All muscle but no class. Spatz stabbed him with his finger. 'Hey punk. Don't mess with me or you'll end up in the morgue. Got it!'

Spatz could tell the man was scared witless.

He hit him with his finger again. 'You Gary Wade?'

The man was quaking as he nodded.

'You got Nancy here, fella? The truth now or your brains will put a new pattern on your wallpaper.'

This time he shook his head. 'Don't know where she is. Don't care.'

Spatz believed him.

Dan's hand was shaking as he knocked hesitantly on Gary Wade's door.

A young man answered. He was big and muscled. An unshaven skinhead. Tatoos up to the eyeballs. Definitely not friendly.

"Yeah...?"

135

"Eh...hello. My name is Dan Foster. Can I talk to you about Nancy?"

"Piss off, mate, before I throw you down the stairs!"

The door slammed shut. End of conversation.

Dan wandered away. Obviously his Hi-Viz jacket with 'Security' printed on it had not intimidated the lad.

All great detectives have setbacks. Remember Kojak? Always in trouble. That's what makes us tough.

Spatz knew he could have easily disabled the punk with his unarmed combat skills, even killed him. A quick jab to the throat, a Karate chop to his neck, but he decided it would not help the case.

Far better to use his sophisticated surveillance techniques to find Wade's associates. Get one of them as a snout. Find Nancy that way.

Brains 2. Brawn 0.

Dan's primrose yellow Peugeot 107 (he called it the 'Tec Mobile) followed Gary Wade's unsuspecting BMW through the town. It stopped to drop off packages at two different places. At the third stop Dan saw the contact come out of a nearby café, take a package through the BMW window and disappear back into the café.

Dan parked and went in, ordered a coffee and waited.

Ten minutes later the man went into the Gents.

Dan left it a couple of minutes and then followed, opening the door quietly.

Spatz couldn't see anyone. But he heard a conversation in one of the cubicles.

He couldn't hear what was being said.

Two men he could handle. He'd subdued more than that in his time. No problemo.

The other man came out first. Spatz floored him with a single punch. Out for the count.

He pinned his man against the wall and frisked him, relieving him of a 9mm Colt Automatic and a flick knife.

Spatz held the gun to the man's neck. His body quivered. 'Don't hurt me,' he pleaded.

'I want information, buster. Co-operate and you'll live to finish your coffee. If not, your lights will go out. Permanently. Got it, punk!?'

The man nodded as enthusiastically as anyone could with a gun in their neck.

'Gary Wade's girl, Nancy. Know where she is?'

He nodded and whispered an address. Spatz knew the area.

'What's your name, son?'

'Randy...'

'Right then, Randy, my son, you work for me now. Understand?' Spatz gave him his card. 'Otherwise. Bang. Bang. You're dead meat.'

The man dropped to the floor, petrified. Spatz didn't blame him.

Spatz Foster rides again...!

When Dan went into the toilet he heard a conversation in one of the cubicles, then a flush.

The door opened and his man came out alone, finishing a conversation on his mobile phone. "Okay," he said, and put it into his pocket.

"Can I talk to you a minute?" Dan asked.

The man was washing his hands. He turned and shrugged his shoulders. His manner was hostile. Dan could see the suspicion in his eyes.

"I want some info. I'm willing to pay…"

"Yeah…?"

"Gary Wade's girlfriend, Nancy. I'm trying to find her. Know where she is?"

"Hhhhhow mmmmmuch?" The man stammered. *Why couldn't the world be simple?*

"Fifty pounds."

"Mmmmake it tttwo hhhhhundred."

Dan paid him and got the address. Also the information that Gary was going to be out of town for a couple of days.

"Any mmmore wwwork, mmmmate?"

Dan gave him his card and wrote the man's telephone number in his notebook.

"What's your name?"

"Hhhherbert. Fffriends call mmme Hhherb."

Spatz sat outside the address in the 'Tec Mobile all night. Food, drink, sleep didn't matter when he was near to closing a case. Come dawn he would slip a catch on the back window of the house, find Nancy's bedroom and sweet talk her into coming with him or strong-arm her into the back of his car. Deliver her to her Momma.

Someone pounding on the window awoke him. It was light. People about. He looked at his watch as he roused himself. Nine o'clock!

He wound down the window and a beautiful young woman put her head through.

She smiled. "You Dan Foster, the famous detective?"

"Sure," he replied.

"I'm Nancy," she said. "Been waiting for you since Herb rang last night. My cases are packed – in the hall."

She got in the passenger seat and Dan hauled himself out of the car and fetched two suitcases.

"You might be the town's best detective, Dan, but this car smells like a sweaty Indian brothel. Ugh. It reeks!"

"Sorry. I slept in it last night. Had a takeaway. Vindaloo. Would you mind if we called at my place so I can have a shower and change?"

She smiled her beautiful smile again. "Okay. You can make me a cup of tea."

So, you're a real Private Eye. Never met one before. Exciting. Fab.

Nancy was obviously impressed by his occupation, by his penthouse apartment and, judging by the way she came on to him in the car, by his suave good looks.

'Call me Spatz,' he said.

He poured them both champagne from his bar and they drifted on to his balcony, looking at the view over the river.

'Magnificent,' she exclaimed. 'I like a man with style and good taste, Spatz. I could learn to enjoy this…'

They clinked glasses and went inside, snuggling up together on the couch.

He had always been irresistible to women. Like a sensual magnet. Like moths to a flame.

But this was different. Comfortable. With an inkling of father-figure-hood. He liked that.

'I must take off these stinking clothes and have a shower, Nance. Won't be long.'

Her voluptuous body was waiting for him in the shower. It didn't surprise him. She washed him down and they made passionate love under the warm water.

And then again on his kingsize. She liked the mirrors on the ceiling. Holy Moly!

Completely satisfied, she whispered 'Can I stay with you forever, Spatz.'

He knew she meant it.

He nodded. 'Sure, babe. Forever sounds good. What about a quickie wedding?'

On the way to Mamma's they stopped off at a downtown jewellery store. Nancy chose a two-carat engagement ring. But what the hell. Not every day you give your heart away.

He let her go ahead of him. Nancy and Mel threw their arms around each other. The ring became the centre of attention and they both started jumping for joy. Literally.

"Me and Dan are getting married," she was saying as he reached them.

Mel beamed at him. "I could tell you were a fast worker, Dan," she said. "Fantastic news." She kissed him on the cheek.

"How about a honeymoon in the Bahamas for us all?" she suggested. "I've got the brochures…"

Dan nodded but a niggling thought flashed through his mind. Was the case <u>too</u> easy? Had he been set up?

No Way, Jose. All great detectives make solving cases look easy. Their skills and superior intelligence did the work for them. Spatz was no exception.

THE DRAGON GIRL

I was excited. Couldn't wait for her arrival. I had everything ready, everything done.

Impatience is such a motivator, isn't it? And fear. What if she doesn't come?

But she will, I know. I have to *will* her hard enough and she will appear, for she lives in my head, you see. Shelters there. Always has done since I was a little girl.

Her name is Saphira. She is a dragon.

Every day she steps out of my head to visit me. That may seem unusual, even strange to you, but it isn't really, once you grasp the notion that your whole body is nothing more than your thoughts, in a form you can see.

Safira is magnificent. Beautiful. With paper-thin silvery wings, sharp claws and a long tail, she breathes smoke down her nostrils and flaming fire can sometimes erupt from her mouth. But not very often.

Despite her appearance she is not heavy as she perches on my arm. Sometimes she puts her wings around me. To comfort me. I feel like a chrysalis, all protected. Warm and cosy. It's wonderful. We talk to each other about everything and her squeaky dragon-like voice gives me lots of advice. No one else can see or hear her, of course. She is my secret.

You probably think I'm off my trolley, don't you? Doolally, mad, insane, or at least seriously deluded. That's what my mother thinks anyway. She took me to see several people in white coats. Doctors, I presumed, but they never bothered to introduce themselves to me. Most were men. They bristled with their self-importance and maintained a quiet hostility as my mother told them about Saphira. She was so convincing they probably thought 'folie à deux' was at work (to some extent this was true – mother has always been a bit of a human dragon). They stared at her incredulously with an intensity which made her drop her gaze to the floor, like a piece of litter.

Most didn't bother to speak to *me* at all and those who did used the tone of voice usually reserved for stupid people and foreigners. I didn't answer.

They prescribed tablets of one sort or another. I pretended to take them and said I was cured. They didn't want to see me again. I was discharged, they said. Another feather in their cap, another line on their CV, another case to flaunt before adoring students.

Only one got it right. A delicate lady in a white coat who looked as though she had been discharged from hospital too early. She told my mother that everyone has such episodes as a child; saw things others couldn't, adopted pretend playmates, usually from stories they had heard.

"They are like a comfort blanket," she explained. "We invent them to keep us safe and secure; to protect us from the Bogeymen, from the dark and from a hostile world." Her face went whiter still. "As we lose our childhood innocence, we don't talk openly about such things. We replace them with obsessions, compulsive behaviour, addictions and fantasies. These serve the same purpose."

The unfortunate face that life had bestowed on her softened into what she probably thought was a smile but looked more like the contemptuous sneer of a schoolteacher addressing a small child.

"Mrs. Parker," she said, in a condescending manner. "Let me give you a piece of advice." She paused to make sure she had my mother's full attention. "Once you realise everyone in this world is a little mad, your life becomes easier."

My mother was having none of it. She told me later that she thought the woman had been seeing too many mad people for too long. But I think she was right, don't you? Look at the people you know. Aren't they all a little mad? And what about you?

When I was eighteen things changed.

Saphira became distant, impatient with me. She told me I should be standing on my own two feet more and not be so reliant upon her. I should move on, she said.

I was confused. There was something in the tone of her voice I didn't understand. That I didn't like.

"What do you mean?" I asked.

"You seem to imagine I belong to you alone." She shrieked. "Do you think you are the only one? I have many people who seek my attention and wisdom. It drains me." Her voice tailed off.

I was shocked. "I don't believe you!" I said indignantly. "You belong to me. You live in my head."

"Doubt my word, do you, girl? Come with me."

Before I could object she had me firmly in her claws and we were flying across the land. I only had my thin nighty on and it was cold and windy. We landed in a forest clearing, near a big bonfire. The place was filled with people. I saw one or two dragons, and other creatures I didn't recognise – ugly frightful things with snarling faces and big teeth.

The people were dancing round the fire, chanting in time to a drum. Saphira told me to join in and I did. We were chanting and clapping, moving slowly around the fire. The heat relaxed me and I was soon in the grip of some form of hypnotic trance, my body swaying to the rhythm of the drumbeat. My head was spinning and my whole body was trembling and becoming out of control. I closed my eyes and let whatever was gripping me take me over.

Through my haze I heard someone shout "Do you believe?" Everyone around me responded "We do!" The drum suddenly stopped. "A non-believer!" I heard someone near me say. Then everyone took up the chant "Non-believer! Non-believer!"

I opened my eyes to see the whole circle chanting and pointing at me. *At me!*

Then an eerie silence. I was shivering, despite the heat of the fire. The silence was broken as another chant began "Sacrifice! Sacrifice!" The mantra was delivered by hostile faces, full of murderous intent.

A blindfold suddenly went over my eyes.

"Saphira, help me, please! I don't know what I am supposed to believe."

"Too late now, my dear, I'm sorry. The sacrificial slaughter of a non-believer must go ahead. You will be devoured by the Dragon King, my father."

I must have fainted. When I awoke, Saphira had her wings around me. "I think I can help," she said. "When he opens his jaws and takes you into his mouth, just before he swallows you alive, tell him you are a friend of mine and ask him to fly you to meet me at the cave."

With my trance-like state wearing off and the sacrificial chant still ringing in my ears, strong arms grabbed me and stood me nearer the fire on some form of platform.

The chanting stopped abruptly. I heard the flapping of wings above me. Enormous teeth lifted me up and I fell back into a wet slippery hole which I assumed was the Dragon King's mouth. It was like a large greasy, smelly, oven. I felt his smooth tongue licking me, cleaning me, ready to eat.

"I am a friend of Saphira," I shouted.

The licking stopped.

"She wants you to take me to her, in the cave..."

A loud grunt came from his throat, deafening me. His tongue pushed me sideways and then completely covered me, protecting me as the roar of a fierce flame emerged from his mouth. Even under his slimy slobbering tongue I could feel its searing heat.

I heard his wings flap as we suddenly took off. I slithered around his mouth as we flew, but he didn't swallow me. Didn't eat me alive.

When we landed, I slid out of his mouth and landed on a soft white bed. I was confused and weary, but otherwise okay.

I opened my eyes. "Where am I?" I asked a lady in a white coat.

She smiled. "You are in the psychiatric clinic again, dear," she replied. "Where they bring you when you haven't been taking your medication. You know very well it lets the dragons take you over."

I hear Saphira's wings flap as she flies away.

"I'll be back," she says.

THE FINAL CHALLENGE

"I would support the introduction of compulsory euthanasia for everyone over the age of seventy."

I put it as forcefully as I could, leaning forward to engage the audience.

"The country would be better off without them."

I heard a murmur ripple through the young audience of the Uni Debating Society.

I couldn't tell whether it was a favourable response, but it didn't matter, I was into my stride now. Into a subject I felt passionate about.

"Friends, we should no longer tolerate these geriatric dinosaurs."

My fist hit the table as I said it. It hurt. I waited for the impact to settle.

"Their pensions are bankrupting the country. Their pessimism and cynical attitude undermine our pride and our progress – drags down this once proud nation. We deserve better."

Keep cool. Keep your tone strong. Scan the audience and make eye contact.

"They occupy the majority of NHS beds, use most of its resources. They demand free bus passes, winter fuel payments and anything else they can get their hands on, as though it is a right." I raise both my hands into the air. "Tell me, just tell me – what do they contribute to our Society? Tell me."

No one moves to speak.

"Exactly!"

I pause. *Smile and lighten the mood.*

"They trudge along like zombies, drive like Noddy on a bad day, in their clapped out ancient cars or mobility scooters and witter on unceasingly about the past. Talk to them about iPhones, Twitter or the Net and dementia cuts in. Their main topic of conversation seems to be their grandchildren and their ailments – it's like an organ recital..."

I pause until the laughter dies down.

"In conclusion, my friends, elderly people are out of date, out of sorts and out of touch. They are pathetic, scrounging dinosaurs. Like their beloved Bingo, the big Seven Oh should mean the needle. It would be as simple as their flu jab."

I nod at the audience to show we are right.

"We would be doing them a favour; showing them we care by protecting them from the pain and misery of old age and perhaps a lingering death. A nicely managed, compassionate and peaceful end to their life. It would be cool."

I pause and scan the audience again to show sincerity.

"It would also be better for their loved ones. The finality could be anticipated. Planned for. Allowing them to tidy up their affairs – wills, undertakers and all that stuff. And, less morbidly, it could be reason for a celebration, for a party – recognising a life fully lived. In short, Ladies and Gentlemen, as a caring society we would arrange a nicely managed, compassionate, quick and peaceful termination of a life."

My eyes pleaded with the audience to understand.

"I know it would be a cultural change for the State to be organising death at seventy, but surely it is only a small step from the regulations we already have. When we start and leave school, when we can get married and when we can go into a pub for a drink, for example."

I pause for the logic of the argument to register before I continue.

"Ladies and Gentlemen, it would be the mark of a truly caring society. The ultimate act of our compassion. Thank you."

I sat down, knowing I had made a reasoned argument. No one could dispute the fact, nor the compassionate nature of my proposal. *Good job.*

I'm Mike, by the way. Mike Yardley. In my final year at Uni studying Philosophy and about to take time off to research my dissertation on Critical Reasoning. Trouble is I can't seem to find a topic that grabs me, one which will stretch and challenge me; one that is enough for my energetic 'change the world for the better' views.

My mate Rob, who is on the same Course, and our house-mates Jo and Ros, are trying to help. After a few jars they feel they can be blunt: "You are an arrogant, ignorant, uncaring bloody pig, Mike!" Jo said, with Ros nodding vigorously. "Too full of yourself and not open to opposing views. A bloody 'Know It All'."

I feel my hackles rising. I was under attack, ready to take a defensive position.

"No, I'm not. I try to take a balanced view of things, to reflect what I see in life."

"HA!"

They said it at once, with feeling, much shaking of heads, and looks of disbelief. Rob spoke for the three of them. "Okay then, smart arse, we'll take you at your word. We dare you to take a balanced view of the elderly."

They stared at me, as though willing me to turn the offer down, just to prove their point. The gauntlet had been thrown down.

"Lost for words are you then, Mikey? Chicken are you?" Ros did chicken wings with her arms as she spoke.

I jumped in straight away. "Okay, you nutheads, what do I have to do to prove my open-mindedness to you?" Too late, the words were already out of my mouth and I saw the grins on their faces. An ambush. A conspiracy, no less.

"Funny you should say that, Mike. We…" she indicated the three of them with her hand, "have given it considerable thought. We want you to role-play an old man for a week. You did 'A' level drama. Didn't you? It should be a doddle. You could use it as the basis of research for your dissertation."

"Absolutely," I responded. There was no way I could back out.

Perversely the idea appealed to me. A week living as an old man would confirm all my views.

The next night we sat around with coffees at McDonald's and knocked about some ideas.

I had no role models so Rob said he would ask his grandfather, Bert, if I could talk to him to get some info about being old, about his life, his beliefs, his fears and his activities.

Jo and Ros mentioned they had some contacts on their Media Course who specialised in creative make-up. All high tech stuff apparently. I could almost have a new plastic face.

Charity shops in town would have suitable clothes.

149

My three so-called friends said they would critique my speech, body language and mannerisms etc.

With my acting experience I was sure I could carry it off for a week. *Absolutely!*

Rob gave me the address of his grandfather. A bus ride out of town. The terraced house looked unremarkable, the small front garden seemed neglected or perhaps it was just the time of the year. I knocked on the door.

I heard a key turn and the door opened to reveal a silver haired old man. I could see the family resemblance – he had the same steady gaze as Rob, the same curiosity in his eyes.

"Come in, lad. I've been expecting you. I'm Bert. Our Robert has told me all about your venture."

The sitting room was over-furnished with a lifetime's collection of furniture, nick-nacks and photos. Little light pierced the room from the small window.

I couldn't detect any source of heat and then realised that Bert had a couple of pullovers on to keep warm.

I briefly explained what I wanted. Bert looked up at me from the armchair he had folded himself into. His face was from the Middle Ages. Used and life-worn. Pallid. In contrast, his dark eyes were bright and searching. He looked me up and down.

"Think you're up to it, son? It's not easy being old." His speech was clear and his manner direct.

I nodded. "Yeah, of course."

As his eyes pierced mine, they seemed to see behind my cockiness, behind my front. It was as though they detected my hidden lack of self-confidence, my insecurity, my weaknesses. I found it uncomfortable and threatening. Scary.

Bert slowly shook his head as if to say although he had seen my weaknesses, he accepted them. His warm smile melted any apprehension I had.

"Okay, son, you're okay. Let's get going, shall we?"

I spent four hours with Bert. Four hours of reminiscences, feelings, experiences – in short, a summary of his past and present life. My notebook was already half full from the Psychology of Ageing books from the library. Bert filled the rest.

"At seventy-six, son, I live my life as if I've only a year to go." His voice continued more softly. "And, as they have just told me I have pancreatic cancer, this will definitely be my last one."

His keen eyes looked at me and I detected sadness in them.

"Each year I make myself a list of things I want to achieve – challenges if you like. If you are serious about all this, son, how about doing one or two things from last year's list. It will give you a focus. You up for it?"

"Love to," I lied, not wanting to seem discourteous to a dying old man.

"Good lad. I've already sorted out some things and given the list to our Robert."

Silly old bugger. If he can do them it will be a piece of cake.

As I said goodbye, Bert touched my arm. "Remember this when you grow old, son – you don't stop doing things because you grow old; you grow old because you stop doing things." He smiled. "Good luck."

151

"How'd you get on, Mike?" Rob asked that night

"Your grand-dad Bert was a mine of information and a real nice bloke. I really liked him."

Rob produced a piece of paper. "And this list?"

"Yeah, I said I would do it all. No problem. It will get me well and truly feeling ancient. What's on it?"

Rob looked at the paper.

"He's made some notes…first, he says he's going into hospital next week so he would like you to live at his house. It will help you keep in character twenty-four-seven. He says you can use his bus pass too."

"Suits me fine." I hoped my apprehension didn't show…..

"He says I've got to confiscate your mobile phone, your laptop and your MP3… Oh …and your iPad and game station. And he says definitely no booze or women in the house."

I closed my eyes in despair. A week without my gadgets… it would be like being sent to Siberia.

"Come on, Mike, it's only for a week…want me to read the list?"

"Okay, cowboy, shoot."

"He says you can do them in any order. You've got to go on a day's outing with his Social Club."

I smiled at him. "No problem, mate."

His face was buried in the paper.

"Then you've got to talk to kids at the local Primary School about the war years."

"Easy peasy."

Rob laughed. "You'll like these, Mike…You've got to shoplift and – wait for it – he's booked you in for a parachute jump."

"A what?"

"A parachute jump. You know, out of a plane. In the sky."

I shook my head. "No bloody way. I can't do that. You know I'm scared of heights. Bloody petrified, mate."

"Grand-dad was too, but he did it." Rob flapped his elbows. "Chicken again, are we?"

I took a deep breath to calm myself. *If Bert can do it at his age...*

A few days later I was kitted out with old men's clothes, including a cap, Jo and Ros's mates did my semi-permanent make-up, including a balding head, and they showed me how to touch it up each day.

When I looked in the mirror I hardly recognised myself. The speech patterns, the bent shoulders, the unsteady walk all slotted into place. The only thing I was unprepared for was the reality of it.

My so-called friends made me walk down the High Street to a café, while they sat at a window table, watching. I caught a reflection of myself in a shop window – a pale, hunched old man in NHS specs, as bald as a kneecap under my cap – just like hundreds of others I had seen.

I ordered a cup of tea and a toasted teacake. OAP rate one pound twenty-five pence. I scrabbled slowly through my money to find the exact change. I even picked up a penny someone had dropped and put it carefully into my purse.

The cheerful young woman on the till, whose large breasts were comforting, grinned at me. Her lips, slightly open, had the promise of ecstasy.

"I'll bring it across, love. Save you carrying it. You look a bit unsteady." She lowered her voice. "Want some jam on it?"

I nodded and she winked. "Don't tell the Manager else he'll charge you extra."

I shambled across to a table, sat down and took my cap and scarf off. I saw Rob give me the thumbs up as they all made a move to leave. Ros touched my shoulder as she passed. "I fancy you like mad, grand-dad. If you want some company, give me a ring." She laughed. "On your mobile."

"Goodnight children," I croaked.

I shook my head and turned to the old lady behind me. "I can't understand this younger generation. A total lack of respect for their elders." She nodded her agreement and revealed a mouthful of toast.

Later, I walked slowly back up the High Street towards Bert's house. I shook my head disapprovingly at the juvenile hoodies and tut-tutted at young women in short skirts. I smiled at the few old ladies I saw, then stopped and leaned against a wall to listen to a domestic conversation between a husband and wife hurling abuse at each other.

I was starting to enjoy this.

That was until I entered the cold, dark house. It had the feel of a deserted bus station at midnight…in winter.

Sitting in Bert's armchair in front of the gas fire, curtains drawn, I felt suddenly desolate. Shut off from the world. Uncared for. I can't explain it. It was like an invisible shroud of despair that saturated the room and wrapped itself around me, penetrating my being.

It was as if the world was happening somewhere else and I was being left to perish. It was quiet, too. The only sounds I heard were the ones I made. Nothing else. Absolutely nothing.

I shook my head to try and rid myself of these morbid feelings by thinking about my first task. Bert had told me that to avoid the punishing loneliness he always had a project to work on.

Mine was shoplifting!

I think I subconsciously chose this first in the hope that I would get arrested and not have to jump out of a plane.

My mind settled on British Home Stores. Big enough for me to be anonymous but hopefully not too much sophisticated CCTV. My thoughts started to gel – avoid taking anything heavy or bulky, or breakable. Nothing too expensive. Clothes of some kind? Yes.

I spent an uncomfortable night in pyjamas. (I usually wear nothing in bed). But at least they were warm. The bedroom had the same creepy, scary isolation of being in the house alone when I was a kid – axemen behind every door...ghosts and nasties. Bogeymen everywhere. Every creak an indication of someone coming to get me!

I looked at my watch – three a.m. – the time when fear rules.

In the morning I had a wash in cold water. I had forgotten to put the immersion heater on. No shower, only a bath. The empty feeling of loneliness still clung to me as I ate my cornflakes, looking at the four walls.

I dressed – thermal vest, shirt and pullover, plus coat – enough layers for the Himalayas. But it somehow felt appropriate, not only to keep out the cold but to insulate me against the despair I felt, like a child's comfort blanket. The clothes reassured me, kept me secure.

BHS was busy. The lady near the door was wearing a sash. She offered me one of those mesh baskets with a practised smile. I took it.

"You must think I'm a fisherman," I grumbled.

Her expression said, "Silly old fool", but she kept on smiling.

Up the escalator to the men's floor. I put a vest and pair of socks into my basket, followed by a couple of pullovers of different sizes, and made my way to the changing rooms. No one at the door. I found myself a cubicle, quickly took off my shoes and then my socks. I was nervous and fumbled with the packaging on the new socks. I stuffed the cardboard packaging into my pocket and put them on, with my own socks over them. With difficulty, I squeezed into my shoes. I then took my cap off, ruffled what little hair I had, crumpled the pullovers, and stepped out.

"No good, sir?" I jumped like a scared rabbit. "Shall I put them back for you?"

"What? Oh no, it's okay, love. I'll do it."

My heart was pounding. *Be careful, walk slowly. You're an old man.*

I was sweating under all the clothes, expecting a hand on my shoulder any minute. I put the pullovers and vest back and went down the escalator. *Nearly there.*

"Excuse me, sir." A loud voice to my left. *Panic!* As I turned, I caught my foot on a display and went sprawling.

My instinct was to jump up and leg it to the door, but somehow I managed to keep in character. A Security man knelt beside me.

"You okay, old fella?"

The male sales assistant with the voice was saying, "I was only asking him if he wanted a store-card. He seemed frightened and tripped…"

They sat me up against the wall. I said I wasn't hurt but played on the shock of it all.

Damn! I could see the stolen socks protruding underneath my own. I scrambled to my feet hoping they hadn't been seen.

The Security man held me firmly by the arm. "You'd better come with me, sir."

It was a plain windowless room, with a metal table and chairs on either side of it. A telephone and a writing pad enhanced the décor. Nothing else. He sat me on a chair.

"I'll get you a drink of water. Just relax."

Relax! You must be joking. I felt as though I was in an electric chair, awaiting execution. I was sure he had seen the socks and had gone for the police. I felt my heart pounding and had to hold on to the chair to stop my hands from shaking. I waited. A worried looking woman came in with a plastic cup of water. She introduced herself as the Store Manager.

"You okay, sir? You sure? I'm sorry. It was our fault startling you like that. I'll arrange for someone to take you home. Yes?"

I gave her a feeble smile. The paper cup shook in my hands, spilling some of the water.

She looked even more worried.

"Sir, as a goodwill gesture, I would like you to accept this small gift."

She thrust into my lap a pack of three pairs of socks. I nearly burst out laughing. Ironic or what?

A trainee manager drove me home. Katie. She was in her early twenties, my age, and gorgeous. Power suit, lovely perfume. Full of energy and enthusiasm for the role of caring for an old man in the line of duty.

She helped me into the car, face close to mine. I clung to her like a limpet. Her shiny, stocking-clad legs and thighs protruded from her short black skirt as she drove. Oooh! I lolled sideways to get a better look every time she changed gear. The term dirty old man slipped into my mind.

In the house she sat me in Bert's armchair and insisted on making us a cup of tea. She noticed a photo of Bert's wife. "She died ten years ago," I said, with a suitably forlorn expression.

"You must miss her and feel lonely, Michael." She put her hand on my arm.

I was longing to hug her, to kiss her, to... *No chance, son, you're an old man, remember?*

"You remind me of my grand-dad," she said. "A real gent. It's nice to find a man of any age these days who doesn't want to put his hands all over you."

Gulp. Oh, if you only knew, sweetheart.

I was sure I was a hit with her, so I chanced my arm. "Can I give you a kiss for your kindness, dear? I'm a bit out of practise but I can pretend you are my grand-daughter."

She looked embarrassed as she leaned over me. "Just think of it as part of the BHS service, Michael…"

Our lips touched and I tried to convey my passion through them. Hers lingered a little longer than I thought they would. *Oh My.* I could see from her expression that she was puzzled.

"Do all old men kiss like that?"

"I wouldn't know about the others, dear. What I do know is that we get terribly forgetful as we get older – did I just ask you for a kiss?" I leaned forward in my chair and puckered my lips.

"You're a scoundrel, Michael, but, as it's in the line of duty, why not."

She placed her full hot lips on mine once again and I felt a passion an old man shouldn't recognise.

She pulled away, breathless and looking flustered.

Her words came fast. "Another satisfied BHS customer, I think. Bye, Michael. You take care now." And she was gone.

Goodness knows what was going through her mind. I knew what was going through mine.

Rob dropped round later and I showed him the socks I had stolen so he could tick his list.

I tried hard to stay in character as I told him what had happened – minus the kisses of course.

"Tomorrow," he said, "is the Social Club outing. I've told them that grand-dad can't make it and that he has asked you to come in his place." He couldn't help gloating. "It's a mystery tour. Full of old ladies, so just behave yourself, old 'un."

I glared at him, pointed to the door and he left, laughing all the way.

I feel a lot more relaxed today after my successes yesterday and I turned up for the coach on the dot. I presented myself to the fluorescent-clad lady in charge. She looked slightly younger than the others. Short, stocky and with a manner suited to a prison warder. She had what you might call an unfortunate face – full of menace. She came at me in the manner of a Rottweiler, one which hadn't been fed for a week.

"You!" She glared at me and pointed to the end of the queue. "Back there!"

I had counted about forty old ladies, most with white hair, looking as though some hairdresser was on piece-work. And three old men, including myself. A nice hubbub of friendly conversations created a buzz of restrained excitement.

I stood next to two old dears. "Take no notice of her, love. Power mad she is. Thinks she's in charge. We let her get on with it."

The queue slowly moved towards the coach door as she ticked off people's names.

"...and you are?"

"Spiderman," I said, with a straight face.

The lady behind me giggled. She looked painstakingly down the list and then at me. I tried a smile. She didn't do smiling.

"We don't have you on the list... wait here."

"Naughty boy," the lady behind me said. I felt like one.

She came back. "I only have Michael Yardley, in place of Bert..."

"That must be me then, love. Spiderman is my hero."

"Oh for goodness sake, grow up!" She looked and sounded exasperated. "Get on the bus, will you, and be quick…"

I climbed on to the bus and made my way up the aisle. Halfway up a lady patted the spare seat beside her. "Yours," she said. "Been saving it for you."

I looked at her – white hair, expensive clothes, gold everywhere, fully made up with lipstick as red as a traffic light. What Bert would call a dolly bird. I sat down and smiled: "Thank you, my dear."

She leaned in closer. Her perfume was expensive and overpowering. Her considerable bosoms pinned me to the seat. A rugby scrum I can handle, but this?

Her voice was sexy in a geriatric way, low and breathless.

"I'm Doris. You must be Bert's friend."

"That's right. I'm Michael. Pleased to meet you, Doris."

It wasn't long before we had a "comfort break" as our leader called it. In the Gents, I bumped into one of the other blokes from the coach.

"Watch out for that one you've sat with." I lowered my head and moved closer to hear him. "She's buried three husbands, worn them out, and she's after a fourth. She'll have your trousers off in no time."

He spoke with the intensity and authority of an unfortunate experience.

I wanted to say "Oh, come on, she's a sweet old lady, going on eighty, not a young bimbo." But I kept my mouth shut.

When we got on the coach again I took off my jacket and laid it across my lap. As we moved off, I

161

felt her hand wander underneath it, exploring – and I don't mean up the Amazon. *Christ Almighty.*

She leaned in close again and whispered, "Who's a big boy then?" and gave it a squeeze. Being touched up by an eighty year old. I would never live it down! Thank goodness *Facebook* and *Twitter* are not in the vocabulary of this lot.

I pretended to have cramp. "Sorry, Doris, I'll have to stretch my legs…" I moved back to an empty seat. Massaging my calf like mad.

Another old dear came and sat next to me. A pale, white haired, kindly faced lady. She saw me pull away. "Don't worry, dear, we are not all like Doris. Just be charitable. We have our needs, some more than others, if you get my meaning."

I did. And I was trying hard to erase the image that came into my mind.

"She's a dear, really. Do anything for anyone. It's not easy for her to adjust; she likes a man around."

"I can imagine," I lied.

She put her frail hand on my arm and there was sadness in her voice as she spoke.

"You men die too early, that's your trouble." Her smile tried to make it a jovial statement, but her eyes gave her away. In them I saw the sorrow she felt and the start of a tear. She started to move back to her seat. "Don't you die on us too…"

"I'll try not to, love. Not today anyway."

As I looked around the coach it was full of happy women, chattering away. Genuinely interested in each other, caring for one another. It was a bond that didn't need men. We were peripheral. My ego found it hard to accept but here it was right before my eyes – a world sculptured and organised very successfully by older women. Caring, communicating, thoughtful and jovial women. The backbone of our nation. They were survivors. They had to be.

I remember Bert saying to me that he noticed funeral directors' offices a lot more as he got older and I wondered whether men, the more solitary of our species, somehow got into a death mindset too early. Pondering and dwelling on it in their conscious and subconscious minds. My psychology student friends might say that men show signs of 'Conditioned Obedience' like some of Pavlov's dogs – conforming to what is expected – that men die before women. Whereas women carry on as normal, getting on with life, taking the rough with the smooth. Enjoying what they have. Just living.

The pub lunch was great. We mingled and everyone acknowledged me in their own way. I danced with a few – the women that is. Everyone seemed happy and joyful. Whatever personal tragedies they had were left behind. Left hidden to be picked up again in the quiet and loneliness of their homes.

They made me feel part of them and I genuinely enjoyed myself. After a few beers and a singalong, my alternative life felt normal. I felt I fitted in. Age didn't matter.

I even saw our jailer smile. Only once.

When we arrived home I was surprised that people thanked me for helping to make it a wonderful day.

Doris grabbed my arm as we were getting off the coach. "Take no notice of me, Michael. It's just my way of coping with life. I find it tough sometimes. Sorry if I upset you."

I gave her a hug and a kiss on the cheek, in fact I gave nearly all of them a hug. I knew now what it would mean to them...I knew what it meant to me.

I left with "See you at Bingo" ringing in my ears as we all returned to that personal hell which is loneliness in old age. No wonder solitary confinement is classed as torture.

G-o-o-d M-o-r-n-i-n-g M-i-s-t-e-r-Y-a-r-d-l-e-y

The practised chant of the thirty young kids echoed around the classroom and lured me into the life of Class Four. I was dreading the prospect of falsely talking to them about my memories of wartime Britain. I felt a fraud.

I had read it all up, added Bert's childhood experiences and delivered my recollections to the kids with as much passion as I could.

At one point I actually felt I was reliving it — how my earliest memory was being carried, wrapped in a blanket, and placed under the stairs, with the thud of bombs and incendiaries all around. The next morning's scene: the holes in the road, the burned houses, the rubble and death everywhere were still vivid with me, as was the relief of the 'All Clear' siren.

Other memories which stayed with me were the landmines that exploded in the sky, causing widespread damage, not having seen a banana until I was ten, Red Cross parcels with their chewing gum and powdered egg. *Larry the Lamb* on the radio, rationing, sweet coupons, buses camouflaged like desert tanks. Barrage balloons and searchlights. The Air Raid Wardens saying 'Put that light out'. The homesickness of being evacuated...

All this I re-enacted to an unusually quiet and attentive young audience. They believed every word, I could tell, that is until I said there was no TV, no mobile phones, a loo down the garden, frozen in winter, gas lighting, a tin bath by the fire... the lack of what they saw as necessities of life floored them. They couldn't comprehend it. I told them to check it out with their grandparents

"I think you were very brave," one little girl said. She had curly hair and the face of an angel.

Her comment made me realise the terror and extreme hardships people had lived through. Their husbands and fathers away fighting. Kids like this little innocent girl. As I began to absorb emotionally how terrible the trauma had been, a feeling of pride emerged for the people who had steered us through this nightmare conflict. I felt humbled.

I said to the teacher when I left that I hoped I had made some connection between their lives and their grandfathers' generation: some crack in the wall of insulated unreality which pervades this electronic age. The death and destruction kids of their age had to endure. But how could I expect them to understand. Even I found it difficult.

I went home today to the cold, empty house. Alone, with no one to talk to, no one to share the triumphs of the day with. I felt depressed. The thought of doing the same routine every day until I die... no wonder this age group of men have a high rate of suicide. They are good at it and I am sure some must think they have already died inside, in a tomb of their own making. Suicide just makes it public.

Funny, isn't it, how men seem to need a woman around them – most feel incomplete without one. Whereas women, although I can't speak for them, seem content alone. Or are they?

This train of thought led me to ask myself, "What if this was my final year." Would I have the emotional strength and courage to get off my backside and do the things that Bert had done? Or would I wallow in depressive thoughts and sink into the slimy pit of self-pity, not even seeking the will to pull myself out? I honestly don't know.

And what if it was my final year in life – me, Mike Yardley. What have I contributed to life? No job, no taxes, no offspring, no deprivation, no caring for someone, no fighting to save my country…in fact, no real struggle at all.

My estimation of Bert and all the men and women of his generation blossomed.

Pull yourself together, Mike, don't let this creepy house get to you. Tomorrow is the biggest challenge of your life. The boy who is terrified of heights is going to jump out of an aeroplane.

I pull the blankets over my head and pray for gale-force winds and thunderstorms. It didn't stop my old friend – the fear of heights – staying with me the whole of the night.

When I opened the curtains the following morning the sky was a pale blue with wisps of cloud that hardly moved. An ideal day, some would say, for an act of supreme folly…

The 'Airport' sign exaggerated its importance. It was a series of huts and hangers at the end of a grass landing strip which was littered with little aeroplanes parked at all angles. The general untidiness of the scene didn't inspire my belief that people knew what they were doing, that I was in safe hands.

Hey, it's my life we're talking about here!

The falling on the mat practise went well, even though I had to make it look painful.

My next session, unscheduled, was to rush to the loo to be sick. Fear gripped my stomach and turned my insides liquid, as well as freezing my mind. I struggled to think straight.

The instructor was a breezy thirty-something bloke with testosterone leaking out of every pore. His voice rose ten decibels when he spoke to me, until I used the time worn phrase, "Don't shout. I'm not deaf." It had no effect.

"Ah, right, mate." I detected a slight Australian accent. "Now, mate, we would normally double up on the jump but Bert told us when he booked you in that you had been in the Paras for National Service, so you'll be used to going solo. Yeah?"

What's he talking about? I couldn't take it in. My frozen look halted his spiel.

"That okay, mate?"

I felt my head nod – a reflex action to his question. To any question.

"Good. I expect you're looking forward to it ...after how many years?"

I did a quick calculation. "Fifty-six, mate. Yeah it'll be déjà vu all over again." He didn't get my attempt at a joke.

"Right, mate, we're going from four thou. So you need to be quick with the rip once clear of the slip. Okay?"

I nodded again having no idea what he was talking about.

Relief. A woman walked by in a tight fitting flying suit. A real good looker. The instructor grabbed her arm. "Sal, sweetheart, this is Mikey. Bert's friend – you remember? Mikey, this is Sal, your pilot."

Things had just got a whole lot better.

"High grand-dad." She gave me a peck on the cheek. "That's for luck." Her bright green eyes were eager and challenging. "At least you know what it's like. The others are wetting themselves at the thought." I did my automated nod again. "You go last. Push 'em out if you have to..."

The old plane bumped and rattled across the grass, its single engine straining to take off. I wondered if it would ever make four thousand feet. I felt lucky I had a parachute, in case it disintegrated.

The other two heroes – a woman in her twenties and a bloke about fifty – were white faced, holding tightly on to anything that remotely looked stable. Nothing was. I have never seen two people so full of second thoughts. They were looking to me for comfort and guidance. Poor sods.

The intercom crackled... "See that green field on the side of the door." We looked out of the window at a patch of green a couple of centimetres square. "That's the one we are aiming for. I'll circle a couple of times. When I call your number you jump straight away. Count one-two-three, then pull the ripcord. Piece of cake."

"Mike, open the door, but hold on tight."

I slid the door back and was unprepared for the strength of the wind. It nearly sucked me out. I clung on as though my life depended on it. It probably did.

"Get ready number one. Think of it as stepping off the kerb. Number one GO NOW!"

She did. No hesitation as she stepped through the door. Whoosh and she was gone.

"Get ready number two. GO NOW!"

He stood by the door, clenched knuckles holding both sides, a look of terror on his whitewashed face.

I moved behind him and shouted in his ear. "Come on, son, be a hero. You can do it. Take your hands off." To my surprise he did and I nudged him out. Whoosh! He was gone. My turn. I felt numb with fear. Nothing was functioning. As we circled one last time, I seemed to stir like a boxer just before the final count. I had a vision of Bert beside me.

"Come on, lad. If I, and thousands in the war, can do it, so can you."

"Off you go number three…"

I let myself fall forward out of the door. Whoosh. The noise of the wind deafened me. It was tearing at my face. I was tumbling. Tumbling. My mind raced. *Pull the cord. Pull the cord.*

I did. A yank on my harness and then a sensation of floating. Floating peacefully like a cork on water. Oh Boy! It felt wonderful. My panic had gone. I was calm. I could go on like this forever. Floating.

I looked around, saw the countryside and the two parachutes on the ground. I tried the steering cords and manoeuvred over the green field.

It was though I was in a trance…calm…relaxed…

I suddenly realised the ground was approaching quickly, too quickly, rushing upwards. Fear gripped me again. *Think. Think.* I pulled hard on both cords as I touched down, almost walking out of the parachute.

Like stepping off a kerb.

I was on a high. Adrenalin buzzing in my ears. Great stuff! I had done it! Mike Yardley had jumped out of a plane. Believe it!

Rob, Ros and Jo ran across the field to where I was sitting. They were grinning and shouting their congratulations.

"Terrific, Mike. Brilliant! You okay?"

They hugged me and we walked, arm in arm, down to the local pub.

"You degenerates need to get the drinks. I can't afford it on my pension."

The following day, after we had sobered up, Rob told me that his grand-dad, Bert, had died during the week while I had been doing the things on his list.

The news hit me like an emotional sledgehammer. Even though I had only met him once, I felt that because I had imitated him, his words, his stories, his mannerisms, done the things on his list, that part of Bert was now inside me. He was part of me.

I couldn't believe he was dead. Couldn't face up to it. Someone had made a mistake. I couldn't believe he would no longer be around. I wouldn't be able to relate my exploits to him, to have a laugh and a joke with him.

For the first time in my adult life, I cried. Ros and Jo put their arms around me but said nothing. There was nothing to say.

"Come on, Mike, it happens to old people. They die. We all will one day."

"I know, I know, but those experiences he had, those memories, his fighting spirit, his dreams...gone forever."

We sat in silence for a while, until Rob finally spoke.

"Look, Mike, I realise this may be difficult for you, but would you like to say a few words at his funeral. Bert liked you and left a note asking if you would…"

I stared ahead, only half hearing the words. Too upset to respond.

"He wanted you to stay in character as an old man. To talk about him as an old friend would."

I nodded without thinking, my voice a whisper. "Of course, anything for Bert."

Ros filled four glasses with beer and handed one to each of us.

"To Bert," she said. "May he rest in peace."

I was crying again. We all were.

A carpet of wet leaves led up to the church door. The inside was lovingly tended, with flowers and candles everywhere. Frank Sinatra was singing 'Send in the Clowns', backed up by a hushed and friendly babble of conversation.

I felt intimidated, as though everyone would know I was a fraud, but then I realised I recognised most people as I made my way towards the front, to where Rob was sitting. I nodded to some of them as I walked down the aisle, the ladies from the social club – even the parachute instructor and the woman from BHS were there. As I sat and took off my cap, she came across and kissed my cheek. "Be strong," she urged.

The atmosphere was necessarily sombre, with some fixed expressions of grief and some tears. They had, after all, come to say farewell to Bert.

Even the music couldn't lighten the mood. Me? I still couldn't comprehend it, still couldn't accept he was gone. I guess everyone felt the same.

We are here one minute, gone the next. What a waste. Our lives brought to a shuddering halt.

It must be a circumstance old people know well when their friends and loved ones pass away. I wonder if their minds have a shutter of denial that filters out the thought that it might be them next? Do they become conditioned to deny the pain and grief of death which now overwhelms me?

Bert's coffin lay on a table in front of the altar. It was open so that people could pay their last respects. Some did. They looked in at Bert. Some whispered something, touched him. Some laid a single flower. I couldn't bring myself to do it. No way. Not even to sneak a view out of curiosity. I had no idea what a dead body looked like and now wasn't the time to find out.

In front of the coffin, leaning against the table, was a large photo of Bert. Taken some years ago by the look of it. Happy. Smiling. Confident. Full of life, as though he would live forever. And now this.

We sang hymns. Subdued, except for the vicar who hammered the words out like a karaoke king. He talked to us in his special vicar-speak voice about Eternal life and Everlasting glory, as though he was trying to protect us from the reality that Bert was dead.

To be fair, he did say he had not known Bert and he invited others who knew him to say a few words.

No one stood up or came forward. Embarrassment was compounded by a silence which should have urged people to overcome their inhibitions and say something. No one did.

Eventually, Rob nudged me and pointed to the front.

I stood up, feeling more of a fraud and a fool than usual as I walked slowly up the steps. The intensity of emotion I felt overwhelmed me. I turned to face the church full of people, many of whom knew Bert much better than I.

Bloody hell, Bert, what have you let me in for?

I had agreed to stay in character because that is how people knew me and that is what Bert had wanted. To 'come out' now as a young man would be to detract from our main task of remembering him.

The sea of faces looked up at me, anticipation writ large on each of them. Eager to hear what I had to say. Willing me to be normal, to bypass the usual funeral protocol about life in Heaven.

I took a deep breath, then several more.

"Ladies and Gentlemen. Hello." I smiled. "Many of you I have met. I'm Michael, Mike. Bert made a request for me to say a few words at his funeral. *Lighten the mood, son.* It was before he died obviously. He couldn't have done it after, could he?" Restrained ripples of laughter.

"He also asked me to jump out of an aeroplane." I paused. "And he arranged for a parachute, so he must have liked me a little." More laughter. I had their attention.

"Most of you will know Bert far better than I so, instead of talking about him, I would like to talk about the things he stood for, the things he believed in and the things he taught me in the short time I knew him."

I saw people nodding their understanding, waiting for what was to come. I felt at ease in my 'elderly' body talking to Bert's friends, knowing they looked on me as a friend too.

"Bert told me that he looked on each year as his final one." I laughed. "Of course he was bound to be proved correct at some time." More laughter. "But none of us thought it would be so soon. Bert told me he wasn't ever going to die – but that one day, for him, the world would cease to exist. That's a good way of looking at it, isn't it?"

I nodded my head along with most of the audience. "Yeah?"

"As we get older there is a temptation to opt out of life, isn't there?" I hesitated until I heard one or two agreeing. "We get stuck where we are when our partner dies, or when we retire. We live on memories. We step back from the excitement and the pressures and take it easy. It's tempting, isn't it, to sleepwalk into hibernation."

I knew I had a rapport with them all, they understood. They were murmuring their agreement. I could hear it bubbling away.

"But that wasn't Bert's way, was it? He went in the opposite direction. He looked for challenges as he got older. This took strength and courage on his part." Some people started to applaud, then others joined in, until the sound filled the church.

I put up my hand to quieten things down.

"Bert believed that we continue to grow stronger because of these challenges, whether or not we are totally successful with them. He felt we were all just grown-up kids at heart, exploring the world and that age didn't come into it. We are the same throughout life, he said to me, whatever our age. We have the same underlying feelings, prejudices, habits, passions and weaknesses throughout and our character is shaped by the unique life experiences each of us has. How right he was, Ladies and Gentlemen. How right he was..."

People were clapping again, smiling and nodding their heads in agreement. The atmosphere was one of a celebration. A celebration of Bert's life.

"Underneath, Bert believed, we are still the little girl skipping or the lad kicking the ball." I had to raise my voice to make myself heard.

"WE..." I almost had to shout, "WE, the older generation, provide the graciousness, the embedded knowledge and the wisdom. We represent the dignity in life that is not driven by money, by ambition, or by power."

I took a deep breath knowing I was nearing the climax of what I had to say, wanting it to have maximum impact.

"Some would advocate – and they are usually the young arrogant men who are out to change the world – some advocate that we should be 'Put to Sleep' at a certain age. They call it progressive thinking." I raised my voice. "Rubbish! The thought is as primitive and as distasteful as cannibalism. What do they know? If they walked in our shoes, they would realise the joys, the achievements, the contentedness of old age, as well, of course, as the struggles we all face."

I moved forward and placed my hand on the edge of Bert's coffin, avoiding looking at him.

"Ladies and Gentlemen. Friends. I conclude with one of Bert's many profound sayings. Something we should all take to heart. He said, 'There is more to life…than death'."

As I moved away from the coffin to face down the aisle, there was an eruption of emotion, of gasping, of screaming. Clapping. It felt like hysteria. It didn't fit – a mixture of joy and fear. It grew even louder, like an express train thundering through a village station. People were animated, on their feet, spilling into the aisle. They were reacting. Looking at me. I was gobsmacked. I knew Bert's words were profound but this reaction is ridiculous. It's bizarre. *Something is wrong.*

A few started to point. I realised they were not focussing on me, but something behind me. At first, fear made me reluctant to turn round, too afraid of what I might see, but the wave of excitement carried me along with it.

I turned…

I wiped my hand over my eyes, not believing what I saw. Oh My God! It had to be a dream, a nightmare…was I going mad?

Bert was climbing out of his coffin, slowly, his face the colour of his white shirt. His silver hair neatly brushed back He was dressed, ready for Heaven, in an immaculate black suit.

Oh God! I thought I could smell death.

I felt faint and stumbled back towards the mayhem. People were dancing, clapping, shouting 'Hallelujah'.

Please tell me it's not real. I looked again. The ghost-like figure was coming towards me. I felt the colour leave my face. I was about to be sick. I was pinned to the spot unable to move. Sweat ran down my face into my eyes, dripping off my chin.

Suddenly Rob was beside me, holding me up.

The figure halted where I had been standing and raised both hands, as though to Heaven. There was immediate silence. The noise replaced by a wave of quiet expectation...

It spoke, the voice hollow but with an intense energy. "Friends. Yes, it is me. Bert. Please don't be frightened. I am alive. I am a living symbol of what Mike just said: 'There is more to life than death'."

His quiet words swept around the church, into every crevice. Echoing.

He waited. We all waited.

"Most of you know that, because of pancreatic cancer, this really is my final year of life. Possibly much less than a year. You also know, with the exception of poor old Mike here – who looks as though he has seen a ghost – that the University has been filming everything. They had heard that the final challenge I had set myself was to attend my own funeral – while still alive."

Bert took a step back towards the coffin, put his hand on it and laughed.

"I just hope you have as much fun at my real funeral!"

The congregation erupted with laughter, loud and genuine.

He held on to the coffin for support as he struggled for breath.

"Most of you also know that because of the extremist views Mike held and demonstrated at the Debating Society, we decided to make him into an old man for a week so he could experience what being old was really like. It will all be in the film, including his exploits."

Bert walked across and held my arm. His smile and touch were real and they brought me to my senses.

"What a good old man he makes, doesn't he?"

Everyone clapped and cheered. I looked up to see a sea of smiling, cheerful faces.

"Well done, lad!" Bert said, as he shook my hand. "And thank you, everyone."

"By the way, lad, I have to come clean – I've never jumped out of an aeroplane in my life."

I put my arms around Bert and hugged him, completely overcome, tears washing the sweat from my face.

THE PRICE OF FAME

'Fly me to the moon...'

The lyrics were legendary, as was Sam Strong, the ageing singer belting them out, much to the rowdy adoration of his female fans.

But none of this penetrated Frank Noble's consciousness. Not the over-amplified sound, not the drab village hall, nor the raucous excitement around him.

All his senses were riveted on one thing – the female guitarist. She was drop-dead gorgeous. Instantly captivated, he had impulsively followed her from the car park an hour ago. That was the only reason he was here.

But now he had seen the glint of her wedding ring, his fantasy was shattered and his ardour had evaporated.

"Enjoying it?" a woman's voice asked.

"No I'm not!" His answer was tetchy.

The voice was that of a woman about his own age, round pale face, short brown hair. She shook her head in agreement and then smiled at him.

"Nor me. My mother's his greatest fan. She's housebound, so I'm deputising."

"Bad luck, love..."

He seized on the opportunity of a conquest. "The interval's coming up. I'll get us a cup of coffee in, shall I?"

His body deliberately touched hers as he slowly squeezed past. "I'm Frank," he said.

"Kate," she replied nervously.

As he came out of the Gents, he noticed Sam Strong in the corridor, off stage for an encore. He was small, with glazed eyes and a heavily made up face. Close up, his stage costume was faded and worn.

"Autograph, mate?"

"I don't do autographs you idiot, everybody knows that."

Sam Strong reached into his inside pocket. "Here's a photo." He threw it behind him as the ovation sucked him back on stage.

Frank picked it up and pulled out his pen. *"Don't do autographs, eh?"* He signed it with a flourish. *Sam Strong.*

"Kate … over here!" he shouted, as the interval crowd poured into the tiny refreshment room. Now that he could see all of her, his earlier enthusiasm declined. She looked plain. More than that, she looked weary, beaten down.

"Thanks." She pulled the cup towards her. "This is a life saver."

He understood. The evening had been a disaster for him too and his pent up frustration crept through in his choice of words. "Yeah, you look all in and, if you don't mind me saying so, Kate, the clothes don't help – specially chosen for that loser on stage, were they?"

She banged the cup down and glared at him, her face reddening. "You don't think this is how I *want* to be, do you?...well *do* you !..."

He felt terrible. "Sorry...I didn't mean..."

She took her eyes off his face and shook her head slowly. "No, you're right. I've been caring for my mother since I left school. No life of my own, no glamour, no boyfriends, and no money."

She waved her hand down her body. "And this is how you end up..." Her shoulders slumped, allowing her sleeve to soak up the spilled coffee.

"Cheer up, there's always a bright side." He smiled apologetically. "Look, I got Sam Strong's autograph for your mother."

"But he doesn't do autographs, never has done."

"I cornered him in the Gents. Gave him an offer he couldn't refuse – a re-arranged face or an autograph, and I'm bigger than he is. So here it is."

As her eyes melted, he felt a fierce emotion stir inside him.

"Thank you, Frank," she said softly, "she'll be so happy."

He didn't know it then, but the emotional stirrings he had felt that night were the first pangs of love. He soon became besotted, couldn't get enough of the woman. His cherished 'Jack the Lad' image lay in tatters. His whole life, every waking moment, was filled with Kate.

After a month he proposed.

"I know it sounds daft, Kate, but will you marry me?"

"Pardon?"

"I love you, Kate – marry me. I have fifteen thousand pounds saved. We can use it for the wedding and our honeymoon."

She was shocked. "Oh, come on, Frank, it's much too early," she said. "We hardly know each other. You could be hiding all kinds of dark secrets."

He smiled, more to himself than to her. "No, only one, love – and it's nothing really. You know that autograph of Sam Strong? Well, it was me who signed the photograph, not him."

Kate exploded. She was furious. "*Nothing*! You call that nothing! It's the most precious thing mother has in all the world. If I told her it was a fake it would kill her!"

"I didn't ..." The words wouldn't come.

She was still shouting. "You want to marry me, Frank Noble, then get his proper autograph. Until then, I think we should stop seeing each other."

"I'm sorry, Kate. I didn't realise. I've let you down big time. I'll get it, I promise I will."

For the first time in weeks Frank's mind was forced to think rationally. His Plan A was to get into Sam Strong's house; he *must* have a signed photo of himself somewhere.

A small, timid looking lady answered the door.

"Hi, Mrs. Strong, I'm Frank Noble. Just joined Sam's road team. He sent me to pick up some promo photos for tonight's gig – said he'd forgotten them."

"Sam didn't mention taking on a new man."

"Well, you know Sam, not the best of memories..."

"Yes, of course I know...you'd better come in."

She led him upstairs. "Probably in one of those boxes over there." She pointed to a corner of the overcrowded office. "Come down when you've finished."

He looked everywhere. He found boxes of photos, but nothing signed.

"Thanks, Mrs. Strong. Oh, I almost forgot – Sam said he had a signed photo somewhere. Wanted it for a special guest tonight."

"No chance, not even *I* have one. He says he's only ever signed one. Gave it to some floozy ten years ago, when he was drunk."

The doorbell cut short their conversation and, when she opened it, two policemen walked in.

"This is him. My husband says he's never heard of a Frank Noble."

That night was the longest of his entire life – the disinfectant smelling cell was cold and the single light bulb pierced through his eyelids like a laser. Next morning he told them everything.

"Pathetic enough to be true, sir," said the sour-faced Inspector who gave him a Caution. He added sarcastically: "Tried looking on the internet, have we, sir? By the way, your friend Strong's in hospital with a fractured skull – fell down stairs last night in a drunken stupor."

"Pointless exercise," he thought as he tried ebay. But no... there it was! The one and only signed photo was for sale! *"Oh, Thank You, God!"* The price was five hundred pounds, so he offered one thousand pounds to clinch it. But it didn't. To his amazement the bids shot up...two thousand pounds...three thousand pounds. He couldn't understand it. Then he noticed the wording had been altered to 'the *late* Sam Strong'.

Frank became caught up in a bidding frenzy; his rational judgement was overtaken by a desperation to win at all costs. He *had* to have it! When the bidding slowed at twenty thousand pounds he made one last killer attempt – thirty thousand pounds – his life savings plus a hastily arranged bank loan. Much to his relief, it was accepted.

"This is how much I love you," he said to Kate, as he showed her the autograph, telling her of the difficulties he had encountered to obtain it.

"Oh, Frank, thank you." She kissed him passionately. "You're a marvel. Come to tea on Saturday. You can now meet my mother with a clear conscience."

Frank felt relaxed and happy as he knocked at the door of the little terraced house, the precious autographed photo safely in his pocket.

Kate's radiant smile welcomed him. "Come on in, Frank, come and meet my mother."

He felt the dagger-like antagonism reach out to him as Kate opened the parlour door. Her mother's face was scowling as she sat there, overweight, in her wheelchair. The flowers he gave her were met with a stiff rebuff: "Don't think you can get round me that way, son. I don't like the idea of my Kathleen having a man friend. Her place is here, looking after me."

Kate cowered as her mother gave her a withering look, as if an icy wind had blown through the room.

"If she marries, she's gonna marry into money; wed someone who will live here and look after us both."

Frank looked anxiously at Kate, trying to convey his mounting apprehension: *"You didn't tell me that...!"*

"You've got an overdraft, haven't you, son?"

Frank nodded feebly, feeling deflated and trapped.

"*And* been in trouble with the police," she stated accusingly, her eyes boring into him. "Think I'd let my Kathleen marry a criminal do you, son?"

He wished she would stop calling him "son". It made him feel like a naughty boy again.

Kate tried desperately to change the subject. "Mother was very grateful for you getting Sam Strong's autograph for her, Frank."

He shrugged, trying to rescue some dignity. "That's okay, I knew you were his Number One fan. It was so sad he died."

"No good to me dead, is he, son? I've burned all his mementoes."

Frank forced a smile. "Not the autographed photo too, I hope?"

"Don't be daft, son. Sam's autograph meant a lot to me. Thirty thousand pounds, to be precise. I sold it on ebay."

THE RED NECKLACE

My mind screamed out *Do it now and get it over with!* as his hand closed around my throat, tightening until I couldn't breathe. He pushed his snarling face into mine, saliva bubbling from his lips. "One day I'll kill you."

I felt his grip loosen. "Get straight back here from work, bitch, or else!"

I began to shake, as I had so many times before. Suddenly it all became too much. Four years living with this possessive, brutal husband had driven me to the edge. I knew I had to get out.

And I did. That day.

I didn't return from work. Left everything behind and disappeared in what I stood up in, with a few pounds in my purse.

I went to a town on the coast and used my maiden name – Amanda Green. It was much easier than I had imagined: a change of appearance, new job paying casual wages, sharing a cheap bedsit, new friends. That was six months ago. Now I am more relaxed and learning to live again.

I do get homesick for the town where I had lived all my life but I know I can't return for fear of meeting my husband, Eric Ratcliffe. And I do mean *fear*. I still begin to shake when I think about him, knowing he would seek his dreadful, abusive revenge for me daring to leave.

The young man in the Library showed me how to get the local paper of my old town on the internet.

"There it is," he said. "Just scroll down the pages like this..." He held my hand gently on the mouse.

"Shout if you want help." He chuckled as he put his finger to his lips in a sign of silence.

'MISSING WOMAN FOUND DEAD' – the headline leapt out at me.

I felt the blood drain from my face as I read her name – Amanda Ratcliffe. It was me! A badly decomposed body had been found in a disused office building. The Coroner had returned a verdict of Accidental Death and released the body for cremation.

On the inside page there was a picture of Eric, dressed in black, holding a wreath. "I'm devastated," he told the reporter. "We were a blissfully happy couple with no problems. I miss her so."

"Are you okay?" It was the young librarian again, hand on my shoulder. "Drink of water?" he offered.

"No... no thank you. Just feeling a bit faint. I'll be fine."

I stood up shakily and made my way to the door, my mind racing. There had been a dreadful mistake, of course there had. I was here, alive and kicking, wasn't I?

I *had* to find out more...who was she? How did she die?

I met the reporter who had covered the story in a pub on the outskirts of town. Said I was researching Coroner verdicts. I suggested we use the Ratcliffe case as an example. He was already on his second pint and I was regretting my offer to buy the drinks.

"Suicide was ruled out because there was no evidence," he said. "No note. Nothing."

I nodded encouragingly before I went to the bar to get him another.

"What about foul play?"

He lifted his glass in a silent "Cheers."

"The same. I know DI Stubbs, thorough as they come. He told the inquest there was no evidence to suggest it."

He gave a wry smile. "Theory was she tripped on the stairs, the rail gave way and she fell five floors."

"Nasty."

"Yeah, but not as nasty as the sight that met the bloke who found her – a down-and-out called Tom Squirrel." He took a long drink. "Nor as nasty as the husband. A right headbanger he was."

"What makes you say that?"

"Well, all that grieving hypocrisy. A load of play-acting, if you ask me. He's put the house up for sale and I hear he's clearing up on her life insurance – two hundred thousand pounds." He shook his head. "Along with the police, I thought he was somehow involved and I went poking around the neighbours. They said he'd disposed of all her jewellery soon after she disappeared and burned all her possessions in the garden – papers, photos, that sort of thing. Even cut her clothes up and burned them too. Weird. The police thought he had something to do with it, but the Coroner's Accidental Death verdict will have put an end to that; he can do what he likes now."

I never want to be Amanda Ratcliffe again, but it's so unfair – my identity, my possessions, including half the house – everything has gone. It's as though I cease to exist. The thought of it made me so *angry*. He had no right to do it! Whatever the personal cost, I knew I must claim what is rightfully mine.

But I also had this re-awakened feeling that it could have been me; that one day Eric would have carried out his threats and killed me.

The Salvation Army knew where I could find Tom Squirrel. He was suspicious of me at first but when I told him I was the dead woman's sister and offered to buy him a meal, he relaxed a little and agreed to talk to me.

"I'll tell you exactly what I told the police, lady, although none of the details came out at the Inquest. Suppose it wasn't needed."

I nodded an understanding.

"Sometimes I used the place to doss down. Knew the code for the back door." His lips opened to reveal smoker's teeth, and the trace of a smile. "C1234 for Christ's sake, how secure's that?" His face hardened. "I struggled to push the door open, something behind it." His breathing became strained. "First the smell hit me, then the flies." He was struggling to get his words out. "Then I saw her squashed behind the door. She was... covered in maggots."

He stopped to take a drink of water. "I don't know why but, as I looked up, the inside of the door caught my attention. Bright green it was with 'Peace' aerosoled on it in yellow letters. Of all things – 'Peace'."

I could see the sweat on his brow as he looked up at me, his sunken eyes finding mine.

"Sorry, lady. Must be rough on you, her sister...to hear all this."

"No, please, go on. I need to know."

He nodded. "Not much more to tell. Police said she'd been there for months." He wiped his hand over his face. "I threw up all over the place. Couldn't get out quick enough." His eyes began to glaze over.

"Notice what she was wearing?"

"What? ... Oh, not really. A dress I think, but I did notice the necklace round her neck. Big red beads they were." He shook his head in a gesture of despair. "Most nights I wake up in a cold sweat, dreaming I'm trapped behind the door with the corpse. All I can see is the red beads...and the maggots!"

I would never know her name, of course, but now I had more details I felt I could move forward; it somehow gave me the added strength to fight for what was rightfully mine.

"Get lost, Amanda, you dim-witted slut." Eric's response to my phone call was predictable, as was my reaction: the fear came flooding back, overwhelming me, my hand shaking as I held the phone. I fought to keep control.

"I'm recording this call, Eric. If you don't meet me, I'm going to the police..."

"You bitch. You'll pay for this," he snarled. I could almost feel the venom.

We met the next day in a café. Eric was hostile from the start; for a while he showed a morbid interest in how the woman was found – I told him all the gory details, including the code, the green door with the yellow 'Peace' on it, and the necklace. But I didn't tell him how I knew.

When I asked for my share of the money he went into a rage, his face red and pulsating. He leaned forward over the table and grasped my arm. "Who are you?" he said. "I don't know you. My wife is dead."

His threatening scowl slowly widened into a tight-lipped smile as he put a spoon into the hot coffee and then on to my arm, at the same time tightening his grip. His face was inches from mine and I could smell his stale breath. His deranged stare numbed my mind. I felt no pain.

"Look here, slut," he whispered through clenched teeth, "if you pester me again you will end up like her." A shudder ran through my body. "A slow painful death, and no one will ever know or care because you're already dead." I believed him.

It was half an hour before I stopped shaking. I felt empty. Empty and defeated. No way was I going to risk my life being ruined again by this monster.

"Forget it," I told myself. "No amount of money is worth that."

As I sat there staring despairingly at my cold coffee, out of the numbness of my mind came a voice – "Get even," it said. "You owe it to yourself."

But how could I? He was so powerful, so invincible.

Gradually my mind provided an answer.

I called Detective Inspector Stubbs from the 'phone box at the railway station. When he answered, my nerve almost deserted me.

"Listen, I don't want to be involved, but I thought you should know," I said. "A weird bloke has just approached me in a café in town. I thought at first he was just chatting me up, but then he kept insisting I was his dead wife. Kept calling me Amanda, and then he threatened to kill me *again*. Scared the life out of me, it did."

I could hear chatter in the background. Stubbs grunted to show he was listening.

"Said he was sorry for pushing me down the stairs and then rambled on about a red necklace. Kept repeating the word 'Peace'. That's all – it's probably nothing…"

I was about to put the phone down when Stubbs spoke: "Wait – did the man give his name?"

"Oh yeah, sorry. Called himself Eric."

I hung up, walked across the platform and caught the train to my new life, knowing that Eric Ratcliffe would never bother me again.

THE FOOTBALLER'S WIFE

She exploded. I knew she would.

I have seen the signs before – the smouldering silence, the glaring eyes, full of disapproval, the grim mixture of defeat and disappointment on her face. Feet planted firmly, in defiance. I looked into her eyes but saw no kindness there. Only frustration, anger ...and blame. The words, when they came, were loud and antagonistic. Spewing out as though her body was being cleansed of some disease.

"You are a disgrace!" she shouted, "with all the charisma of a wet lettuce." She shook her head dismissively and lowered her voice. "You are a total waste of space, no good to anyone."

I am always at a loss for words in this situation. What could I say? Chloe was right, but to agree with her will just prolong the unpleasantness. Nevertheless, I couldn't help it...

"You're right," I murmured.

Chloe threw up her hands in despair. "See, there you go again! Not only are you incapable of getting a well-paid job, you can't even have a decent argument." She pointed accusingly at me. "Everything washes over you like a tsunami." She stamped her foot. "You know how it infuriates me, yet you won't change, will you." It was a statement of fact rather than a question. "I don't know why I stay..."

But I knew why she stayed. I was a convenient stepping stone, a rung on the ladder to her dream of marrying into wealth. She stayed expense-free in my flat; I had bought her a car – okay, it *was* a clapped out old Renault Clio but, even so, better than my old van, and I paid for the petrol. *And* I bought her clothes galore.

I think we are incompatible. Me – anything for a quiet life. I'm still in bachelor mode, I suppose. A self-employed bricky. I work when I need the money, not otherwise, but no debts. Chloe is Princessy. A bit of a drama queen too. She longs for designer clothes, exotic holidays, expensive jewellery. Anything expensive. She is completely 'Celebrity' obsessed. Thinks she should have everything they have. She takes me to *Harvey Nichols* and shows me the people lashing out hundreds of pounds.

"See," she says.

"You ought to be a footballer's wife," I tell her. "With access to a bottomless pit of money. Life isn't like that, Chloe."

"Oh yes it is!" she shouts. "I know it is. And I want some of it. All of it!"

I'd love to oblige because, other than this obsession with money, she is a lovely woman. But it's not my style and all this Celeb stuff leaves me colder than yesterday's cup of tea.

I know I will lose her. She will find some rich bloke and have everything she wants.

"What then?" I say to her. "When you have got everything you want. You won't be any happier than you are now!"

She looks at me as though I am mad. "Absolute rubbish! Spoken like a true loser."

Then one day it all changed.

We were shopping in Walsall, in Park Street. I had gone into the card shop and Chloe into *New Look* further up the road. It was busy, a lot of people about, as usual.

As I came out of the shop I saw her strolling towards me, some distance away. I don't really know what came over me but I hid myself in the crowd, walking towards her, and just before we met I jumped up in the air and shouted BOO! She was startled. Only a bit of innocent fun. Unfortunately, because I was trying to conceal myself and had my eyes firmly fixed on Chloe, I failed to notice a G4S Security van parked nearby and its Guard, who was about to walk across our path, delivering a Cash Box to a nearby bank.

When I jumped out and shouted, the Guard thought he was under attack. He flung the Box across the pavement and dashed back into the van, pushing the panic alarm. The sound was deafening and, to make matters worse, the bank alarm went off a few seconds later. The crowd around the van panicked, rushing about in all directions, some trying to get away, others dashing to see what was happening. People were screaming and two women fainted. It was mayhem. Chaos.

Everyone's attention was focussed on the van. Everyone but me, that is. I had watched as the Cash Box slid across the pavement, under some railings, dropping out of sight into a pile of rubbish. It took me less than a minute to retrieve it and wrap it in my coat. I walked away with it under my arm, through the arcade and into the bus station. As my bus pulled away, I could see the police starting to clear away the crowds and cordon off the area.

Chloe was furious when she returned home. Incandescent. "You stupid fool!" she shouted. "Why did you leave me? I could have been killed in that stampede, trying to find my way back to the car."

Ignoring her, I smiled and offered her a glass of champagne, nodding to the Cash Box. "Know what that is?"

She stopped in mid-flow. When she realised what she was looking at, I saw her mouth drop open as she gave a silent nod.

"It's a Box full of money!" I said, raising my glass. "To us, my flower, and our new life of luxury."

After her third glass of champagne, and once the initial shock had worn off, Chloe put her arms around me. Wide-eyed, she whispered, "How much?"

I shrugged nonchalantly, as if about to guess. "Nine hundred thousand." The label had given me the exact amount. "In used twenties."

Chloe collapsed on to the sofa. I thought she had passed out. "Give me another drink," she murmured, and then, unable to contain herself, said, "Let's have a look."

"It's not like a suitcase, Chloe. It's protected. Says so on the label."

"Then unprotect it."

"It's not that simple. Cash in Transit Boxes contain explosive dye which ruins the banknotes."

"There must be a way." She was starting to sound desperate, as though I was depriving her of spending the money right now.

"Yes, of course there is. Each bank has a special key. We just need to get hold of one."

Chloe sat upright. "I know someone who works in a bank," she shouted triumphantly. "Tracy... you remember, that red headed tart who was all over you at Adrian's party. You couldn't take your eyes off her."

"Can't remember, too much to drink." I lied. Tracy was gorgeous. "Talk to her, offer her money. We can afford it."

Chloe found Tracy's number and rang her straight away. They arranged to meet at lunchtime the following day.

I couldn't rest. Spent most of the day pacing up and down, looking at the Cash Box. Willing it to open.

When she came home I expected Chloe to be bubbly and excited but she was subdued and I feared the worst.

"Did you get it?" I asked, willing her to say "Yes."

She nodded and mumbled, "Yes, more or less."

I was confused. "More or less? What's that supposed to mean?"

Chloe's tight smile did not reach her eyes. "Yes, Tracy got the spare key from the bank. As it happens they were delivering the money to *her* bank. She will have to return it as soon as she has unlocked the Box. She's outside, in the car."

"And?"

"And I had to draw out all my savings. I paid her two thousand pounds." She hesitated.

My look must have told her I knew she had more than that stashed away.

"I put a big deposit on a new Mini with the rest..." She still looked glum.

"That's chicken feed, love."

Chloe came over and stood close to me, something she often does to get round me. "And..." she hesitated again; I could see she was almost in tears. "I'm sorry, I had no choice. The cow had me over a barrel...I had to agree that you would sleep with her." I could feel her body bristling with anger. "I mean *right now*, before she will unlock the Box."

Silence drifted between us. I tried hard to suppress my excitement and see it from Chloe's point of view. "Was there no other way?" I tried to sound as miserable as she obviously was.

"No, she was adamant. No you – no key." She began to cry and I put my arm around her.

I shook my head in mock dismay. "Okay, it looks as though I shall have to do it. But I shan't enjoy it and I will be thinking of you all the time."

But I did enjoy it, and I didn't think of Chloe once. When we were dressed again, Tracy took the key from her handbag and unlocked the Box. She smirked at Chloe and winked at me. "Thanks for everything, guys," she said, as she left. But we hardly heard. All our attention was focussed on the Cash Box.

"Stand back, Chloe," I urged. "In case of anything unforeseen."

But she didn't. We stood shoulder to shoulder. I felt her warm cheek close to mine as I threw open the lid. We peered in eagerly...inside was a bundle of newspapers Sellotaped together. It had a large printed label on the top which read: FOR TRAINING PURPOSES ONLY.

We stared, unable to believe it. The Cash Box was part of a training exercise! The sirens, the police, the bank. All of it just an exercise in which I had become innocently involved. Even Tracy must have known.

I couldn't help it. I burst out laughing. Uncontrollably. Chloe pulled away sharply, gave a shriek and ran out of the door shouting insults at me, saying she never wanted to see me again. I still couldn't stop laughing.

MORGAN

In the distance a dog barked, its sound muffled by the mist and rain.

The two men approached silently in the darkness. They were alert, adrenalin pumping through their bodies, hardly noticing the rain lashing their faces. The oars of the small rubber dinghy plopped quietly in and out of the water as the incoming tide carried them swiftly through the narrow mouth of the Looe river, towards the harbour.

Muted music escaping from the nightclub floated overhead as they moved beneath the banjo pier and beached on the shingle, just beyond the lifeboat station. The rower started to drag the dinghy towards the harbour wall, the scraping of the boat on the shingle breaking the silence. The other man stiffened. "Quiet, you fool!" he hissed. His glare more demanding than words.

Their eyes searched the harbour wall, dimly illuminated by the street lamps across the river. The second man pointed to a grating about fifty metres away.

"There…that's the sluice – got the key ready?"

The rower nodded.

They flattened themselves against the wall as a prowling police car moved above their heads. It stopped, its headlights rifling through the rigging of the pleasure boats on the river. It moved on.

The padlock on the barnacled grating was stubborn. When it opened, they entered a dark narrow tunnel, bent double, water up to their ankles. Rats and crabs scurried for cover as they edged towards a dim light up ahead – a sign that they were expected.

The slit of light was overhead now, at the top of a rusty iron ladder. The men climbed up, their sea boots slipping on the slimy rungs; the first up slid the hatch fully open. Bright light flooded down, momentarily blinding him. A strong hand reached down and pulled him into the cellar of the *Ship Inne*, then the second, his backpack tight in the opening.

"Welcome, sirs." The gruff voice echoed as it bounced off the walls. When the men straightened up they saw no one; the cellar was deserted.

"What the hell…" They drew their pistols and looked around cautiously. Nothing moved. Silence. They were alone.

Up in the bar, the landlord of *The Ship* laughed as he handed his Dutch visitors a whisky.

"Ah, that'll be Morgan, our resident ghost. Don't worry, he's harmless."

The men didn't share his joviality; they were stony-faced, uninterested in his delusional fantasies. They were here to do a job.

"Skol." The man with the backpack downed his whisky in one gulp. "Enough of this foolishness – you have the money?"

The landlord nodded. "Of course…and the stuff?"

The man hit the harness and unzipped his backpack. He threw a sealed package on to the bar: "Five kilos of the best cocaine…"

"Good. I'll test it, then you'll get the money. We'll do the deal right now."

They did.

"Wake up, Zoe! Wake up!" The voice was urgent.

Warily, the girl opened one eye and looked up at her brother. She was used to his tricks and teasing.

"Get lost, Michael!"

He was looking out of the window.

She yawned and stretched, then, more awake, she mellowed her tone. "What's up?"

"I heard a dinghy scrape as it landed – two men. It's them, Zoe, I know it is – I have this feeling…"

"Let *me* look." She pushed her brother aside and leaned out of the window. The dinghy was tied up below.

"Let's go and see…bring the torch." She put on her coat. "We'll take Scruff too."

They both knew their soft dog wouldn't protect them, but he had a reassuring presence and they were a team.

Cautiously they crawled into the dinghy, inspecting the inside with the torch.

"Look…here." The boy was looking closely at a painted sign 'Tender To'. "Someone's tried to scratch off the rest." He pointed. "See…it's two words, I can just make out a P and an E in the second word."

Zoe looked, then whispered the name angrily through clenched teeth. "It's *Prince* Michael. *Black Prince!* Their boat must be out in the bay." She looked at her brother anxiously. "What happened to the men?"

Michael nodded in the direction of the harbour. "They walked along the shore up there and then disappeared."

Zoe turned to step over the edge of the dinghy, trying to avoid Scruff darting to and fro. But the dog stood still, his fur standing up, his tail down. Puzzled, she followed the direction of his gaze – and then she, too, froze.

A few metres behind her brother, as though standing on the water, was a shadowy figure. She closed her eyes tightly, thinking she was seeing things. When she opened them again she saw the figure move away.

Mesmerised, Zoe slowly lifted her hand. A quivering whisper came out of her mouth. "Michael, it's a ggghost. A ghost."

Michael sighed and shook his head slowly in a resigned "not again" gesture.

Every boy knows little sisters can be a pain – drama queens the lot of them; never do anything wrong, and everyone's favourites. Ugh! So for a sister to tell her older brother that she's seen a ghost, well...

"Don't be stupid, Zoe, there's no such thing."

Michael turned round to reassure himself...no, nothing.

Zoe was walking away. "I bet it *was* a ghost, Looe's full of them. Scruff saw it too. I'm going to follow it and see...Come on, Scruff."

The dog reluctantly obeyed, but kept several paces behind.

Michael gave in, as brothers always do, usually to avoid the embarrassing tantrums that otherwise could erupt. He was fourteen, worldly wise enough to know how to keep the peace with his twelve year old sister. So he followed her...

Then he stopped dead. *He* saw it now, floating across the quay as though on a skateboard, a long coat flowing behind. It stopped, its back to them.

203

Zoe, clinging tightly to her brother's arm, hesitantly moved them closer.

"It's a man, see...dressed as an old sailor."

Without warning the man wheeled round, his arms outstretched like a giant bat.

"Aaaah!" he roared.

"Aaaah!" he roared again, his grey hair and beard shaking, making his head seem enormous as he moved towards them.

The two children were rooted to the spot, petrified; a trembling Scruff cowered behind them.

"What, me hearties, never seen a ghost afore?" The voice was softer now. They could see his discoloured teeth as he smiled: "Do not ye worry yer pretty little heads. I mean ye no harm. I be Morgan...and you be?"

Zoe who had, for the first time in her life, been speechless, looked at her brother. His body was rigid, his unbelieving eyes staring. She took control as she always did in times of crisis. Girls are more mature. They have this inbuilt ability to deal with difficult situations. Big brothers don't have a clue. Nor, it occurred to her, do dogs. They're rubbish too.

Zoe found her voice. "I'm Zoe and this is my brother, Michael." She pointed behind her. "This is Scruff, our dog."

Michael let her get on with it, as he usually did, allowing her to believe he could have dealt with the situation just as well, if not better. Secretly he was relieved.

The ghost nodded. "This be my haunting ground – between 'ere and *The Ship* hostelry yonder."

He pointed to an old pub standing back from the Quay. "'as been for nigh on two hundred years."

Despite the bizarre situation, Zoe's inquisitiveness – a forte of little girls – broke through: "Two – hundred – years?" She exaggerated the words. "Don't you get bored? I know *I* would."

The ghost's huge head shook again as he laughed. "Nay, missy. It's not like earth time. Some go to the other world drekkly. Others, like me, get to rest awhile where they be struck down."

Zoe thought he looked sad.

The ghost turned to Michael. "Cat got yer tongue, lad?"

"Er...no..." Michael spluttered.

"Tell me then, what you doin' 'ere, matie?"

At last Michael found the courage to speak. "Er, we live above the lifeboat station, we're looking for our par..."

Morgan cut him off. "Nay, nay, lad. What you doin' searchin' that thar boat?"

Seeing how hopeless her brother was going to be, Zoe stepped in. "It belongs to two horrible men. Their motor-yacht is in the bay," she said.

"They have disappeared," added Michael. "Will you help us find them, Morgan?"

"They be Dutchie smugglers, me dearies, and they be in yonder *Ship Inne*. They bring in opium and be leavin' with their bounty on the early mornin' tide."

Michael and Zoe looked at each other. Then Michael, his fear overcome by excitement, said: "Can we capture them, do you think, Morgan?"

"Aye, we'll scupper 'em maties, but not without the Customs men."

It was six in the morning when the police raided *The Ship*, sweeping noisily up the stairs to apprehend the landlord. Their over-zealous entry alerted the Dutchmen who were preparing to depart. They quickly made their way down through the cellar into the sluice. With water up to their waists, they battled their way out into the river and to their dinghy.

The early morning hubbub of the busy fishing harbour meant they were able to leave without causing suspicion. This time they used their small outboard to push them rapidly out into the choppy waters of the bay. Now they were in sight of their motor-yacht, and safety...

Almost immediately the swell brought water into the dinghy. It became obvious to them that the bow section was deflating – the hole Michael had cut in it half an hour earlier was becoming effective. The power of the outboard forced the collapsing bow deeper into the waves and within seconds the whole dinghy was awash. To continue was hopeless. They were an easy target for the waiting Customs' launch.

Customs officers disarmed and apprehended the two men. Their motor-yacht was impounded and towed into harbour.

The front page in the *Cornish Times* reported the story in detail: cocaine and a large sum of money had been seized, and three men arrested. It said the Harbourmaster's keen eye had noticed that the name of their boat had been painted over another name, and some painstaking work revealed the original to be *Black Prince*.

It was further reported that the Police and Customs had acted on an anonymous tip-off from two children.

The Curator of the Looe Museum, an expert on ghosts in the town, was interviewed on *Radio Cornwall*. He said the *Black Prince* fitted the description of a vessel which, one stormy night two years ago, had holed a small yacht in the bay.

The larger vessel made away without attempting a rescue and the yacht sank.

Four bodies were recovered from the sea by the lifeboat – a Mr. and Mrs. Roberts, and their two children, Michael and Zoe, together with the family dog.

HOW TO PLAY CHESS

Will Owen hesitated. A tremble ran through his body.

Not with fear but in anticipation of the unknown threat lurking ahead. He sensed it clearly.

In the deep shadow of the shop doorway a large figure bided his time, watching, waiting. His breath disappearing into the darkness surrounding him. His hand clasped a knife.

He was ready. Ready to retrieve a piece of information which, should it fall into the wrong hands, would cost him and his friends a fortune. And probably lead to a stretch inside.

Will Owen normally enjoyed his solitary walk home from work; an antidote to the stress of constantly dealing with damaged people in his occupation as a hypnotherapist and his part-time recreational job at the Casino. There, at the Casino, he was trying to learn the scams, the tricks of the trade that one day, he hoped, would bring him a fortune.

But tonight he felt ill at ease. He didn't know why. It bothered him.

Without a sound, the hand came from behind, tight around his throat, cutting off his breath. His attacker was menacingly close as Will struggled to turn his head; close enough to smell the stale beer on his breath. His battered face momentarily illuminated by the lights of a passing car – the flattened nose of a fighter, a white scar down his cheek, the shaved head. Ugly.

The words were barked: "You Will Owen?"

Will tried, unsuccessfully, to nod. The man spun him round, pinning him against the shop door with a huge hand.

"I want the DVD." It was then that Will saw the knife. "Or else."

Will wasn't normally rattled in a tight situation; it was his job to deal with disturbed and difficult people. But this was different. He felt a tremor of fear run through him. His brain was spinning, his mouth dry.

He stalled for time, fighting to regain his composure. The cold unresponsive eyes of his attacker told him the hypnotic route was out.

"Okay, okay. Tell me what you mean and we can talk about it." The huge hand pushed him harder against the shop door.

"I want the DVD you got from Sam's video shop yesterday. 'How to Play Chess'. Remember it?"

"Why, you interested in learning as well, then?"

Before the words had left his mouth, Will knew he had made a mistake. The point of the knife came up under his chin. He could feel it pressing, piercing the skin.

"Don't mess with me, son," the man hissed. "I'll hurt you, if I have to."

There was little doubt in Will's mind that the thug meant business. Oh, if only he had a weapon – one of his trusty golf clubs would do – but no, he'd have to find some other way out of this mess.

"Okay, okay, don't hurt me. It's back home. I haven't watched it yet."

For some reason his mind flashed to Mary, the well-endowed girl in the flat next door... The thug

209

cut short his image. "Right, let's go and get it, shall we?"

The hand on his chest eased off. The man folded the clasp knife, put it into his pocket, then stepped back. Will took his chance; his shoe found the thug's kneecap.

The man's fist came faster than Will had anticipated, but he was ready. He moved to the right and it glanced off his shoulder, hitting the wired glass of the door with a crunch. Will's second strike hit the thug's other knee. He crumpled, his weight taking him down like a sack of potatoes.

"Checkmate," Will said, as he hurried away to the security of his flat.

As he put the safety chain on, he realised it would not stop a forced entry, and it occurred to him that the thug may know where he lived…or would he? Best not to take chances.

As he threw some essentials into a holdall, he slotted the DVD into the machine. A couple of minutes into the introduction the screen went blank and a badly shot home movie appeared. Recognising the outside of the local Ford car factory, Will moved closer. The DVD gave details of a planned robbery – dates, times, layouts and even the names of people involved, including the insider, a contract cleaner named Sid Lines. It was all there.

Now he knew why they wanted it back! And he could see why they would use force to get it.

Will froze. The knock on the door sent a spasm of fear through his body. He rushed to the window and pushed up the sash, ready for a quick exit on to the flat roof below.

"Just a minute," he croaked.

Another knock. This time followed by a soft voice: "Come on, Will. Open up. It's me."

He took a club from his golf bag, undid the chain and turned the key, then stood back. "Come in …"

Mary smiled as she stood framed in the doorway, holding up a bottle of wine. "It's for us," she chirped, "for afters."

Will grabbed her wrist and pulled her roughly into the room. "Quick!" he snapped, pushing the door to with his foot.

Mary stumbled forward, unsure. "What's happening?"

The door flew open. Will recognised the large hand preceding the body as it lunged towards Mary. The golf club hit him accurately on the back of the neck with a thwack. He was senseless before he hit the floor.

Mary stood rigidly looking down at the man, mouth open. Will guided her through the door: "Go… Lock yourself in your room. I'll explain later."

Before he exited through the window, he rewound the DVD and placed it by the thug's hand, hoping it would keep him off his back for a while.

If the crooks were happy with the outcome of their thuggery, Will certainly wasn't. He didn't like his life being rudely interrupted. "Payback time!" he snarled into the mirror of the B&B he had booked into.

By morning he had a plan of action in his mind: he would thwart the robbery himself.

He skipped breakfast, found Sid Lines' address in the telephone directory, and caught up with him just before he left for work at the engineering factory.

Fortunately, he was an ideally receptive subject for Wills' hypnotic skills and he soon revealed his daily cleaning routine as well as the whereabouts of his house and van keys. He left the man in a deep sleep.

Self-consciously looking the part in logo'd overalls and cap, and driving the liveried van, Will had no difficulty gaining access to the factory. No one seemed to notice that he wasn't the regular office cleaner; perhaps they only ever saw the uniform. Or perhaps they didn't care.

He was just getting into a routine when one of the office women screeched down the corridor, "Your name Sid Lines?" Warily, he waved an acknowledgement. "Phone call...in here." She wiggled her bottom back into an office. Will followed. "It's your boss." She put her hand over the mouthpiece of the phone and smiled. "Glad he's not mine..."

He tried to sound casual: "Sid Lines here."

"About bloody time. Why didn't you ring in this morning, Lines?" The voice was hostile.

"Sorry. Got up late. Rushed here. Completely forgot."

"You okay, Lines? You sound strange..."

Try to remember Lines' voice, imitate it. Will deepened his voice. "Yeah. Under the weather, a bit croaky."

"Right. When you've finished there get yourself over to Reflex Logistics." Will grunted. "Clean and polish the corridors like last time. I'll meet you there at two... And don't go off sick!"

The phone went dead.

Fifteen minutes after the Security van had made its wages delivery, Will walked casually to open the security door between the yard and the Wages offices, as described on the DVD, but he found it unlocked and ajar. Through the crack he could see two of the office women having a cigarette. Will concealed himself in the nearby cleaner's cupboard, leaving the door sufficiently open to observe the corridor.

Shortly afterwards, two men in balaclavas, one with a shotgun, entered the Wages office, pushing the two women, who were outside, in front of them. The one with the gun rounded up all the staff and pushed them down the corridor into another room. No commotion, no screams, no resistance. The shotgun was doing its work. He gave his orders: "On the floor, arms outstretched, and don't move!"

The other man came out of the Wages office carrying two bundles of notes. As the man took his first load out to the van, Will broke cover and slammed the Security door shut. He heard the man hammering on the outside, followed by silence. Then the van's horn sounded three times, repeatedly – a pre-arranged warning signal.

It took the man with the shotgun a couple of minutes to realise something was wrong. He rushed out of the room where he was holding his prisoners, locked the door behind him, and almost ran into Will. The man raised the sawn-off shotgun and waved it in Will's direction. Will could see the hesitation in the man's eyes. He could also see his huge hands.

Will put one hand to his face, the other in the air: "It's me," he whispered. "The inside man."

Fortunately for Will, the man took more notice of the uniform than his features. He turned, rushed to the security door and threw it open, just as the van was driving off. "Christ bloody Almighty!"

Unsure what to do, he turned, only to receive a charging Will Owen's head in his stomach. As the man fell back into the yard, there was a deafening roar as the shotgun went off, the pellets smashing the windows on the floor above. Will slammed shut the door, his ears ringing.

When Will released the relieved staff, they said he was a hero. The robbers had taken only half the money, leaving one million pounds behind. There was sure to be a reward, they said.

Because Will was shaking, genuinely upset by the shotgun blast, the Manager sent him home. He left Sid Lines' name and address for them to pass on to the police, loaded his equipment into the van and drove off.

Under hypnosis, he told Mr. Lines exactly how *he* had been involved, detailing his every movement. He also told him about the reward. Will erased all memory of his 'insider' involvement from the man's mind and set him to wake up two minutes after he had departed.

Will left by the back door at the same time as the Police arrived at the front. They were obviously satisfied with the story because the following day the local newspaper headlined Mr. Lines – the man who had faced up to the shotgun and thwarted the robbery – as a local hero. It had a photo too, fortunately taken from a distance, showing him, in uniform, standing beside his van. A reward of ten thousand pounds was on its way, the paper said.

Mr. Lines, sounding like a model citizen, was very convincing: "I only did what anyone would do. I'm happy I could be of help."

And Will? Oh, he's a happy man too. He's moved to Spain, curing the ills of rich women with his hypnotherapy; living modestly on the seven hundred and fifty thousand he managed to stuff into the industrial vacuum cleaner before he released the staff.

He never did learn to play chess.

HAPPY BIRTHDAY

The funeral was a simple affair. What he wanted. No sense spending money on the dead, he had said. Cremation. Followed by a wake. At the local pub, if people wanted.

They did. Just a handful. They drank his health. Talked about the good times. Ate the sandwiches.

A life over. A chapter closed. Bridges burned.

'Friends' vanish as if they were dead too. Too busy living their own lives. Done their duty by coming. Good times shared, conveniently forgotten.

Numbness. Feelings shout out: Disbelief. Guilt. Anger. The isolation of loneliness. Its vice-like grip. The cold silence. Emptiness.

Reaching out…to find no one there. No arms around shoulders. No comforting words. Nothing. Resentment. Being unloved. Abandoned. Life standing still. Each day a struggle to comprehend.

Jobs to do. Tell Utilities, Banks, Pensions. Sift through papers. Where is his Passport? Linger over photos. Sort out clothes. Possessions. Offer family first, then down to charity shops in black bags. Christ, where has it all come from? Got to be done.

Then gradually, very gradually, it all passes. Life moves on. New routines. New people. New things to do. Projects. Hope emerges and looks around for encouragement.

Muted excitement. Guilty laughter. Cautious happiness. They creep back. Like air filling a balloon.

Uncertainty at first. Interrupted by memories. Sadness. Like a see-saw, up and down. Up and down. Occasional tears. What ifs. Insecurities. Will I cope? Do I want to?

The ups slowly get a foothold. Positiveness. Joy. Ambition. All seep through. Thoughts for the future crowd out the melancholy.

Then suddenly I am out the other side. Released. From grief. From sorrow.

Another me. Moulded by the past. But reborn. A new spirit making bow-waves through life.

What the Hell. Why Not? Let's get on with it.

I do. Tentatively. Carefully. Confidence growing. Taking control.

Solo holiday. New friends. New home. Things start smoothing out.

Six months on. It happens. WHAM! A text from the dead, From beyond. From the Afterlife.

'Hello love. Don't forget.

It's my birthday today. x'

Everything churns. Heart thumps. Mind stands still.

Cauldron of emotions. The coldness seeps in again. Back to square one. At the funeral.

Unthinking I text back:

'Why did you leave me alone? I need you!'

Then one each day for a week:

'Where are you?'

'What is the code for the burglar alarm?'

'Where is your passport?'

'When and how do I prune the roses?'

'What shall I do with your gold Rolex watch?'

'What is the password for the computer?'

No replies. Nothing.

217

In desperation I send:
> *'Give me a sign you are listening.'*

I become obsessed. Looking. For Signs. For messages.

Searching – on TV. In shops. On the bus. On posters.

I pray for sightings. Attend Psychic events. Consider reincarnation.

Still nothing. Only silence from beyond.

Am I going mad? Balance of mind disturbed?

Get a grip, girl. You are distraught. It just doesn't happen. Dead means dead. No ghosts. No miracles. No Afterlife.

Use rational thought. Common sense. It was just a message left on the phone *before* he died.

Friends confirm this. Shake their heads. "Don't be bloody daft," they say. "Move on," they say.

I do. Again. Just a silly episode. Part of grieving.

Memory is dispersed. By torrents of activity. Back to normality. Keeping positive. Pursuing dreams.

Settled again.

Be prepared next year. Say "Happy Birthday" and then forget it.

Twelve months. Of serious and hectic living. Making up for lost time.

Sun, Sea and... yes, that as well. Happy and contented. Time for myself.

Ready for message this time. Not anxious at all when it comes:
> *'Hello love. Don't forget. It's my birthday today. Need money c/o Post Office, Vallarta, Mexico. New life here. Send Rolex also. Alarm code 4724. Password – "Escape".'*

Be calm. Stay in control. Difficult…
New Life?…"NEW LIFE!!" I shout. "I HAVE A NEW LIFE TOO!"
Calm down. Then a smile…
"Oh yes, I do," I say.

SIM into rubbish bin. Phone into canal.
It's over. Lie down, mister. You are dead.

DOUBLE DUTCH

Michael Burnside lived in a remote house on the outskirts of Amsterdam. He was burned out by his past and oppressed by the present. The fingertips of his mind desperately clung on to reality, not quite succumbing to the drug-induced oblivion his doctor sought.

He longed to rejoin the mainstream of life and a compartment in his mind held plans to reach out from the futility that surrounded him. All he needed was a sign; a spark to kick-start his life again. Just a sign...

The words in the English newspaper leapt out at him:
>Pen Friends Wanted for Women Prisoners
>Send photo & details to: P.O. Box 674
>Wilmslow, Cheshire.

This was it! A reborn enthusiasm forced its way through the fog that enveloped him as he realised this could be the escape route from his personal maze.

He sent a photo; said he was a thirty-eight year old businessman too busy making money to meet people socially. His only deceit was to give his surname as Michael Bell. He did this to protect himself; there are some unsavoury people about.

Three agonising weeks later it came – a return letter.

'*Michael,*' it said. '*I'm so pleased you wrote to me. I am nearing the end of my time here at Styal Prison.*'

He raised his eyebrows and smiled to himself.

The letter went on. '*I'm forty-one in September.*'

A photo of a pleasant dark haired woman fell from the envelope on to his lap. Michael picked it up.

"Nice, very nice," he mused as he went on reading. '*I made a mistake and I've paid for it. I'll never let myself down again. If you could write to me, you'll make the time go quicker.*'

The dark haired girl with a wide pleasant smile in the photo signed herself '*Veronica Owen*'.

They corresponded weekly for six months, revealing more and more about themselves and their feelings. All the time becoming closer. Tentative romantic phrases gradually led to professions of love. '*I love you, Michael,*' she wrote.

He couldn't believe people could fall in love through letters, but *they* did. It happened.

As his mood lifted, the fog and futility began to evaporate; he felt he was stepping out of a shadow into the glow of life again. Even his doctor recognised the rapid improvement and drastically reduced his medication.

"Yes, Michael, my lad," he said to himself, "you are on the way back."

"You did bloody what, Vee?"

Veronica smiled at the question. "I just told you, Pauline: Stevens was an illiterate snivelling no-hoper, the dregs. So when I wrote a reply to her new pen-pal I used my own name and sent my own photograph."

She nodded gleefully. "He thinks I'm a bleedin' prisoner! I told Stevens he must have lost interest – silly cow believed me."

Pauline took a drink of coffee and put the mug back on the table, allowing her mind to settle, to take in what her friend had just said.

"I don't understand you sometimes, Vee. Isn't being a Prison Officer enough? Why, Vee, why?"

"Why?" Veronica was smiling again, her excitement escaping as she spoke. "'Cos he's loaded, that's why...and dishy too. His name's Michael, lives in Holland, big house. Too good an opportunity to miss, Pauline."

She paused and her mood changed, as though a dark cloud had passed over her.

"I can't stand working in a prison any more, it's crushing the life out of me; the endless routine, the boredom, the grime – it really drags me down, Pauline. It's no life for a woman." Her face and eyes hardened and she almost spat the words out. "What I hate most of all are the prisoners. They are sewer filth, the scum of the earth...I *detest* them." She took a deep breath. "I can't get out of this godforsaken hole quick enough, Pauline. And when I do, I never want to see another prison for the rest of my life."

Pauline slowly shook her head, not in disagreement, for she understood only too well; it was in silent recognition that *she* wouldn't have Veronica's courage.

"You've got guts, Vee, I'll give you that...So what now?"

"It's been going on for months, Pauline, and now, with a bit of encouragement and a few juicy letters, he's fallen for me. Would you believe it? Fallen for *me! Me!*"

She held her head to one side, briefly closed her eyes and, as if talking to herself, softly said, "Little old me...Michael will do anything for me. He says I'm his reason for living."

"I'm happy for you, Vee, but you are a scheming bitch; always have been."

Veronica shrugged. "Sure I am. Anything to get out of this stinking place. I've told him I unexpectedly came up for early release and will be out in two weeks. Then I'll hop on a plane to Amsterdam and start living it up." She lifted up her mug in a toast. "Here's to my new life."

Good News! Veronica is being released early. He had agreed to buy a small house for them both in Volderdam and a villa in Marbella. *'It will put some colour in your lovely cheeks'* he wrote to her. She was thrilled.

Michael's safety deposit box in a London merchant bank contained some extremely valuable securities, the contents of which he now needed to fund his future life. The bank agreed to release them to Veronica; she will bring them to Amsterdam one at a time at weekly intervals. They are too valuable to bring all together.

He told her to hand the securities to Paul, his chauffer, on the first two occasions as he will be in Spain but on her third trip he will meet her personally. He sent her a bank draft for three thousand Euros for expenses and explained that Paul will give her more.

Veronica felt jubilant. It was the best day of her life. Even the prisoners commented on how cheerful she looked.

"That's my last shift done then, Pauline, love – free at last! Tomorrow I'm going to Amsterdam to take Michael some papers, and again next week. Then we're off to Marbella."

Pauline gave her a hug.

"I'll miss you, Vee. The place won't seem the same..."

"Come off it, you Nelly. This dreary dump hasn't changed in fifteen years. Me not being here won't make any difference – they'll continue to serve up the same pig swill, and the dim-witted, pale faced scum will still have to be banged up."

She hugged her friend. "But I'll miss you, Pauline."

Veronica found the trip to Schipol Airport a breeze. She immediately recognised Paul from Michael's description. Over coffee she gave him the package and he handed over another three thousand Euros. He seemed a warm and friendly guy, a little flirty but she didn't mind that. In fact, if it hadn't been for her attachment to Michael, she may have strung *him* along to see how it worked out.

Paul said he had known Michael for many years; a good guy, caring and trustworthy. He apologised for his absence. He was in Spain finalising the purchase of a villa. She already knew that.

The following week the same procedure. Paul asked if he could treat her to dinner – she could stay at the airport hotel overnight and fly back the next morning, he said. She realised he had other things in mind. No thank you, not while Michael is away, it could ruin everything. She asked him to pass on her love to Michael; she was so looking forward to meeting him when she came over next week.

Veronica had never been so excited. At last she would meet Michael and they would set up home together. Heaven. She had given notice on her rented flat, sold her car and other bits and pieces. On this final trip she took three suitcases fully loaded with her worldly possessions, knowing that Michael would soon be buying her anything she wanted.

The carousel at Schipol Airport trundled and squeaked sleepily around. Her impatience willed it to go faster. At last her first case came, then the second, then... then nothing. Eventually she was standing there alone.

"Missing the bag, Madame?" the porter asked in broken English.

"Yeah. They were all put on the plane together. Where do I go to find it?"

He smiled. "It happens much...follow me."

She wheeled the trolley after him, annoyed at the delay.

"Here..." He opened the door for her and gave a smile as she walked past him into an office. On the table was her missing suitcase. Standing nearby was a man and a woman. They looked like Customs Officers.

"Thank God," she declared, reaching for the case. "Where did it get to?"

They didn't speak; just stared at her.

"The dog thinks it contains drugs," the woman said. "Please unlock it, Miss Owen, and sit down."

She had nothing to fear and did as they asked.

In the middle of the case, wrapped in her underwear, was Michael's package. When they cut it open, she saw sachets of white powder. They stared at her, waiting silently for an explanation. When none was forthcoming, the man said, "Can you tell us what this is, Miss Owen?"

Her voice responded in its usual no nonsense Prison Officer's tone. Well why not? *She* hadn't done anything wrong. She remained in control, as always.

"I have no idea. It doesn't belong to me."

"You put it in suitcase, yes?"

"Yes, but it belongs to a friend of mine. I am just delivering it for him. He said it contained securities..."

Then the questions. "Who you work for?" "'Av you brought packages here before?"

"Yes ... He's a wealthy businessman, an Englishman living here called Michael Bell, lives in a large house, here in Amsterdam."

Their silent stares made her feel flustered. She rifled through her handbag with nervous hands.

"Look, I have a photograph. His address is on the back." She handed it to the woman.

"Thank you, Miss Owen."

She wished they would stop calling her that.

"I will check." The woman paused: "Now you will tell the whole story, yes?"

And she did, every single detail. She felt she had no choice, it was the only way she could get out of trouble, the only way to clear her name. The man taped it all.

An hour later the woman returned, carrying a brown folder. Her cold stare was fixed on Veronica as she whispered a few words in Dutch to her colleague. Then her mouth relaxed into a half-smile.

"I'm sorry, we have no records of your Michael Bell. But you are right, Miss Owen, the address *is* a large house."

Veronica felt relieved as the woman continued to smile at her... "It is part of Amsterdam Prison, the Unit used for psychiatric prisoners."

They were both standing over her now. Veronica felt vulnerable, she was in a daze, struggling to reconcile the reality fixed in her mind with what she was hearing.

"No...no... it's impossible. You have made a mistake...or you are trying to trick me."

"We tell you truth, Miss Owen."

The woman sat at the desk and opened the folder.

"An English prisoner in the psychiatric house was called Michael Burnside." She paused and looked up at Veronica. "Same first letters as Michael Bell, eh?... *And* same handwriting. He also had many letters from an English prison. He made good recovery and was released some weeks ago."

Veronica's face showed she didn't understand, she was shaking her head. "I..."

The woman cut her short. "But your photo is not of him."

She reached into the folder and slowly turned a photograph to face Veronica. "This is Michael Burnside. Do you know him, Miss Owen?"

Veronica froze as she picked up the photograph; she began to feel faint and her mind went blank – she was looking at the face of Paul!

"No... it can't be...," she muttered, and then her words started tumbling out. "Yes, yes...I have met this man, he called himself Paul, he was Michael's chauffer. He was the one I gave the packages to."

Her words stopped suddenly, her pale face expressionless. She sat still for a few moments as the truth percolated into her brain.

Paul was Michael!
It was Michael she had met at the airport!

Her disbelief oozed away as the truth became apparent. She became angry with herself, realising she had been completely taken in and outwitted.

"The bastard!" She half-heartedly thumped the table with her fist and looked at the Customs Officers, seeking their sympathy. It didn't come.

"He has made a complete fool of me, hasn't he? I feel so stupid."

The man and woman laughed. Then, as suddenly as they started, they stopped. Their eyes hardened, their faces became stern. The woman spoke, her voice full of contempt: "Ah, so you feel stupid. A good English word, eh?"

Veronica recognized the attitude they displayed. Hadn't she always treated prisoners like that?

The woman's voice was clipped and crisp with authority when she next spoke.

"You have been caught, Miss Owen."

She bit her lip and shook her head; she tried to say "No" but the words wouldn't come. Her stomach somersaulted and she could taste vomit rising in her throat. She made a supreme effort to regain control of the situation.

"I told you, I don't know of any drugs."

She could see from the expression on their faces that they didn't believe her.

"That is your case, yes?"

Veronica nodded.

"You have admitted you were carrying a package for a friend, yes? And that you were paid."

Veronica didn't move her head this time.

"And we know the package contains drugs."

A silence that seemed to go on forever dropped over the room.

Veronica began shaking, but for what she wasn't sure. She was in a mess but it could be cleared up, surely.

"I'm innocent. I didn't know they were drugs," she said weakly.

The woman stood up. Veronica thought how small she was beside her colleague.

"In Holland, Miss Owen, ignorance is no excuse. There is a five year mandatory prison sentence for anyone bringing in drugs."

The man added: "There are never any exceptions."

The silence ebbed back as the Customs Officers waited for the seriousness of her position to strike home. Veronica felt dizzy and sucked in air to clear her spinning head.

"What's going to happen to me?" she whispered.

They didn't answer. Instead the female officer pulled out a pair of handcuffs.

As her world fell apart, the man completed the demolition.

"As a British Prison Officer, Miss Owen, I think you will be popular with the other prisoners...very popular."

JONAS

"Don't talk bloody daft. It's bullshit!"
"No, it's true. Trust me."
"You must be seriously deranged to believe that, mate."
Kev shook his head. "Just because we are doing a Psychology degree doesn't mean we have to buy into all that crap about everything having a rational explanation...and anything that doesn't being a product of our overactive subconscious – or is it unconscious? – mind."
"Well, it makes sense to me."
"Not to me. I tell you again, Tom, *the place is haunted.*"
Bollocks!

The women were becoming restless. Pulling faces at us.
"Why don't you carry on as though we weren't here," said Sally sharply.
Liz joined in. "Yeah, whenever we go out, you always spoil things by bloody bickering."
She put down her drink and looked at us.
"Why don't you just go there and prove it one way or the other. We'll referee, won't we, Sal?"
"Yeah, of course." She laughed. "I've never been laid by a ghost before..."
"Ha. Ha. Very funny. You up for it then, Tom?"
I was.
I figured that a ghostly mystery was more appealing than dull academic certainty.

The four of us – Kev, Sal, Liz and myself – Tom – are on the same Uni Course which started a couple of months ago. Nothing more than mates, but you never know…

Kev had been banging on about this old hospital in the town being haunted and, one way or another, we kept taking the piss. The hospital was built for the Crimean war and had been closed for years; a listed building apparently.

After a few more rounds of drinks it was all fixed. We each pledged on our mothers' lives that we would stay there for twelve hours, whatever happened. Nothing *would,* of course, but it would keep Kev quiet and would be a good laugh.

Sal and Liz would make sandwiches, I would bring a bottle of whisky and some Pepsi and Kev some candles.

By the time we had finished our drinking session, we could have taken on the SAS let alone that figment of Kev's vivid imagination.

It ended with Kev saying "I can find a way in, people. Leave it to me."

I have never known such a bullshitter, but he gets away with it every time.

It was dark when we met.

The old building looked like a fortress, grey and forbidding. It had the sort of ambience that Dracula would have been proud of.

In the cold mist we huddled together next to the big entrance doors, cursing Kev for being late. We had agreed not to bring our mobiles, so I couldn't ring him.

The sudden creak made us jump.

One of the heavy doors slowly swung open as though inviting us into the long dark corridor which lay beyond. As soon as we entered, the door clanged shut. The sound had the finality of permanence.

To me, the place had a peculiar smell. It reminded me of a butcher's shop.

The corridor was dimly illuminated by a single candle half way down and, as we moved nervously towards it, we realised Kevin was holding it.

We were too surprised to speak as he led us into a small room.

He had put newspapers on the table and dusted off four chairs. Half a dozen candles gave an eerie light.

The mood was sombre. Morbid. But the three of us, although a little scared, were determined not to get sucked into Kevin's paranormal world.

"This reminds me of my room at Uni," said Liz, with a nervous laugh.

I joined in. "Yeah. When's the television being delivered, Kev?"

We laughed but I noticed Kev seemed edgy and quiet.

"Right," I declared, "let's have a drink to start the proceedings."

I poured whisky into four paper cups. "Here's to ghosts and ghoulies…"

"Specially the latter," joked Liz.

We touched cups.

"Shush," Kev whispered. "Hear that?"

We looked at him as though to say "No, Kev, we didn't."

The sound of a clanging door in the distance coincided with two of the candles blowing out.

"That," said Kev.

I felt a cold shiver run through my body.

Sal spoke for the three of us: "How come you heard it before it happened?"

Kev raised his shoulders. "I don't know." he murmured.

He produced a small wine glass and a folded board from his rucksack.

"Anyone ever used an Ouija board before?"

None of us had.

"The idea is that we first summon a spirit, then we all put one finger lightly on the glass and it moves around, stopping at the letters on the outside of the board. Someone," he looked at me, "you, Tom, write down the letters and they should make a telepathic message from the spirit."

"Ghost Busters 'R' Us," said Sal. "Sounds a great party game to me, Kev."

I shook my head in disbelief.

"A load of bollocks. I told you he was crazy, didn't I?" I replied.

"Chicken then, are we?"

"Let's humour him," Liz suggested, and we pulled our chairs close into the table.

Kev looked at each one of us. "Look, children, we have to take this seriously. When I summon the spirit, if you laugh or make fun of it, it won't materialise. Just try to believe, eh?"

We said we would try.

Kev stood up, eyes closed, his hands in the air. "Is anybody there?" he said loudly, in a melodramatic voice. "We wish to contact you... give us a sign if you wish to make contact."

Nothing happened.

Sal and Liz were almost wetting themselves. I had to look away to stop myself getting a fit of the giggles.

"Are you there?" continued Kev sombrely.

The glass, which had been upright on the board, suddenly toppled over.

"Ah... a sign that the spirit is ready," said Kev.

Liz stood up. "Come on, Kev, stop trying to frighten us. You must have shaken the table."

"How could I, Liz? I'm standing too far away."

He was right.

Kev put the glass upside down on the board and we all lightly rested a finger on it. I had a pen and paper at the ready to go along with the pretence.

"Are we ready?" asked Kev.

We nodded and smiled at him like children about to listen to a fairy story.

"Tell us your name," said Kev loudly.

To our amazement the glass spun around the board as though propelled by an unseen hand, stopping at various letters.

I noted them down. J-O-N-A-S.

"Thank you, Jonas," continued Kevin. "How old are you?"

T-W-E-N-T-Y.

My scepticism was quickly disappearing.

It was as though we were in a spell. Totally absorbed for about two hours.

We could not believe the phenomenon we were experiencing.

But come on...a spirit talking to us? A dead thing communicating?

There was no other logical explanation.

I summed up our findings – Jonas had been injured in the Crimean war. By the time he had reached this hospital his arm was so gangrenous that it had to be, in his words: S-A-W-N-O-F-F

As these words were spelled out, there was a piercing scream, a scream of agony and torture, from somewhere down the corridor. It was accompanied by a sawing sound, followed by a terrible groaning.

We were petrified. Our faces gaunt in the candlelight.

This can't be happening. It is unreal.

Our fingers were still on the glass and it started to move again. Very slowly this time. D-E-A- The glass stopped in the centre of the board and then shattered.

I put in the last 'D'.

Jonas had died after having his arm amputated, without anaesthetic.

I knew we all believed it.

A dead person had been talking to us…

What could we say?

We sat in hushed silence as I poured us another drink.

Liz's hands were shaking as she raised her cup to her lips. Her face was white, her eyes staring and her words hardly audible.

"I don't like this," she sobbed. "I can't do it. It's my worst nightmare."

Sal put an arm around her.

"Christ, Kev," she shouted at him. "Look at the state of her. She's frightened to fucking death…and she's not the only one."

As I went to pour more whisky, an almighty agonising scream echoed around the building. It seemed to go on forever. It was horrible. .

I sat down rigid in my chair and felt the hairs on my neck and arms standing up.

I looked across at Kevin.

His shoulders were slumped but for some reason he didn't seem scared shitless like the rest of us.

"Look," he said, shaking his head, "we must not give in to this. There is a logical explanation."

I think he was trying to convince himself, as well as us.

"This was a busy hospital, dealing with horrendous battle wounds in terrible conditions. The sawing, the screams, the noises of panic and death are what would have happened on a daily basis. Everyone learned to live with it."

Kev looked at each of us in turn.

"And that is what we have to do, not let it get to us. Otherwise…"

He didn't have time to finish. The candles blew out and we were left in total darkness.

"Let me out," shouted Liz. "I can't stand it." She began to sob uncontrollably.

As Kev relit the candles he whispered, "We are invading their territory…we have upset the spirits…"

"I need the toilet and I want to be sick," muttered Liz between sobs.

"It's just down the corridor, not far. I'll come with you. Yes?" said Kev.

He helped her up and she clung on to him as they left the room.

I shut the door tight.

Sal moved her chair next to mine and held my hand.

"I'd rather wet myself than go out there," she said.

"Me too."

"What's going on, Tom? Do you think Kevin has set this up to frighten us?"

I shook my head. "No. It's too elaborate, Sal. I think it's really happening and Kev is scared as well. It's a nightmare and we are powerless to stop it."

Another blood-curdling scream echoed in the corridor. I felt a shudder go through my entire body. We stood up and held each other.

"I'm scared shitless, Sal," I said. "Really frightened that something nasty will happen to one of us."

The next scream was Liz's. High pitched and hysterical.

We hesitated, but then rushed to the door as she collapsed into the room, shaking all over. She was a quivering wreck.

"He… he's …g-gone. Left me alone with those…those Things."

I held her by the shoulders and put my face close to hers.

"Liz, what do you mean…gone?"

She slipped through my hands on to the floor and curled up in a foetal position, rocking to and fro, muttering incoherently.

I looked out into the corridor but couldn't see much in the dark. I thought I saw a glow in the distance, with figures moving through it, but it may have been my imagination.

"Kev," I whispered, but nothing stirred.

Then I heard a sawing sound followed by muted screams and groans. A door banged shut.

I ran back into the room, slammed the door and gulped down the rest of my whisky with shaking hands. I looked at Sally and shook my head to convey I hadn't found him.

We sat Liz on a chair and sat close together in quiet desperation for a long time.

No words could convey how we felt. The petrifying clamp of fear held us like a vice, paralysing the body and numbing the mind, trying to crush us into quivering pulp.

Slowly but surely it was happening to us all – Liz was already in its grip, no longer a rational being; I knew my turn would come.

I tried to urge my mind to think.

Think psychology, Tom! What happens when we are under threat? Pounding heart, clammy skin, blood moving to the muscles for 'fight' or 'flight'. Neither of these options was open to us. Think of a third – Freeze! It was inevitable this would happen.

We would tie ourselves to the stake and wait for the ghostly beasts which inhabit this place to come and devour us.

Shuffling footsteps outside, in the corridor, broke my thoughts.

The door slowly opened and the intake of air blew out the candles.

I waited for the monster to pounce on us. I was sure we were all going to die.

Sal screamed. "Oh my God," her voice choked with fear.

Then a match illuminated Kevin's face as he relit the candles.

He was a mess – his hair was all over the place, his face dirty, his breathing laboured. He looked totally drained.

His coat was gone and the sleeve of his shirt was torn off, revealing a bloody arm.

Sally shouted at him. "Christ Almighty, Kevin, where have you been! Liz was frightened to bloody death."

"I'm sorry." Kev's voice was hoarse and weak. "I don't know what happened. I think I lost consciousness." He clung to the table and began to ramble. "Lying on a table...blood everywhere...it was horrible...the unbearable pain."

He slumped into a chair then looked me straight in the eye, for a moment regaining some composure.

"Tom," he said, "we must get out of this place. Things will happen to us."

He rested his head on the table and closed his eyes. He looked exhausted.

My fury cut through the fear I was feeling. I grabbed his shoulders and shook him hard.

"You got us into this shithole, so wake up and get us out before we all go stark raving mad. Think man! There must be another way out."

Kev raised his head. His words were slow and uncertain. "I think there's a back entrance through the kitchen...but I can't...I can't go back down there. Don't make me...please, Tom, don't make me."

He looked deranged and was clearly in the grip of some delusional force.

"Okay, mate. You stay in this room. There's plenty of food and drink. You'll be safe. We are going to try and get out before Liz suffers some serious mental damage. Okay?"

I was talking to myself. Kevin had passed out.

Between us, Sal and I managed to get Liz on to her feet and we half carried her shuffling incoherent frame to the door.

I put my hand on Kevin's arm to say goodbye, but he didn't stir.

We picked up a candle each and made our way slowly, hesitantly, down the corridor, half dragging Liz. In the deathly quiet I thought I saw figures moving about in the gloom. I closed my eyes and kept walking.

Suddenly a door flew open near us and with a crash it slammed against whatever was behind it. We stopped dead, frozen with fear. Liz slid to the floor.

I was on the edge of losing control, shaking all over, panic stricken.

Then something strange happened – it must have been my survival instinct kicking in.

It was as if something had taken control of me, neutralising the fear.

"Come on, Sal," I said calmly. "I think they are showing us the way out..."

We picked up Liz and made our way through the door that was open – into a huge kitchen, with stoves and pots and pans. As we moved further into it, we could see there was a door at the far end, half open.

We flew through it, like mad people, and collapsed on to the grass outside, completely spent.

The door closed with a mighty crash.

How long we lay there I don't know.

We found our way to our familiar all night café, not far away from our ordeal. We kept up a continual conversation with Liz, talking about holidays, clothes, her family, anything pleasant. To our delight she gradually came back to normality, although her hands were still shaking a little as she held her mug of coffee.

Mario brought our bacon sandwiches from his kitchen. He looked worried.

"How's your friend?" he asked.

We stared at him, uncomprehending.

"You mean..." the word would hardly come. "Kevin?"

Our three mugs clattered on to the table in unison.

"You have not heard? Two hours ago he was found by the old hospital. His arm was severed, hanging off. Someone brought him here and I called an ambulance."

We looked at each other, then back to Mario.

"Are you sure it was him?" Sally asked.

"Well, it looked like him. Funny though, he was calling himself Jonas or something like that. Probably delirious. He looked in a bad way."

Mario sat down to join us, clearly upset.

"I was very worried, so I rang the hospital a short while ago to see how he was." He shook his head. "I could not believe it. They said they have never heard of him."

I looked down at my mug and saw the bloody finger marks on it from where I had touched Kevin's arm.

Next day Sal, Liz and I reluctantly attended a compulsory lunchtime lecture, entitled 'Paranormal Myths'.

241

We were completely shattered. Subdued and hardly talking.

"Hi there, people!" A voice boomed behind us. It was Kevin.

We turned and stared at him in disbelief.

"What?" he said.

We were too stunned to respond.

"Okay. Okay. So I'm a bad boy. I did try to contact you – but no mobiles, remember? – to say I couldn't make it last night. Last minute emergency. How did it go at the old haunted hospital?"

A GIRL'S BEST FRIEND

A footstep...then another.

My eyes open and I raise my head. Alert as always.

I sit up on the threadbare blanket as the door slowly opens, its rotten wood scraping on the stone floor.

I see his large boots first. Size twelve at least.

They approach and plant themselves in front of the bed like two immovable objects set in concrete.

I look up in the dim light to see what they have carried in, expecting a giant.

Instead I see a man whose extreme thinness exaggerates his height.

He has drainpipe legs and wears a long Nehru-type jacket which swamps his thin frame. It is a faded orange. A battered Colonial–style hat perches on his head.

He resembles a human matchstick.

Even in this light I can see the skin drawn tight over his face. It is the colour of the Tropics rather than Africa.

As he looks down at me he smiles and I see his teeth. White as toothpaste.

When he speaks his voice is soft and silky with a slight upturn at the end of words.

"My name is Nikita," he says. "I knew your mother, Rosa..." He pauses. "No, much more than that...I adored her."

I nod, for I already knew.

He puts his hand on my head. "You must be Mistral, yeah? As fast as the wind and just as unpredictable, your mother said."

I nod again to acknowledge my name, still wary of this peculiar looking stranger touching me.

His hand, with its long thin fingers, feels soft and warm as it strokes my head. I shake it off, but not unkindly.

The man gives a small apologetic laugh. "I've been searching for you," he says. "Looked everywhere, all your mother's old haunts…and here you are." His voice fades away.

I look up at his face and see a tear run down his cheek. For the first time I look into his pale grey eyes as they stare down at me. I guessed then.

I move silently to his left but his eyes barely move. He is almost blind.

"She's dead, isn't she?" he whispers, his voice grief-stricken.

As I nod, he cradles my head again as though to comfort me, or perhaps in sympathy.

"Poor Rosa…" He is lost in thought.

After a while he breaks the silence: "And poor Mistral, having to survive alone at your age in this squalor…"

He continues, as though he now has an urgent need to dispense his thoughts. To tell me his story. I let him. It seems the right thing to do.

"The last time I saw your mother we were on a capsizing yacht off Land's End, in a filthy raging storm." He hesitates as though reliving the moment in his mind.

"I grabbed her and threw her into the half inflated life raft." He shakes his head. "That was the last I saw of her… at that moment the boat turned over and I was knocked unconscious. They found me days later clinging to wreckage, at death's door. The salt water had taken most of my sight."

He looks exhausted and sits down on the bed. I feel so sorry for him and put my face close to his soft hand.

He takes a deep breath, as though summoning strength, then continues: "Before I placed your mother on the life raft, I put a pouch around her neck. It contained a small fortune in diamonds."

I feel his hand move beneath my face.

"I have searched everywhere I think she may have put them, but nothing. I need them to pay for an operation on my eyes, so I can see clearly again. You haven't seen them, have you, dear?"

Diamonds. The word means nothing to me. I shake my head. I wish I could help, I really do.

I am on my feet now, walking with him to the door.

Anxious to get back to my exciting sparkling playthings under the bed which I push this way and that with my nose and my paws.

"Meow," I say as he closes the door, my whiskers twitching.

BEAUTIFUL, ISN'T SHE?

Aaaahh! Every muscle tensed, then tightened as she was slammed back hard against the seat. The guttural roar of the TVR sports car drowned her involuntary cry as it accelerated away at high speed, forcing her into the contours of the upholstery.

Her anxious hands found the edges of the seat and her fingers locked on to the frame.

As the driver turned into a sharp left-hand bend, her stomach seemed to continue forward. Then he put his foot down again.

Physically and mentally overwhelmed she gulped in air – only to retch as the putrid smell of leather filled her lungs.

At last he spoke, his hands nonchalantly caressing the steering wheel: "Three and a half litre. Nought to one hundred in nine seconds. Top speed one hundred and eighty – want to try for it?"

She heard his boastful words as though from a distance. Her mind was numb, uncomprehending.

He smiled. "Beautiful, isn't she? The love of my life."

The intensity of his passion was lost on her.

As he turned his head towards her, her condition registered – the face drained of blood, the fear in her staring blue eyes, a rigid body with white knuckles grasping the seat. She was terrified.

"Oh, sorry, love. Bit of a shock, eh? I'll slow down, shall I?"

He chuckled, sliding through the gears as the next corner rushed towards them. The wind through the open top ruffled his hair and he took one hand off the wheel to sweep it back. She closed her eyes. Tight.

"Barry."

"What?"

His hand, accompanied by a smile, reached across. "My name. It's Barry."

The tightened skin on her face wouldn't allow a smile.

"Olga," barely escaped her lips.

He nodded.

"Where are you going to, Olga?"

A reasonable question to a hitchhiker, he thought.

She dared to loosen her grip and open her mouth now that the speed had reduced.

"Down south."

He couldn't place the accent – certainly foreign. A touch of Eastern Europe perhaps?

Barry shook his head. "Sorry, love. Not going that way. I only live five miles down the road. But I'll drop you off at the M5 Junction, if you like."

He felt the need to explain. "Can't be late home. My tenth wedding anniversary. Big night out."

Olga was thinking fast now that the fear had subsided. She tugged at her skirt to try and show some thigh, but it was near impossible sitting almost on the floor. She put her hand on Barry's knee and in her most sexy voice said, "Sure you don't want to go further with me, Barry?" She paused for effect. "We could go all the way."

The exhaust note filled the silence as he turned towards her, taking in her knees sticking out from a crumpled skirt. He shook his head.

"Not easy being a seductress in a TVR, eh?"

247

He laughed. "Thanks for the offer, love, but, no thanks, not this time. I've a lovely wife waiting at home."

His thoughts drifted...she had been sitting in his car as he came out of the supermarket with some flowers. The TVR had always been a good bird-puller.

Normally he would have been upset, someone daring to mess with his precious car. Not even his wife was allowed to do that. But he could never refuse a pretty woman and, boy, was this one pretty...

The gun poking him hard in the ribs brought his thoughts to an abrupt end. Again and again she rammed it hard against him.

Her voice was urgent, threatening. "Pull over and turn off the engine!"

He did.

"I am with Russian Embassy. An Agent. We have received a coded message to round up all the TVRs we can find and take them to Soviet freighter in Dartmouth."

She allowed herself a tight-lipped smile. "Just like old Lada cars we collected in your country for spares. Yes?"

He remembered, but was too bewildered to answer. He turned his head slowly towards her. She was staring at him fiercely, her eyes ice-blue, cold and uncompromising as she spoke.

"This my first assignment. Failure not an option. Either you drive me to Dartmouth, or I shoot you in the knee and drive myself. You choose!"

A void opened up in his stomach. He felt sweat on his brow as he shook his head involuntarily. There was a tremor in his voice as he spoke: the words had a deep intensity: "No one. *Absolutely no one* drives this beauty." He struck the steering wheel to emphasise the point and stuck out his chin. "No one!"

His attachment to the car amazed her, being shot in the knee was not an issue – it was *her* driving his precious car that worried him. She turned to smile at him. "Good. Now drive. And not so bloody fast!"

Nearing Bristol he pulled into a service station for petrol and, on the pretence of checking the oil, he dislodged two of the plug leads, ensuring the car wouldn't start.

The RAC man lifted the bonnet.

"She's a beauty, sir…"

"I know. Three and a half litre. Nought to one hundred in…"

"No. I mean your girlfriend. A real stunner…"

"Moron. She's not my girlfriend. She's a Russian Agent, and she's got a gun!" Barry grabbed the man's arm, his voice low and demanding. "Contact the police. Tell them I am being held prisoner. You've got all my details. And let my wife know. Understand? Do it, man. NOW!"

Without comment the man reconnected the leads, slammed down the bonnet, leaned into the car and started the engine. He looked at the woman, got an eyeful of leg, and was beguiled by a beautiful smile. No gun.

"Just sign here, sir…"

"Do it now, you idiot!" Barry whispered.

The RAC man waited an hour before he phoned.

"Mrs. West? Your husband asked me to phone. Says he's off down south in his TVR with a Russian woman. Beautiful she is, a real stunner. Wanted you to know."

Silence.

He heard sobbing…then a quiet, exasperated voice. "This is the last straw. He thinks more of that car than he does of me. Missed our Wedding Anniversary and now this! I'm leaving him…"

"Good move, if you ask me, lady. Not very likeable is he? And now going off with this woman…"

The line went dead.

Olga had seen the whispered conversation with the RAC man. She asked Barry to move her seat further back for comfort and, as he bent over, she hit him on the head with the gun. Unconscious, she pushed him down until the seat swallowed him. She fastened the seat belt around his unconscious body. Click.

Olga jumped nervously as his mobile rang. A text message from his wife. *'I've left you, you bastard!'*

She dumped the mobile and Barry's wallet into a rubbish bin and checked the map for the best way off the motorway. Then she roared away.

Sometime later Barry stirred. His head was pounding; he couldn't focus. Where was he? Yes… in his beloved TVR. Alarm!…the woman was driving…*the woman was driving!* As his eyes gradually focussed he saw they were going too fast down a country lane.

"What?…" His voice sounded feeble and hollow. It echoed in his head.

Olga glanced across at him and saw the large bump on his head. As her eyes returned to the road they widened. She saw it...Too late. A tractor turning out of a field.

The driver, confronted by a sports car hurtling towards him, swerved on to the verge, but his large tyre caught the rear of the TVR and ripped it off.

The car skidded sideways from the impact, demolishing saplings and leaving glass and fibreglass debris strewn across the road.

There was a thud as it came to rest in the ditch, the front-end caved in. Engine roaring.

"You okay, Miss?"

Olga moved her arms and legs to make sure.

"I think so. Give me tow out, will you?"

He did.

Sparks trailed behind the remains of the TVR as she drove off.

She noticed Barry had his head on his chest. He was crying.

"Oh come on, Barry. It's *only* a car."

It didn't help. Tears continued to run down his face as he murmured, "My TVR. My beautiful car."

"You should be more worried about your wife. She has left you."

It didn't register; he gave her a blank stare, before his head fell once again on to his chest.

For the rest of the journey Barry was in shock, holding the bump on his head and rocking to and fro, a soft incomprehensible muttering coming from his lips.

It was almost dark when the wrecked TVR pulled up at the dockside next to the Russian freighter. Olga, excited and full of herself for completing her first mission successfully, took the car keys and rushed up the gangway.

As Barry climbed unsteadily and wearily out of the car, he could hear Olga and the Captain in a heated exchange. He watched as Olga stormed down the gangway and rushed towards him.

"Bloody coded messages!" she raved, hurling the car keys at the ship. They hit the side and dropped into the water. Splash. She was furious. Boiling over with rage.

"My first assignment and I have failed! Failed!" she shouted, fists clenched. "Failed! Aaaahh!..."

She stamped her foot and banged her fist down on the wing-mirror which, already weakened, fell to the floor with a smashing of glass.

She suddenly noticed Barry, standing forlorn and dispirited by the car, and her tone calmed. She gave him a sheepish look. "I owe you apology," she said. "The Captain says I have to go with him to Russia."

She tried unsuccessfully to find a smile. "I decoded the message all wrong. The Captain tells me it wasn't TVRs I was to bring but VTRs – video tape recorders. I am sorry."

Olga walked slowly away towards the ship, shaking her head.

As though in a dream Barry collapsed into a heap beside his once beautiful car, sobbing. Unbelieving...

THE BUTCHER

The flash of the blade was unexpected. Hostile. Quick.

Torrents of blood sprayed across the wall.

He blinked, uncomprehending. It was *his* blood!

He put a hand to his throat and, covered in blood, saw it dragging down the white emulsion as he fell, his fingers searching for a grip on the smooth surface.

His face showed a mixture of shock and bewilderment as he saw his red fingers sliding down. A symbol of his life slipping away.

On the floor, his cheek settled in a pool of warmth. He tried to breathe but was only aware of the gurgling of his blood-filled lungs.

It was the last sound he ever heard.

Charlie Baker was good at his job. A trained butcher by trade, he worked for one of the big supermarket chains. It would never bring in a fortune but it suited him.

Also, he had never had ambition or an urge to 'get on' and now, at fifty-four, he was settled. Comfortable.

Some would say in a rut, but he didn't care.

His wife Gloria, on the other hand, had always had a dynamic driving force within her.

She had long since given up trying to coax him to do 'better things', as she called them.

But she had always pushed herself hard.

She was now the CID Police Inspector in charge of Pelsall Police Station.

The station had been threatened with closure in the money-saving scramble. If this happened, Charlie knew she would quit. He also knew that their relationship would not stand the strain.

Gloria was forty-five, young enough for another career and still pretty enough to attract admirers. He knew that those admirers would be women. She had gone right off men. He blamed the macho image of the police force; having to struggle endlessly, even now, to prove herself because she was a woman. The constant sexual talk behind her back and the innuendos to her face. It sickened her.

Charlie knew he hadn't helped. In their early years he was insanely jealous. Possessive too. Not wanting to let her out of his sight; not trusting her. He would have worn her down to a submissive nobody had she not been so strong willed. All this because she was pretty.

They sleepwalked through their marriage, never discussed their relationship or other important issues. Just got on with their lives. Separately. In their own space. Even their work patterns were separate – hers, daytime plus anytime. His, mainly evening until early morning.

But it suited them both to fulfil the pretence of being husband and wife.

They smiled, joked, said 'love' and 'dear', shared domestic chores, ate meals and watched TV together occasionally.

They tolerated one another, tried not to antagonise. A relationship? Well, yes, of sorts but they were no longer emotionally 'connected'. There was no romance.

The Pelsall Police Station had been given a reprieve the previous year when the mutilated body of a local man had been found.

And, today, another.

"In Commonside, Charlie," she told him when she took the phone call at six a.m. "Looks like the same MO – butchered. No name yet. Gotta go, love."

Charlie opened his eyes to look at her. "That's two local murders you're involved with. Should ensure that the station doesn't close."

"Thank God for small mercies. Although the biggest loss of life in Pelsall since the mine disaster is not something to be happy about."

"Go back to sleep, love, you've only had an hour," she continued.

He did. He had been on the night shift cutting up meat for today's customers.

Inspector Gloria Baker arrived at the crime scene at the same time as the Duty Pathologist, Dave Siletto. It had already been taped off.

"Good morning, Gloria, my darling. The gruesome two-some meet yet again."

"Too early for jollity, Dave. I've had no breakfast. Not even a cup of bloody coffee."

She ducked under the tape.

"Let's go and have a look."

The uniformed officer at the door pointed up the stairs. "Up there, Ma'am. Not pretty."

She pulled a face to show she wasn't looking forward to it.

"Lead the way, Constable..."

The bedroom door was half open.

The first thing she saw was the blood soaked carpet. The man was naked. His throat had been cut. Another cut sliced down from the throat to the genitals and another across his stomach at the height of his navel.

An ear was missing. The left one. Sliced off and nowhere to be seen. On his forehead was carved the letter 'C'.

"Exactly the same as the last one." Dave Siletto knelt to examine the body. "Poor bugger. All signs point to death about twelve hours ago. I'll know more when I get him on the slab."

"Thanks," Gloria said. "No sign of a struggle or being tied up. Suggests he knew the killer." She paused. "Or didn't feel threatened by him," she added, almost to herself.

She took a couple of paces back towards the door while Siletto did his work.

"Any info yet?" she asked the Constable in the hallway.

"Some, Ma'am. He lived alone. Neighbours didn't see or hear anything but we're still checking…"

"Well done. Any name yet?"

"Yes, Ma'am." The Constable looked in his notebook. "Joseph Montgomery White, aged forty-seven. Single."

Gloria stiffened. She recognised the name Joe White. One of her old boyfriends from many years ago. The previous victim, Tim Sherwood, was also an old boyfriend, although she had not disclosed the fact to anyone.

Why hadn't she? She didn't know. Perhaps an involuntary act to protect Charlie.

He had known both of them and because of his extreme jealousy had threatened them both. But that was long ago.

Gloria instructed the Scene of Crime team when they arrived. Then she talked to the Uniforms doing the door to door, which didn't add any additional information. When the body had been removed for post mortem, she popped across to *The Railway* pub for a quick sandwich and a drink.

"I'm going to have a close look around," she told the Uniform keeping a watch on the property when she returned. "Don't let anyone in, please. Phone me if you need to. Got my number?"

"Yes, Ma'am, I have."

Gloria looked carefully around the house. Every room.

She looked through photo albums but as far as she could see there was nothing linking her to the victim.

The knife drawer in the kitchen yielded a sharp knife that looked similar to Charlie's set. She put it in her handbag.

The next day the Scene of Crime Officer briefed her: "Nothing significant, Inspector. No finger prints would indicate the perp. used gloves. No weapon. No DNA – all just like last time. The only thing we have is this." He pushed a photo across the desk to her. "Looks like a trainer has trod in the blood. Unusual tread pattern. See...there on the heel... a distinctive cross tread pattern as though it has been damaged."

He shook his head. "Nothing else, I'm afraid."

Gloria remained silent about the conclusions she had drawn. She kept it to herself until a month later.

The fridge had mysteriously gone on the blink after Gloria had gone to work and Charlie set about mending it. First he had to clear everything out. Like most households, they hoarded out of date odds and ends – pickles, jams, jars of this and that. Right at the back was a small container with some kind of meat wrapped in cling-film.

"You looked whacked, my dear," Charlie said, when Gloria arrived home. "Had a hard day? I'll make us a cuppa. By the way, I've fixed the fridge."

Gloria nodded as he went into the kitchen, then she collapsed on to the settee, exhausted.

"Thanks, love." She took a mug of tea from him.

"Now, what are you looking so worried about? Is it the murder case? Still no suspects?"

Gloria looked at her husband long and hard.

"What …?" he asked.

"Funny you should say that, Charlie. If I were not your wife, we would have."

Charlie looked puzzled as he took a drink of tea. "I don't understand…"

"Don't you, Charlie. Let's look at what I need to nail a suspect."

This was a process they had shared for years. It helped her. "First?" She looked at him expectantly.

"Well," said Charlie, "the first thing would be motive."

"Quite right. I have two – the first is jealousy. Both the victims had been boyfriends of a lady, long ago. The lady's husband was the very jealous type. He had told her once that he would kill the man if ever she had an affair."

"Okay. A good possibility. What's the second?"

"It's more obscure but, suppose a local community facility is threatened with closure, the two murders may prevent this happening."

"No, I don't think so. Too flimsy, dear."

Gloria could see that Charlie had not yet made any connections. "What next, Charlie?"

"Clues, of course. Direct or circumstantial. Do we have any?"

"Yes, Charlie, we have one or two. First. I have the murder weapon – an extremely sharp knife. No prints. Second. I have identified the owner of a heel print found at the scene. Third. The letter 'C' was carved on the victims' foreheads. What do you think that might be?"

Charlie thought for a minute. "Could be a symbol of some sort, or an initial perhaps."

"Yes, I would think an initial. And, fourthly, probably the clincher for a jury – I have found the ears from the victims in the suspect's house with his fingerprints on the container."

Gloria sat up straight, took a gulp of tea and looked across at her husband.

"It's you, Charlie, isn't it? *Your* knife. *Your* heel-print. 'C' is y*our* initial, Charlie. The ears in *our* fridge. Add the motive of jealousy and the fact that you are a butcher. It all adds up, doesn't it? An open and closed case, wouldn't you say?"

Charlie banged his mug of tea on the table so hard that it splashed everywhere.

"No, surely not, Gloria, you can't think I had anything to do with it…can you?"

He was shaking his head vigorously.

"You tell me, love. I have seen the ears, and the heel of your trainer is an exact match. Now, show me your work knives."

Charlie reached behind the settee. "Here." He passed the box to her.

Gloria flicked the catches, opened the lid and pointed to a space where a knife should have been.

"Where is it?" she asked.

"I don't know," Charlie whispered. "I lost it weeks ago."

Gloria opened her handbag and pulled out a knife.

"Is this it?"

Charlie nodded.

"It was found at the murder scene."

Charlie's mouth dropped open. He closed his eyes and shook his head in disbelief.

"It wasn't me...," he said, his voice hardly audible.

"I know it wasn't, my love," replied Gloria.

He opened his eyes to look at her but only saw the blade flash towards his throat.

There was no sensation. No pain. Only spurting blood.

He would never know what happened next.

CHARITY BEGINS

Mine is like any other charity shop – warm, friendly and usually crowded. Filled with quietly focussed bargain hunters, chirpy gossips and 'special' people, not unlike me. My Manageress calls them weirdos. They come in to shelter from the cold and to be among people. They are lonely. Like me. Everyone is welcome; we are like one big family. The family I don't have.

Myself, I am tucked away in the back room, sorting stuff that people have brought in, usually in black bags. I make things presentable if I can. Iron them or sew them. The rubbish, and believe me there is a lot, I throw into the bins.

I don't get paid. I am what they call 'a volunteer'. But I love it.

My job isn't as glamorous as serving in the shop, but I am in and out of there all the time, restocking – clothes, books and DVDs. In any case, I don't think I could work the till. Even some of the old people who work in there get confused.

One of our regular weirdos seems to have taken a fancy to me. And, to be honest, I like him too. Romantic, isn't it? His name is Boyd. He is about six foot seven inches tall, roughly my age and talks half in French and half in English.

My Manageress, who knows about these things, says it's only pretend French. She says he lives in a special hostel for psycho…something or other.

He sometimes talks with an American accent, just like President Obama. We have a good laugh together. He keeps saying "Amour" to me – that's 'Love' in French, you know.

I know he would do anything for me.

Sometimes he sneaks into my room through the back door and we have a cup of tea together. I tell him stories and he speaks to me in French.

I have made up stories since I was a little girl. Mommy used to call me Dolly Daydream. Now I make up stories about the stuff that comes into the shop. I can see things that others can't. I am sort of psychic. That's what I think they call it. It's a gift I have.

Oh, it's lovely. Every bag has a story to tell: a house-move, a Duchess, a Lottery winner, a Divorcée, someone murdered. I can read something into them all.

My friends who work in the shop think it's great fun when I tell stories about the clothes and belongings. They think I'm silly really but we all have a good laugh and it makes the day go quicker.

Then one day it became real.

I opened a couple of bags and recognised some clothes and cheap jewellery.

"Oh, goodness me..." I said to myself.

They belonged to my cousin, Barbara. We are about the same age – mid-thirties – and we spent a lot of time together when we were younger. "Straight" and "Curly" we used to call each other, which described our hair. Mine is curly.

We lost touch about five years ago. It was after her Mommy's funeral. Her Mommy was well off and with the house to sell Barbara must have come into a fortune. I heard she had married soon after. I think he was the possessive, jealous type who didn't want her to have any friends. A bully too, I shouldn't wonder.

And now…*this!*

What brings her belongings into my charity shop? Had she died? Or – I couldn't stop the thought – been done away with, murdered?

What puzzled me most was the jewellery. Bits and pieces I knew had belonged to her Mommy and a necklace I had bought for her twenty-first birthday. Surely she wouldn't throw these away? My Manageress said I could keep them until I solved the mystery.

I shared my fears with Pauline, my friend in the shop, and with Boyd. All Pauline did was raise her eyes to the ceiling in a "Here we go again" gesture. She thinks it's weird that I can't tell the difference between what is real and what is fantasy. But I am really worried.

Boyd listened and then jabbered on in French. *C'est famille,* he kept saying … *C'est famille.*

The first thing I did was to ring the last number I had for Barbara. Pauline was right. She may have thrown the stuff out herself.

A man's voice answered. "Tom Sharp," he said. *The husband!*

"Can I speak to Barbara, please?"

"She's not here. Left six months ago."

"Where to?"

"No idea, love."

He put the phone down.

He didn't seem concerned. My suspicions grew.

Next I went to Tesco, where Barbara worked.

I saw the nice Personnel lady.

"She was due in on Sunday 3rd December," she said, "but she didn't show up. Unlike Barbara not to phone, if she was ill or anything. Nice girl."

I shared my concerns with her. She looked worried.

"Yes, I see what you mean. Her husband did come in. I didn't like him. He was surly and arrogant and only interested in any money owing. There was none."

We looked at each other and I could tell she was thinking, like me, that something gruesome had happened.

"Look," she said, "I shouldn't do this but, as you are a close relative, can I give you this envelope to give to her if you find her…?"

I nodded.

"It's a cheque for five thousand pounds. Barbara's share of the winnings from our Pools syndicate. If you don't trace her, bring it back. Okay?"

I nodded again and smiled my thanks.

My next day off saw me knocking on doors, talking to Barbara's neighbours. A lovely girl they all said, didn't deserve that monster of a husband. They hadn't seen her for a few months. Just disappeared, they said.

One told me that a flashy redhead had moved in with Tom Sharp. *Oh no…the Other Woman!*

Another man told me Sharp had spent a lot of money having a new patio built. Lots of concrete, he said. His tone was grave and I could read between the lines. *Oh my God, Barbara, what has the beast done with you?*

I talked to Pauline and Boyd in the back room.

264

"It looks very bad," I explained. "I think he's killed her. Should I go to the police?"

"Non gendarme, Non gendarme. We fix it." Boyd seemed agitated.

"She might have just left him," said Pauline. "Started a new life somewhere else."

I pulled a face.

"It happens. I know it's not what you want to believe but you do build up these fanciful stories. You know you do."

"But this isn't like that. It's real. It's family. I have to do *something.*"

"Oui," agreed Boyd. "C'est famille."

Pauline put her hand on mine, then Boyd did the same.

"Why not put an Ad in the paper?" she suggested. "See if anyone knows where she is."

I did: '*Anyone with information as to the whereabouts of Barbara Sharp (née Pearce) please contact Box 7856. The Yorkshire Echo.*'

Shock Horror! Later that week I read in the evening paper that Tom Sharp had committed suicide. He had put a pipe from the exhaust into his car in the garage and breathed in the fumes. Obviously the guilt of his horrible deed had got to him and he couldn't stand to live any more. It said the police confirmed it was suicide. He had been drinking and they were satisfied that the message '*Je suis mort*' written in the dust on the back window was a form of suicide note. The dust was on his fingers.

The following week the newspaper sent me an envelope. In it was a mobile telephone number.

A woman's voice answered when I rang. I didn't recognise it immediately.

"Is that you, Barbara?"

"Who wants to know?"

"It's me, Curly. Are you okay?"

"Oh hello, Curly, love. Yes, I'm fine. I saw the Ad. What did you want?"

"I was worried. You had disappeared and your clothes and jewellery came to my charity shop – you know, MIND, in the High Street."

"Tom must have dumped them there when I left him."

"There's something else: you've won five thousand pounds on the Tesco Pools. I have the cheque for you."

"Wow! That's great news. I'm living on the coast. Leave it for me at the shop and I'll come and collect it."

I was mightily relieved.

"I work Mondays and Wednesdays from about ten," I told her. "It will be lovely to see you again."

I didn't tell her about Tom Sharp's suicide. I'll do that when she comes in.

I told Pauline and Boyd all about it. Pauline was pleased, I could tell. Boyd was out of it, in his own little world.

When I reported for work the following Monday, my Manageress told me that Barbara had called just after nine. She said we could keep the clothes and jewellery, but she took the envelope.

"Did she leave any message?" I asked.

"No, she just said she was in a hurry as she had to see a solicitor before she caught the eleven o'clock train back. I checked her ID of course – a bank card in the name of Barbara Sharp." She smiled. "What lovely curly red hair she's got, hasn't she?"

An *Emergency* meeting in the back room with Pauline and Boyd.

"*Oh no!*" I explained to them what I had just heard. "His mistress has got red hair. She came in and took the money. She has stolen Barbara's identity. Has her bank card and everything."

They looked at me as I started to cry.

Boyd rushed out saying *non famille* and then *au revoir*....

Pauline helped me to open up some bags and tried her best to comfort me.

"It'll be all right," she said. "You'll see."

That night when I was washing up my tea things in my warden controlled flat there was a knock on my door.

It was a police lady. She had some bad news she said.

Barbara had been killed. A tragic accident.

She had been waiting for the train back to the coast, standing at the front of the crowded platform, when a non-stop express train came speeding through the station. Witnesses said that its turbulence dragged Barbara's red wig over her face. She had lost her balance and fallen under the train. They were trying to trace a tall man who was standing next to her and he would no doubt confirm the story. He was French, they thought.

The nice police lady made me a cup of tea because I was shaking. She tried to cheer me up by saying that as Barbara's only living relative I would inherit her considerable fortune. I asked her whether this would mean I would have to give up my job at the charity shop but she didn't seem to know.

"I had a feeling something bad was going to happen to her," I told her. "I am psychic you know. It's a gift I have."

MIRROR, MIRROR...

It happened when I was looking in the lounge mirror, combing my hair. A normal mirror, nothing special, round with bevelled edges.

"You don't look too bad, Jonathan," I thought as I looked at myself and stroked the comb through my hair.

As I continued to gaze at my reflection, my lips suddenly moved. "Politicians, kill the bloody lot of them!"

It was a deeper voice than mine, somehow familiar but definitely not mine.

The words had come out of my mouth, but they were not *my* words. Not *my* thoughts. I was not connected to them in any way.

My mind froze and an unfamiliar fear gripped me. *Am I going mad?*

When I looked away from the mirror I felt my normal self. Was it just my imagination playing tricks? It happens. I push the comb through my hair again as I look back into the mirror. My face is staring back at me. Yes, it is me – the eyes, mouth, hair, the ears. All normal. All mine.

But something is wrong. I know it. I sense that the inner person looking back is not me. It is different somehow. I look like me but I don't *feel* like me. I feel strong, powerful, boiling over with an aggressive spirit. The raw exciting power of it fills my body. I stand proud, steady as a rock.

No, that is definitely not me. I am a shy, reserved, introverted person. I lack confidence and self-esteem. I am afraid of people and life in general.

In the mirror my mouth speaks again, as though it belongs to someone else. "Too right you are, my son. You are one of life's losers. Look at the way you dress and those terrible NHS specs. You're a right shambles. A nerd. A complete waste of space."

I stare at my image, not believing what I am hearing and seeing, unable to control whatever is possessing me. Unable to comprehend what is happening.

I summon up the courage to speak. "Who are you?" I ask, hesitantly.

"I'm offended that you have to ask, Jonathan. Don't you recognise me? We lived together for a while. I'm Billy, your twin brother."

"But...but you died at birth."

"Too right I did. But now I'm back. Couldn't stand to see you making such a hash of things. Missing all life's opportunities. Life is for living, not for hiding." He (or was it me?) smiled. "I've come to show you how life should be lived."

I shook my head in disbelief and bewilderment. A little frightened. "But I don't understand...?"

"You will, my son. Now, listen carefully. As soon as you look in this mirror each morning you will become me, Billy. When you go to sleep at night it will wear off."

Next morning I did as he had said and each morning after that, until I gradually *became* Billy, leaving my old life behind.

It felt fabulous. I was powerful, in total control of my life and every situation I found myself in.

I threw out my old clothes and bought up to the minute fashion. I dumped my Honda 50 scooter and bought a flash VW sports car as well as a Harley Davidson. I went clubbing every night, chasing all those desirable women, amazed that most of them *wanted* to be caught by the new me.

I became the life and soul of the party and soon teamed up with a group of guys with similar lifestyles. It was great!

Money was no object – until all my savings ran out.

Fortunately, I had kept my job as an accounts clerk at the GXS Security firm. They weren't happy with my new image, nor with my confrontational behaviour and frequent absenteeism.

Before they sacked me, I used my inside knowledge to defraud them of two hundred and fifty thousand pounds, transferring it to my own bank account. I knew the loss wouldn't be detected until next year's Audit.

"Serves them right, the money-grabbing capitalists. Should have had better security systems."

One night, when I was out of my mind with booze and amphetamines, I told some of my new mates the security entry codes for the vans which delivered cash.

Shortly after, there was a spate of armed robberies and after each one a packet containing twenty grand landed on my mat. A just reward, I'd say.

Now I am Billy all the time, except for a short spell between waking and looking in the mirror. It is absolutely fabulous!

I feel like him, act like him. *I am him!* An out of control, hell-raising extrovert. Brilliant!

The *Legs 2 Heaven Club* turned a bit nasty one night after we took liberties with a couple of the hostesses. The Manager was most offensive, calling us "scum". That, and the indignity of being thrown out by the bouncers, really wound me up. I was determined to get my own back. We all were.

We found out where he lived, poured petrol through the letter box, and torched the place. We didn't hang around.

I heard on the early morning news that he, his wife and their three children had been taken to hospital. One of the children had died of burns. The police were treating it as murder.

I felt the colour drain from my face. I had done some bad things as out of control Billy, but killing a child? An innocent child…

My mind was in turmoil. This couldn't be happening to me. But it was. I resolved to put an end to it there and then. I rushed downstairs in a panic determined to smash the mirror which was the cause of it all. As I frantically grabbed it off the wall I looked fleetingly into it and saw the warning word "No!!" leave my lips.

I held the mirror over my head ready to smash it. Strong invisible hands struggled to stop me, to wrestle it from my grasp but I eventually broke free, bringing the mirror crashing down on to the floor. It smashed into a thousand pieces, glass flying everywhere.

As it smashed, an agonising scream filled the room. It was horrible.

At that precise moment Jonathan ceased to exist.

THE PLOT

The thought of death unsettled her. It always did.

She felt vulnerable, as though death was stalking her, watching her every move.

Yes, Marjorie Fielding was certain that the grim reaper was close by, ready to strike. Ready to trap her, as he had her mother, who had hanged herself aged forty-two.

Marjorie's age.

Her hands were shaking as she looked again at the contents of the envelope she had just opened. The document was headed 'Plot Certificate'. It was made out in her name and gave details of Plot 513 in the local cemetery. It was signed by the Cemetery Superintendent.

She clung to the kitchen table for support, her heart pounding. There was a note attached to it: 'You will be needing this soon, won't you?'

She knew it was her husband's work. His latest attempt to break her, to force her to the edge of desperation, to where she could see no way out but to follow her mother into the release of suicide.

The hate mail, the silent phone calls, the noises when she was alone in the house at night, the dead cat on the doorstep – she was sure Duncan Fielding was behind them all. Slowly and relentlessly he was trying to destroy her. She knew the insidious grinding down was designed to erode her will to live. In her darker moments she thought he would succeed, knew it was only a matter of time before she fulfilled his wish.

Her wealth had bought the house, his sports cars, his business, and his extravagant lifestyle – the golf, the gun club, his expensive clothes. She had mistakenly thought this would buy his affection, his loyalty. What a fool! She knew now that all he wanted was her money, nothing else.

Through her wealth, Duncan Fielding had become a conceited and arrogant spendthrift who enjoyed the good life. He believed he could do anything, if only he put his mind, and his wife's money, to it.

They had married ten years ago. No children. In his view, his wife had stood still, while he had moved on; he had left her behind, outgrown her, intellectually and socially. She was part of the past, not the present – and certainly not his future.

He wanted to be free of her, to enjoy the trappings of her inherited wealth, to have a glamorous, jet-setting lifestyle, with an intelligent, beautiful woman on his arm.

Duncan Fielding had enjoyed several affairs with younger women during their marriage, but the excitement, the sexual thrill, hadn't lasted long. He had not yet found the exceptional woman he was searching for – until now...

They met at a charity event. He noticed her at once, pretending to listen to some overweight charmer. She was stunningly beautiful, and looked about thirty; slender, with bobbed blonde hair. No wedding ring – not that that ever deterred him.

He couldn't take his eyes off her. His whole being was instantly attracted; his insides were churning, his heart pounding, and deep down he felt an irresistible yearning, as though his very soul was aching. He knew beyond doubt that *she* was the one.

Gathering up two glasses of champagne, he wandered across the room. "Your drink, my dear?" he said as he approached.

She looked relieved, took the glass and smiled her gratitude, holding his arm as they moved away.

"Thank you, Duncan," she whispered.

He frowned. "Yes, I do know who you are. I run the Charity so I make it my business to know about people, especially the ones with money."

She held out her hand to be shaken. "I'm Fiona. Fiona Mitchell."

Duncan lifted her hand and kissed it, his gaze drawn to her breasts beneath the simple black dress.

"I'm impressed," he said mischievously, his eyes meeting hers.

"I'm sure you are. But it's hands off. You're married." She paused. "Read my lips – I'm not interested."

Duncan thought her body language told a different story. "Oh, come on, Fiona. I can see you don't believe that, do you?"

She took his arm, guided him into an alcove, and lowered her voice. "Listen, Duncan, I'm a single, independent girl, not wealthy like you, but I'm working at it." Her eyes searched his eyes. "Okay, I admit it would be fun to go out with you but nothing more. I repeat – you're married, so it can't go any further. Understand?"

He did. Only too well.

Duncan Fielding became obsessed with Fiona Mitchell. She was everything he was looking for – lively, intelligent, beautiful. Even though her manner was casual and off-hand, he knew she was attracted to him. Her resistance only served to increase his desire, his passion, for her. *She* was the one he wanted to spend the rest of his life with.

Marjorie had seen the signs many times before, but this time it was different, more intense. She knew it was serious: he had met someone and fallen head over heels in love. His whole persona changed. He became civil to her, tried his best to be friendly. It made her nervous...

She became extra vigilant and kept a close eye on her husband's movements; she even followed him, discreetly, on several occasions to his beloved gun club, where he spent more time huddled in the bar with one of his cronies than on the shooting range.

Twice she saw him with his new love – young, attractive, well dressed and self-confident. When they were together, she noticed it was Duncan who was the more attentive; it was he who stroked, touched, or initiated a kiss. Unlike the others, she thought, this one is in control. *She* calls the shots, dictates the pace. Marjorie even discovered her name and where she worked.

Now that she knew the new love was in charge, she somehow felt less threatened, more at ease. She could foresee a long term 'mistress' situation developing. Proof of this, she felt, was Duncan's increasingly relaxed behaviour. No more threats or arguments. He seemed contented and they talked from time to time. He rang her occasionally from work, and even took her out for a meal – something he hadn't done for a long time.

She didn't like the idea of him having a mistress but she could tolerate it. It took the pressure off.

One morning, as Marjorie was finishing her coffee, Duncan phoned her from work. He wanted to talk.

"I've been a fool, Marjorie," he said. "I'd like to explain...but not over the phone."

He appeared hesitant and anxious, and Marjorie could sense the genuineness in his voice. She felt tears of relief forming in her eyes.

"It's a nice day," he continued. "How about afternoon tea? That new bistro at the end of the High Street looks good, the one with tables outside. Three o'clock okay?"

"Yes, of course, dear." She pictured the place in her mind. "*La Bohème* I think it's called. I'll see you there at three."

She felt happy as she walked leisurely along in the sunshine, glancing in the shop windows, admiring her reflection, as she always did. Up ahead, on the corner, the tables and chairs of the bistro spilled out on to the pavement.

She recognised the back of Duncan's head immediately. His mop of well-groomed hair was unmistakable. She came up behind him, put a hand on his shoulder and gave a cheery "Hi" as she sat down beside him.

It happened so quickly, so silently. The single bullet hit the side of her head with a faint thud. As if in slow motion, he saw her smiling face jerk sideways before flopping forward on to the small metal table, her blood oozing slowly on to its shiny surface.

Fiona Mitchell, the love of his life, lay dead.

Duncan Fielding, half standing, went limp. Then he fainted, sliding slowly and lifelessly on to the pavement.

Screams alerted Marjorie Fielding as she crossed the High Street to meet her husband. She found him lying on the ground and a woman splayed across the table, facing away from her, blood tinting her blonde hair.

"I can't believe it. Can't take it in." She was practically inaudible as she spoke to the Detective inside the now empty bistro.

"I was coming to meet him…"

Marjorie held on to the chair for support. "Who was she?" she whispered.

His response was gentle. "A lady called Fiona Mitchell. We think she knew your husband. Just happened to be passing and stopped to say 'hello'."

He hesitated and looked directly into her pale face. "Wrong place, wrong time, I'm afraid."

She faced him anxiously. "My husband, how is he? I thought at first he was dead too."

"He's okay, Mrs. Fielding. Fainted, we think. Hospital is just a precaution. He's extremely shaken up, naturally, but he confirmed he was waiting for you when this woman he knew stopped by unexpectedly."

Marjorie Fielding suddenly put her hands up to her face. "Oh my God," she said quietly. "Oh-my-God!"

The Detective knew she had made the connection. He filled in the words for her. "Yes, that's right, Mrs. Fielding. A couple of minutes earlier and it could have been you." He let the thought hang in the air. "Of course we can't rule out that Ms. Mitchell was the gunman's target, but it seems unlikely."

Duncan Fielding returned home a broken man. He looked ten years older – a shuffling, physical wreck.

"I've killed her," were the only words he mumbled to his wife.

A friend accompanied him to the funeral. He was ashen-faced when he returned, his red unseeing eyes staring into space. Marjorie put an envelope into his hands. "This is for you, dear," was all she said before she left the room.

Slowly, his fumbling hands opened it and pulled out a sheet of paper: it was the Certificate for the grave plot. Still attached to it was his own note: 'You will be needing this soon, won't you?'

Two hours later, Duncan Fielding hanged himself in the woods next to the house.

Marjorie was upset. Upset because he died without knowing the truth, believing it was his fault that Fiona was shot. Not knowing it was Marjorie who had arranged for Fiona to keep the three o'clock appointment.

ARTISTIC LICENCE

"Carlos Vitara 'ere. You know me. I play for United and España. Best footballer in your country, si?" He laughs.

Unimpressed, I stifled a bemused yawn. "Yeah...well...what do you want?"

"I marry fantastic girl next month. You best artist in town. I want you paint her in your famous modern art way. Money no object – say twenty thousand, si?"

My mind clears instantly.

"Like you, Carlos, I do not come cheap. Double it and we have a deal."

"Okay, double. I know you busy but I must 'av in three weeks – for this I pay ten thousand extra. All money, 'ow you say, 'up front. In cash."

"Anything else?" I ask.

"I want like Picasso, very modern...and big, very big."

"I'll make it as big as I can," I said, as I put the phone down.

The guard let me into the driveway of his out of town mansion. Carlos was right. His girlfriend, Shirley, was fabulous. As he introduced me, he gave me fifty thousand pounds in a big envelope.

"I go for training now in my Aston Martin. You want see?" He winked at me as he laughed. "You buy one now, eh?"

I shook my head, preferring to take the coffee Shirley was offering.

She produced a lovely smile. "My Carlos says you are famous. I've never met a real artist before but I hear you can be very sexy. Do you make a lot of money as well?"

Thinking I was in with a chance, I gave her my alluring look. "Yes, to both your questions."

Her vacant expression told me she had forgotten the questions.

"Yes, I'm rich *and* sexy...and I think you are beautiful." She blushed. I could tell she had taken a fancy to me. Or was it my money?

I said it was essential to sketch her in the nude. She didn't bat an eyelid and seemed to enjoy the attention, particularly when I stroked her skin. I explained it was important for me to capture the texture so I could reproduce it on canvas.

I think me being a rich and famous artist really got her going. She called me hot blooded. I didn't deny it.

We ended up in bed. I knew we would.

I must have impressed her because she asked me if I would like to join her for a week in Barbados. She would tell Carlos it was a pre-wedding holiday with a girlfriend. His credit card would foot the bill, she said. Sometimes it's a hard life being an artist.

I re-arranged things and off we went. Just like a honeymoon it was. Glorious!

We came out of the airport separately and I watched him meet her in his macho 4x4. They kissed passionately. *"She's just a trophy to him,"* I thought. But then who was I to talk.

A couple of days later I showed him the picture. The symbolism confused him at first, but when I explained it to him he was jubilant. "Wonderful! Wonderful! It will impress all 'a my friends and 'ang in our new home." I thought he was going to cry. "You make me very 'appy," he enthused as he put his arms around me. "Come to dinner with us tonight. We celebrate."

I knew the restaurant well. Lavish surroundings, sumptuous food, impeccable and discreet service. Cost the earth, but I wasn't paying.

On the way back from the Gents, I ducked into the kitchen. "Perfect meal and service lads. Well done."

"Oh hi, Sid. You been ill, or what?"

I shook my head.

"Gone up in the world haven't we? *And* with Carlos Vitara. What happened?"

"You'll never believe it. I got a phone call from him saying could I paint a picture of his bird for fifty thousand pounds."

"Wrong number?"

"Yeah. He thought he'd phoned some famous artist. So I bought a picture from a gallery for a couple of thousand quid and signed it. He was over the moon."

"Back waiting on the tables tomorrow then, Sid?"

"Yeah, I guess so – unless I get another commission…"

BILLY NO MATES

My name is Bill.

I'm your archetypal grumpy old man. Only much worse. I'm nasty with it.

To be fair to old men, I should tell you that I have been like this all my life. Consequently I've no friends, no interests. In fact I've nothing worth getting out of bed for – except to bitch at life. *That* keeps me going.

"Shame," I hear you say. "Poor sod! Probably deserves it." And you would be right.

God put nightmares like me on earth to make the rest of you feel good. To appreciate all His gifts – nature, human kindness, the wonders of the world and all that crap. That stuff makes no impression on me whatsoever. Zilch. Unless of course there is something in it for me. Somebody I can take advantage of, or an angle I can make money from.

I've only three moods – intolerant, irritable and angry.

Anti-social is what they would call me these days. Anti – correct. I am anti everything. And I haven't got a social bone in my body. What's the point of that?

A conscience? Don't make me laugh.

As God in his wisdom intended, my life has always been a disappointment. Big time. To me. To my parents. I don't know why everyone tries to dress life up as something special. Something to be interested in, to get excited about, happy about. Absolute crap. They should have seen through all that nonsense when they gave up Father Christmas and the Tooth Fairy.

It's only people like me who give you lot a glimmer of hope that things are not as bad as they could be. But somehow you go on deluding yourselves that things will improve. No chance.

Face up to it. This is as good as it gets. And it's total crap.

The weather is crap, relationships are crap, people are crap, living alone is crap, retirement is crap. Politicians, the economy, TV, mobile phones, doctors – all crap.

And the biggest pile of crap is your adoration of so-called 'Celebrities'. What's all that about then? No one in their right mind would be interested that some talentless slag from *Big Brother* has yogurt for breakfast, shags five different men a week and wants to look after orphans in Malawi. Get real! You must be pathologically deranged to swallow that lot. OMG! Has the world gone mad? Well, has it?

After much thought I have decided to end my relationship with this pile of shite called life. I'm going to a place where people don't talk drivel all the time, don't hype everything up to the level of the second coming of Christ. I'm going into a wooden box, six feet under, where I won't be disturbed by all this tedious bloody nonsense.

Some preacher-man, who I have never met, will talk to an empty church as though he had known me forever. He'll say what a good bloke I was and what a loss I will be. Total crap. Well, I won't miss you, you hypocritical nutheads, that's for sure.

I have made the preparations. Made them in my head when I'm awake at night after the recurring nightmare I've had since I was a kid, where I am falling, falling...falling into the blackness.

I thought I would end it all in Cornwall. By jumping off some cliffs. Newquay perhaps, with no ID on me. Give them maximum trouble recovering my body and identifying it. I won't stay overnight in the town and I'll travel down from Brum on public transport on my free bus-pass – the only thing our self-serving political masters have got right in my sixty-seven years in this dump. In fact, come to think of it, the only good thing that's happened in Parliament since Guy Fawkes. They won't be able to trace where I have come from and the bumping, rattling, perishingly cold buses, full of the meaningless chatter of old ladies and young girls with their pushchairs and iPhones will just reinforce my hate relationship with life.

Of course, if you didn't all delude yourselves about how good life is and how it's going to get even better, I could charter a train and we could all jump off the cliff together, holding hands and shouting "Oh My God"!! Just think of all the OMG headlines...

I've already stopped taking my beta-blockers and the other rubbish my gormless GP has given me for my heart condition. No point, is there? And I've taken all the cash out of my bank. I'll throw it in the sea before I jump to deprive some greedy bugger pocketing it and feeling happy at my expense.

So off we jolly well go then. If I make it through the first day without throwing myself under the bus I shall be surprised although, to build up maximum obnoxiousness, I shall probably see it through to Newquay. Might as well upset as many people as I can on my final journey, eh? I look forward to it.

I catch the bus from Brum to Worcester and sit on the front seat upstairs. The best seats on the bus, I always thought as a kid, but my Dad always made me stay downstairs.

No leg room, so I soon move back.

Just before Droitwich, an army of jabbering little French froglets come upstairs and surround me. All big coats, even bigger bags and screeching voices. Bloody foreigners. Their two teachers didn't look old enough to get out of their prams let alone take responsibility for kids away from home.

As we pass Chateau Impney they all point to it and go "Oooh" with a French accent. Probably thought they were back home. Pity they're bloody not.

Oh hell. One of the girls across the aisle from me is having a seizure. Shaking and quaking all over the place she is, eyes rolling about like a pinball machine. Too many full English breakfasts, I shouldn't wonder. The teachers don't have a clue what to do so, much against my better judgement, I grab the girl to stop her falling and lie her in the aisle in the recovery position, holding her safely until the jerking has stopped.

Poor girl didn't know where she was when she came round, with some ancient Anglais leering down at her, but at least she escaped the indignity of wetting herself.

I helped her sit back on her seat. Her smile was weak but her eyes spoke a language of their own. Full of gratitude. I smiled back reassuringly. The first time I remember smiling for a long time. I suddenly felt all protective.

Christ, what is happening to me. Get a grip, Bill. Be nasty to somebody.

That wasn't hard.

The two embryonic layabouts posing as teachers were faffing around mumbling something about hospitals in my most hated language.

"Non!" I shouted at them. "Medicine. She needs to take it."

They looked sheepish. Obviously didn't know the girl was on medication.

"You silly French buggers. She could have been injured or even killed."

They went all pink. At least they had the decency to blush.

"Merci, merci…"

The girl was okay now, back to normal. She offered me a sweet and in a weak moment I took it. I smiled at her again. *Ah well…*

Two buses later I arrived in Gloucester. It was piddling down with rain. And cold. Nothing to do but go round the shops before they close. Same shops as everywhere else, pretending to be different. Same fifty percent off signs. Same glut of mobile phone shops. Same half-hearted shop assistants looking as though they wanted to be elsewhere. Same dreary shoppers trudging round, collars up, eyes glazed, looking bored. Same dolly birds with their swanky Selfridges and Harvey Nichols carrier bags, flaunting it like *X Factor* judges. Ugh! Pass me the sick bag. I reckon they bring the bags from home and stuff their sandwiches in them. Oh, sorry – they don't eat, do they. No one can possibly afford the prices those shops charge, can they? Two hundred quid for a pair of jeans. They must be joking!

At least M&S is always nice and warm. It's full of the usual middle-aged women, sedately swaggering about in their best M&S bras and knickers as if to say "Look at me, I'm as gorgeous as ever. And I still believe I'm only thirty."

I notice a lad with a peculiar gait shuffling along with his Gran. Cerebral Palsy, I guess. About sixteen. From the waist up he is normal, chatting away and smiling, obviously enjoying being out with his Gran. From the waist down he is having terrible trouble moving his legs along; it is as though they belong to someone else, someone who isn't co-operating

A pang of sympathy shoots through me. How can he be so cheerful, so happy, with a disability like that which rules his life. And here's me, relatively normal, as miserable as sin most of the time, intolerant, angry and disappointed with life, seeking to end it all. The lad would give everything to walk normally like me. Perhaps I could exchange my legs for his happiness?

What kind of person would I be, I wonder, with his handicap. How would I cope with life?

Would I be like him – cheerful, even though life has been so unfair, giving him crap legs.

I look at him again, battling for every step he takes, and for the first time in my life I feel like crying. *What's happening to me?* I felt so upset I had to walk out into the rain and cold to bring me back to my senses. I just couldn't face up to the pain I felt for him.

The next day was a mammoth journey. Gloucester-Bristol-Exeter-Camborne. By the time I got to

Camborne it was dark. And miserable. That misty non-rain that soaks you had done just that.

Have you ever tried to find a B&B in Camborne in the dark? I wouldn't bloody bother. At the end of the trek I felt like a bloody tin miner trudging home after a long shift, exhausted and soaked through. I swear the seagulls were squawking with delight at my plight, the buggers. I would have gladly jumped off a cliff there and then but there weren't any around.

At long last I managed to find a place.

I leaned heavily on the bell. Nothing. Again. Nothing. I turned away and let fly a mouthful of foul language into the night, just as the door opened and a head appeared.

"After a room, are you?"

Are you mental or what? What do you think I'm doing ringing your B&B doorbell at this time of night, you silly cow!

With great restraint I remained civil. "Yeah," I said, "just one night."

"Come in, fella, you look drenched. I'll make us a cup of tea."

I followed her down the hall and into the kitchen. *Nice figure and pleasant with it.* Although I was in no mood for niceties, the warmth of the kitchen and her welcome melted a little of my antagonism.

"Off with your coat then. Get by the fire."

She pulled a chair up near the roaring fire for me.

"I'm Carla. Carla Nelson. Known to my few friends as Nel."

She smiled as she held out her hand. I took her warm hand in mine. "Bill."

Carla made a cup of tea, put some whisky in it and brought it to where I was sitting. "My husband died five years ago but I've still got some of his clothes. If you don't mind wearing them, you can change when I show you your room, and I'll dry yours."

I nodded my thanks.

The bedroom was small, sparsely furnished, but colourful and warm. Carla Nelson brought dry clothes for me, including a dressing gown, and then returned later for my wet ones.

"If you don't mind eating with me, the meal will be about twenty minutes." She looked for a reaction and when she saw none she added with a shrug – "there are no restaurants open in the town in the winter."

"That would be nice. Thank you." I think I even managed one of my rare smiles again.

I must be going soft as I get near the end. Well, what the hell. It will all be over tomorrow.

I had a quick shower and shave and went downstairs, wondering what I was letting myself in for. I usually eat alone, in silence. The thought of a mouthy woman chattering away sounded like purgatory. But I was ravenous. It had to be done.

I sat at the table in the kitchen and watched her preparing the meal. This was my first close encounter with the female species since I was in my twenties. She looked in her late fifties. Tallish. Medium brown hair in a bob and dangly ear-rings. Pretty, or at least I could tell she had been in her day. She had that glow of beauty about her. And she took care with her appearance, I could see.

As she put the meal in front of me, she turned and put a bottle of red wine on the table and then two glasses.

"I don't do this for all my guests, Bill," she joked, "but you look as though you need cheering up. This is the stuff to do it. Trust me."

The food was good.

A full stomach, the warm fire and the wine started to relax me but even so I'm not a good talker. I asked her to tell me about herself.

She and her husband had bought the B&B eight years ago when they moved down from the Midlands. They ran it together for three years before he died. They had no children.

It had obviously been a struggle for her on her own without a network of family or friends to support her. It surprised me that she was still so resilient and cheerful, still outgoing, still bearing no grudges about the way life had treated her. I felt really sorry for her while at the same time admiring the way she was embracing life.

How can she do that? Whereas I, without her bad luck, was just holding on by my fingertips, about to let go. To quit.

The paradox seemed as obscure as a Dylan Thomas verse.

Lifting her glass, Carla leaned across the table. "My problem, Bill, is that I'm stuck in a rut. I don't know how to move on."

She looked at me with big green eyes. I could see the pain, the desperation in them but, at the same time, they seemed to sparkle, to be alive.

"Oh I know I seem okay on the surface but underneath I'm slowly sinking into oblivion. My flame has almost gone out." She gave a big sigh. "I often think I'm losing it; losing my grip on life. Know what I mean, Bill?"

I nodded.

I did. *If only you knew, girl!* She wandered across to get another bottle of Côtes du Rhône and refilled our empty glasses.

"It's nice to have someone to talk to...drinking alone drags you down. Believe me, I know."

At the end of the second bottle I told her about myself. About how I had given up on life, although I didn't tell her about my intention to end it all.

"You can't give up just because you don't get on with life, Bill." She shook her head and looked directly into my eyes. It was as though part of her was entering my head, part of her spirit seeking to shore up mine. "You've got plenty going for you. You're good looking, interested in people, well, in me, anyway. You would be a good friend for anyone to have. You have to put up a fight. Show life who's the boss." She waved her fist in the air. "Things will change for the better. They always do if we let them. Life is what we make it, Bill. It's all about our attitude to things, so just relax and make up your mind to be happy."

She was really animated now, face flushed, her hands urging her point of view. I know she was trying to convince herself as well as me but her words opened up a crack in my armour. *She's bloody right you know, Billy Boy.*

I began to feel something unfamiliar: an inner warmth from sharing emotions with another human being. More complicated than that – a female type human being. I had an urge to care for her, to put my arms around her; a mixture of sympathy, attraction, empathy and goodness knows what else. Lust, I suppose. It unnerved me but at the same time I felt excited. I also felt angry that I had let my inner feelings escape, let my defences down.

It was all too much. It was also midnight. A big day tomorrow. I stood up unsteadily to move to the door and, as I passed her chair, her perfume hit me.

We kissed.

I'm sure neither of us intended it. But we did. It seemed the most natural thing in the world to do. Two lonely souls reaching out to each other. Forming some sort of bond. A bond I had thought was impossible to find. Tonight we had each found an anchor and the kiss seemed a way of saying "thank you".

Carla actually said it but I couldn't quite force myself to say the words.

I don't know what happiness feels like, but I am sure this is as near as I shall ever get. Here. Tonight. Now.

Sleep wouldn't come. My insides were churning. I felt confused, unsure how to react to this evening's events. But why should I react? Why not just pay the bill, move on and finish the job. Forget tonight. Go back, for tomorrow at least, to being a distrustful, pathetic old git fighting the world. Back to my comfort zone.

It's a bit late in the day to think about change; too late to do what Nel suggests – go with the flow and let the warmth of the situation tonight envelop and corrupt me.

If I did that I would lose control. Lose the familiar security I have built up over the years – disliking people, the intolerance, the cynicism, the pessimism ... it would all have to go. I would have to build another life. I'm not sure I can.

My mind had mellowed and my inhibitions eroded by the wine. As I lay there half asleep, I began to sense for the first time in my life what had happened to me. To see, as Nel had said, that my attitude had carved my path in life and steered me down it. It had kept me on the straight and narrow path of disliking life. Every step had reinforced my negative attitude. It had become automatic. I was like an addict. I got a fix from the rubbish things in life, I fed off them.

I lay back, mentally exhausted and sweating. I kicked off the covers. Why hadn't I seen this before? More importantly, what had made me take this path in life in the first place, seeing the bad instead of the good things in life?

I felt tense and uneasy. Anxious. Fearful even. As if I was being threatened. As though a barrier in my mind was trying to close off these unfamiliar thoughts. It was slamming down, trying to suppress them. An inner voice, commanding and insistent, was shouting in my mind *You don't want to go there, Bill. It's all nonsense. Forget it. You're okay as you are.*

It was tempting to agree. To close off the thoughts and to drift into sleep. But something else inside me awakened, equally strong and insistent. I don't know what it was; it felt like another me, a force urging me to explore this black hole which had opened up inside me.

You're no bloody good at anything, boy. Never will be!

The words, uttered with venom, exploded inside me. It was what my father repeatedly said when I was young. All the time. I could hear his voice as though he was in the room with me now. Malicious. Mocking. Belittling.

You have always been a big disappointment to us, William.

My mother's words, cold and deliberate, also echoed around the room.

I realised now they didn't want me to exist. They treated me like I was nothing. And that's what I have become – a nothing. A nobody ...

It all came flooding back...an emotional tidal wave crashing over me. Suffocating me. I felt myself withdraw into the security of my childhood shell – feeling totally alone, unloved, rejected, and frightened – just as I had throughout my childhood. It is real. I can feel the intensity of it right now, gnawing away inside me.

Instinctively I curl up into a ball.

For the first time, I began to see how I had reacted to this threat as a boy. I had become distrustful of everyone. I was no good. Therefore, being disliked and a nuisance was something which couldn't hurt me. Something I could take pride in. It was my only reward in life. My badge of honour.

I was at war with the world. My parents had forced me down that path. Their behaviour had chosen it for me. At such a young age I had no choice but to follow it. It was what I had to do to survive.

I was an unwanted child and they had scapegoated me for their own failures, bullied me to prop up their own rotten, miserable lives. I saw it clearly now…

My head suddenly cleared. The haze was gone. The fear and pain of my childhood was being unleashed. I could feel it leaving my body. It was as if I was *seeing* for the first time. My mind shouted out *Well, sod you, Ma and Pa. Get out of my life once and for all. You are not going to pull my strings any more. I'm going to get a bit of happiness for once. Hallelujah! I've escaped.* I wanted to shout it out loud. To scream it from the rooftops. I felt elated. The demon was gone. Gone forever.

I stayed a week with Nel. No strings, we said.

We went for meals out of town, to a dance, to the cinema. We walked, we talked, we made love. Mad passionate love. OMG!

Above all, we laughed. Oh boy did we laugh! It was as if we were laughing the past out of our sad lives. 'Billy No Mates' and 'Nel No Knickers' we called ourselves when the wine was flowing. It was all abandoned and hilarious. Another world to me. Wonderful!

When I left, we knew our lives would never be the same again – we had well and truly moved on. I had experienced the happiness I had never let myself even dream about.

I had finally told Nel of my earlier plan to jump off the cliffs at Newquay but, as I had written my intention down on a piece of paper, I would throw this off the cliff instead. It would symbolise the end of my former life.

I was now back in the real world, eagerly seeking the happiness I had denied myself all these years.

"You're a good man, Billy Boy," Carla said, as she kissed me goodbye. "I'll still be here if you fancy giving it a go." She squeezed me. "And don't worry about me. This week has taught me that I can move on with my life, whatever happens."

I didn't want to raise her hopes as I needed to think my new life through a little more before I made any commitments. Coming back to Nel was top of my list.

I left her with all the money I had withdrawn from the bank and asked her to keep it for me until I returned.

An hour and a half later I was in Newquay.

Aren't seaside towns the pits in winter? No tinsel and turkey this far south. Deserted streets, closed shops. It was like a ghost town. The rain didn't help. But I knew in a few months it would be warm and thronging with chattering youngsters and music. I can visualise it.

I feel like a new man, at the start of an exciting life-changing adventure. I can even see colours more vividly; people, places, everything is so interesting and new. It's like a spiritual revival. I feel uplifted inside. I can't wait to get going.

I'm starting by erasing every pessimistic, prejudiced thought as soon as it enters my head. I feel great! It must be what the slaves felt when they had their shackles removed. With Nel by my side, I know I can't fail to find true happiness.

These thoughts race through my mind as I climb breathlessly up the steep muddy path from the town to the top of the cliffs. I am having to take a breather every hundred yards or so but I don't care, I am on a mission and I know my new life will start as soon as I toss the paper over the cliff. The despairing blackness of my old life will be gone forever.

I can't wait.

I had an urgency in my step pushing me on as I struggled up the last sleep slope. Here I am at last, gasping, exhausted, but happy, at the edge of the cliffs looking down at the sea below. My goal is almost achieved. I am elated. Overjoyed.

Struggling for breath, I search for the piece of paper that will determine my future.

Where is it?

I can't bloody find it.

Get a grip, Bill! It's here somewhere.

I start to panic, tear through my pockets like a madman. *My life depends on this...*

I throw my jacket on the ground and stamp on it, enraged, then search all the pockets again.

Now my wallet. I spread the contents over the wet grass, desperately sifting through them. Not there. I am becoming very agitated. Frightened. I can't think straight.

WHAM! It hits me like a sledgehammer. A searing pain in my chest.

I feel paralysed.

Again. THUD! This time into my chest and arm.

It's my heart...Oh God!

Can't breathe. Sweating. Dizzyness...

No, Nooo...not now...Please God, not now.

WHAM! The pain doubles me up.

Can't think. Losing control...falling forward...

Collapsing...hands on wet grass.

Body, sliding, sliding...

This is what you really wanted, Bill, isn't it?...
Eyes closing...
I'm falling, falling. Falling into the blackness...

MY PERCY

"Your mother worships you."

My hand strokes the smooth black fur.

"Yes, she does, she worships you."

The cat's penetrating green eyes seem unimpressed. Purring yes, but otherwise emotionally detached as she sits sprawled across my lap.

Her position stops me getting up but, to be honest, I don't feel like rousing myself at present.

Why should I?

I have just read a chapter in this self-help book that tells me to take control of my life; to stop rushing about for other people and do what *I* want for a change.

'Enlightened Selfishness' it's called. So right now I feel enlightened to sit here, cat or no cat, visualising chocolates, and my boyfriend.

I wasn't always like this. Before my 'Enlightened Selfishness' phase I was a human dynamo, a veritable supercharged whirlwind. Here one moment, down to the shops the next. Always walking. Walking my legs off. I think it's because as an impressionable teenager I was taller than my friends and my subconscious saw walking as a way of wearing my legs down so that I didn't protrude above the crowd. And it stuck.

With hindsight, and after reading my self-help book, I now know that if I had 'visualised' myself being shorter then my body would have corrected itself.

My boyfriend…there I go again, it's that book, telling me to be 'young brained'. How can he be my boyfriend when we are both sixty-odd? Although he may be some day because he insists on counting backwards when he has a birthday. In ten years' time he'll be fifty and I'll be seventy, and when I'm a hundred he will be twenty. So perhaps the term 'boyfriend' is okay.

As you can tell, he's even crazier than I am. Well, that's my opinion. He may have a different view of my craziness rating. The book isn't helpful in this respect; it doesn't mention what to do to be less crazy.

His name is Percy. He's not a bad guy. Tries to tell me how to run my life, of course. Well, don't they all? It's the 'I Love You, You're Perfect, Now Change' male philosophy. I think it's built into them. They don't know what a hard life we women have, do they? Running half a dozen lives at once, at everyone's beck and call, including theirs.

But I mustn't grumble. At least he's taller than me, so I don't have to get on my knees to kiss him – I find that very humiliating, you know. I really cherish him for being a proper man-size.

How did I meet this flotsam of a man, I hear you ask.

Not only that, you may be curious about how I came to cherish him. That's probably a good description of my feelings right now. My 'your girl-friend worships you' feelings are still gathering somewhere in the realms of fantasy. But you never know about these things, do you?

Anyway, I was on a ramble, one of the ones I go on to make my legs shorter. At five miles we stopped for lunch in a graveyard. I don't know why, but we always seem to stop in a graveyard. It's not because we are worn out and seeking a quick exit to the next world or anything like that, or even that we've got religion. It must be for the ambience.

I sat down on my treasured piece of oilcloth and opened my box of beetroot and Marmite sandwiches. To be honest, I was feeling a bit miffed because further back some kids had shouted "Here come the Zombies." I suppose they had a point – a single file of slow trudging figures with their eyes on the ground. But it's degrading, isn't it, to be called a Zombie? I'll readily admit to being one first thing in the morning, but not when I have spent time doing my hair and putting my make-up on. It's disrespectful, wouldn't you agree?

Admit it, you probably feel this is all a bit weird, don't you? The graveyard, my oilcloth, beetroot and Marmite sandwiches, Zombies, the ambience … but, in the circles in which I move, this is perfectly normal. I do have aspirations to move in other circles, hence the self-help book.

As I contemplated the scene before me, wishing I had put my 'Bridget Jones' knickers on because the icy cold oilcloth was penetrating my vitals, I heard a grunt. It was quickly followed by a spade-full of earth landing around my legs. Before my reactions took hold, another grunt, followed by a second spade-full. This lot descended into my lap, bang in the middle of my sandwiches. That was too much!

"Look what you've done, you fool!" I shouted.

This was much to the dislike of my fellow Zombieites who were clearly upset by my outburst. I heard them tut-tutting.

Then a head popped up from the hole. It spoke: "Talk to me like that again and I'll lay you flat out in this hole."

Now that was the best offer I'd had in a long time but I didn't want to jump at it until I saw how tall he was. And you know men, they'll say anything to impress a woman, won't they? I could only see his head. Not bad. Not good either. But beggars can't be choosers.

"I'd take you up on that offer if you weren't a foot high earth shovelling pygmy," I said.

"You daft bat," he replied.

Oh joy! An instant attraction. Bats are my favourite animal, particularly fruit bats.

"And I'm not stunted," he retorted. "I'm standing in a five foot hole."

"A likely story. Would you fancy a beetroot, Marmite and earth sandwich on wholemeal thrown in your hole, Mr...?" I was trying to forge a meaningful relationship.

"No thanks. I prefer granary. And my name is Percy. Percy Smith."

My eyes lit up and my Mills and Boon bosoms began to heave. Percy is my favourite name. I tried hard to control myself.

"I'm Allison," I said. "Are you digging a grave?"

"No, I am trying to escape from one, you daft bat... er... sorry."

Swoon, I nearly slid off my oilcloth with joy. Bat again.

Percy rose up from the ground, stuck his spade into the loose earth and walked across.

I noticed his highly polished shoes, the sharp crease down his black trousers and his immaculate

303

white shirt with a blue silk tie. He looked tired and pale.

The word incongruous sprung to mind.

"Here," he said, "have one of my sandwiches. Smoked salmon, with watercress on granary."

They were cut into quarters with no crusts.

What a match, I thought. He's even odder than I am. Well, nearly.

I looked him up and down.

"Gravediggers going up in the world then, are they?" I chirped.

"Not exactly. Only me. The others are going down, I should imagine."

The rest of my Zombie colleagues took no notice of him; acted as though he wasn't there. That they didn't even look at him I found surprising given most are man-less too, like me, but try desperately not to let it show.

We walked into the Church together, Percy and I, (oh joy! he was a few inches taller) and sat in one of the pews. We ate his sandwiches.

"I know you like fruitbats," he said. "What else? Tell me all about yourself."

His dark eyes beamed like two black buttons and his smile encouraged me to talk.

I realised later that he had let me gabble on about myself for what seemed like hours, but must have been only minutes.

Next thing I knew, my friend called me through the church door: "Are you coming, Allison? We're nearly ready to go."

"You'd better join them," he said. "I'll catch up with you later. By the way, you are beautiful."

I blushed.

"And take notice of that book of yours – take control of your life, live it to the full. Have fun while you can. You are a long time dead."

He kissed me on the forehead as I left. I can still feel it there, even now.

"What did you go into the church on your own for?" my friend asked. "And who were you talking to? I didn't see anyone."

"It was the gravedigger. He came out of that grave there…"

I pointed and walked towards it but there was no hole, just a new grave with artificial turf, flowers and wreaths around it. Lying on top was an official-looking piece of paper in a cellophane envelope. I picked it up. It said: 'Percy Smith. Buried 10/03/2015'. Yesterday's date.

"You okay, Allison? You've gone all pale and your hand is shaking."

She looked at the paper. "Did you know him?"

"Yes," I said. "I think so."

The cat stirs on my lap.

"Your mother worships you," I murmur.

"Me too, I hope?" Percy says, his hand grasping mine.

305